Jennifer Word

Once More

ALSO BY JENNIFER WORD

<u>Novels</u>

The Society Book One: Genesis
The Society Book Two: Transcription
The Society Book Three: Regeneration
Higher Love
Once More
The Desert's Green

<u>Poetry</u>
Lyrical Tales: Collected Poems

<u>Collections</u>

Five Tales of Fear
All Because of the Cat & Other Tales

Jennifer Word

Once More

EMP Publishing

EMP PUBLISHING
Oak Park, California

Once More
Copyright © Jennifer Word
All Rights Reserved

ISBN: 978-0-6924658-7-5

This book is a work of fiction. Names, characters, places and incidents are products of the author's imagination or are used fictitiously. Any resemblance to actual events or locales or persons living or dead is entirely coincidental.

Without limiting the rights under copyright reserved above, no part of this publication may be reproduced, stored in or introduced into a retrieval system, or transmitted, in any form, or by any means (electronic, mechanical, photocopying, recording, or otherwise), without the prior written permission of both the copyright owner and the above publisher of this book.

EMP Publishing
Find us online at www.emppublishing.com

Cover design by Fatlind Colaku © Jennifer Word by Licensing Agreement c/o 99designs.com

Printed in the United States of America

Dedicated to all the writers who have tried to describe and capture *love* on the page.

You will be…
The death of me.
Yeah, you will be…
The death of me.

—Muse

The shotgun blast sounded off like thunder. The clap echoed across the flat lands and surrounding hills. It was close. Too close. She had a bad feeling. It could be Farmer Garnett shooting his own rabbit for supper, but she didn't think so.

She flew off the porch, dropping her potato only half-skinned. It rolled down the steps with hollow pings and landed in the coarse grass. She felt a terrible pain in her chest. She knew things. Thoughts flooded into her head like a river overflowing its banks. A dam had broken somewhere inside her soul.

Her feet and long cotton dress noisily scraped through the overgrown Buffalo grass. She was on a straight course, her route aided by the light of the moon. She ducked under branches and waded through the dark shadows of the evening that had crashed the twilight away so quickly, this time of year.

*As she reached the place where the fence should have been, it barely registered on her that the barrier between their land and Garnett's was now wide open. She briefly had time to flit a thought, **Storm brought it down yest'day**, before the tug pulled her to a lone, shadowed figure standing in the adjacent pasture. The shotgun in his hand did not concern her at the moment, but it soon enough would.*

She fell down upon her knees in the pebbled dirt and patches of grass. He wasn't gone yet, but he was leaving fast. She could feel it. Her hand instinctively went to the hole in his belly and covered it in a vain attempt to slow the blood. In the dark, there was no color – only a tactile sense of touch and vague sensory awareness.

Impossibly warm liquid gushed from his insides. It covered her hands, feeling like warm molasses. He was too weak to speak; yet he did. Two words. It should have confused her, but it did not. She immediately understood.

"Follow me."

"Yes." She nodded in the dark, though he did not see. He heard her answer with his last conscious thoughts, however, and he was comforted.

She felt him go. The ache inside her was immense. There was a ripping apart of her insides, as if her soul and his had been melded together with hardened tree sap, and they were now being torn apart. She felt as if she was being broken apart into shards and fragments, like dried autumn leaves crumpled in a fist and scattered in bits upon the ground.

She cried out in pain. The anger and desperation were immediate. She stood and faced the farmer.

"Shoot me!"

"Wh-what?"

"Do it now, hurry!"

"Now look here, this was an accident, you know? He shouldn'ta been on my prop'ty. You know that."

"You done killed one nigga, so go haid, shoot me!" She marched up to him, and he raised the barrel of his gun on instinct.

"Stop!"

But she kept on coming, 'til the barrel stuck into her chest. He stumbled back a foot, and she quickly made up the distance with her own stride, grabbing hold of the barrel with her hand in a vice grip.

"Go on, shoot!"

"No!"

"Do it now, please."

He frowned in the darkness. She was pleading, her voice no longer angry. He shook his head and this time, it was she who could not see the motion. She was out of time and in too much pain.

"I...I cain't..." he stammered.

It was a long reach, but not impossible for her. She held the barrel in place with her left hand, and quickly slid her right along the stock, feeling for the cold metal. Her finger glided over his. He was frozen in shock, paralyzed.

"No!"

Her finger forcefully pushed down upon his, depressing the trigger in an instant. Bright muzzle-flash of light; a quick fire lit up the dark pasture. Then all was dark, once more.

He stood shaking, as her figure crumpled to the ground. She died quicker than her lover. It was nearly immediate at this close range. The farmer did not see it in the dark, but she died with a smile on her face.

Her pain was over.

1. October 21, 2009 –Adria

Adria Allan awoke, gasping from another nightmare. She got up, went into her bathroom and brushed her teeth, sighing at the sunken flesh beneath her eyes. She raked her fingers through her long hair, examining the new strands of dark mixed in with her now dirty-blonde, then applied her makeup, attempting to freshen her complexion to something remotely resembling a sixteen-year-old girl in good health. She dressed then headed downstairs to eat breakfast.

In the kitchen, Emily Allan was fixing her daughter some scrambled eggs. She was already in uniform, her short, brown hair tucked behind her ears. Adria sat down and stared at the table in front of her, dazed. Emily piled the eggs onto a plate and set them down in front of her, then sat down. She gazed at her daughter for several moments, her eyes creasing in concern, but Adria did not see this. Not meeting her mother's eyes, she picked at her food with her fork.

"Another nightmare?" Emily said.

It was more a statement than a question. Adria nodded, almost imperceptibly, still not speaking. Emily frowned and reached her hand out to touch her daughter's hair.

"Did you color your hair?"

Adria jerked her head away and Emily pulled her hand back, as if an animal had snapped its jaws at her fingers. She looked at her daughter again, this time with concern and shock.

"Sweetie, please talk to me. What is going on?"

"I don't know," Adria said. It was the truth.

"Do you want to talk to Dr. Morrow again?"

"No," Adria said.

"He really helped you after Aunt Lynn."

"No, he didn't," Adria said. "He helped you."

"Adria," Emily started.

Adria rolled her eyes. Her mother grew frustrated and sighed.

"I get it. You're young. You're trying to figure out who you are. You want to reinvent yourself. That's fine. What's not fine is your attitude. It needs to change."

"I can't help what I dream about, Mom."

"No, but you're still a kid," Emily said. "And I'd like it if you would ask me before doing things, like dying your hair."

Adria turned a dark glare on her mother. She was still lost in the morbid gloom of the events that had unfolded within her latest dream.

There was a darkness inside of her that she had no idea how to get rid of, and it was taking its toll. She didn't know how to explain these effects to her own mother. In the back of her mind, she thought, at times lately, that the darkness was a living thing, consuming her from the inside out.

"I didn't dye my hair."

There was no emotion in her voice. Then, suddenly, as if a cloud had been blown off the sun, Adria's face livened. It contorted. It went from flat, emotionless apathy, to urgency and feeling, flooding her face with sudden personality.

Her empty eyes filled with tears, and Emily could see her daughter fighting to keep her composure. She was moved to tears herself, at seeing her daughter fight this raging battle. She'd been fighting it for over a year now, and Emily was at her wits' end as to what to do about it, how to handle it, and most importantly, how to fix it.

"Baby, please."

"Mom, I," Adria began, but couldn't finish.

"There is a darkness inside of you, and I don't why. I don't understand what's causing this," Emily said.

Her voice cracked with emotion. She wiped a tear away, standing up. Meanwhile, Adria did her best to ignore her mother's pain. She couldn't handle that on top of everything else she was enduring. Emily glanced at the clock, sighing.

"Shit, it's time to go," she said. "We're both going to be late."

"Mom, I'm sorry," Adria said. "I'm trying, I really am. It's just, every time I have a bad dream, it's like, I just can't snap out of it. I'm sorry."

"I know you are," Emily said. "But I think you should really consider talking to Dr. Morrow."

"How is that going to help?"

"I don't know. But something is causing these nightmares. This has been going on long enough. Look what it's doing to you, Adria."

She gave her mother a perturbed look, again rolling her eyes. The darkness was beginning to fade, however, replaced by teenage annoyance and apathy. Emily sighed again, but managed a small smile, appearing grateful and relieved; relenting.

"I only care," she said. "Can you try to be patient with me?"

"If you'll do the same for me."

"Deal."

The sound of a car's horn drifted into the kitchen from the street out front. Emily smiled.

"I guess Sam's here," she said.

Adria broke into a broad smile. Her mother laughed. Her daughter looked much more livened now, a bit of color filling in her cheeks, taking her pale-white complexion away and replacing it with a look of rosy health. She stood and left the kitchen.

"I'll see you tonight!" Emily called after her.

"Okay," Adria yelled over her shoulder.

2. October 21, 2009 –Sam

Adria ran, grabbing her bag. She flung her front door open, slammed it shut, and skipped down the steps of her hilly yard. Despite the fact that all the windows were closed on her friend's Prius, Adria could hear Sam laughing wildly inside, as well as music blaring. She ran around to the driver's side window. As Sam rolled it down, Adria laughed.

"You like it?" Sam said, grabbing a large hunk of her own shoulder length, flaming-red hair.

Adria nodded. Her smile was contagious and Sam laughed again.

"I figured if your hair's going to change, so is mine."

She looked at Adria then, still smiling, but there was a serious edge in her eyes. Adria saw the look and recognized it for what it was; her friend was concerned about her.

Adria was overcome with emotion. She sighed, her eyes welling up with tears. Sam was not fazed. She only gazed at Adria with sympathy, smiling in understanding.

"And I see you've gotten darker, again," she said, her voice gentle.

"My mom thinks I dyed it."

"Rationalizing," Sam nodded. "A reasonable explanation. We're going to be late. Let's get going. Channel eight?"

"As always."

She quickly got into her used Saturn and grabbed the walkie-talkie on her passenger seat, turning it on and tuning it in to channel eight.

"Testing, cunt," Adria said, smiling.

"I know you are, but what am I," Sam said.

The girls sped away from the house, and the two-car caravan soon left Cannon Beach, heading north on the scenic Oregon coast Sunset Highway, into Seaside. The entire drive took twenty minutes. Along the way, the girls walkied each other back and forth.

"What song are we listening to this morning, babe?" Sam asked.

"Jaded, Open Hand," Adria said, smiling.

The radio in Adria's car was silent, however. She always heard music in her head. Sam knew this. She'd learned to ask, out of curiosity. It made Adria who she was, and Sam loved her for it.

"So, what happened this time?"

She waited for a reply, her walkie remaining silent.

"Your dream," Sam pressed. "Drop it while it's hot, hon."

"The usual; happy couple, madly in love. Then suddenly, blood and gore."

"I want details."

"It's the same one I've had before," Adria replied. "You've heard them all, remember?"

"Yeah," Sam said. "So which one was it?"

There was no response from Adria, again. Sam sighed.

"I'm sorry," she said. "I'm just worried about you, that's all."

"I know," Adria said. She paused briefly, collecting herself. Then she sighed and spoke into her walkie.

"It was the one with the black couple."

"And the gun?"

Adria nodded. Then she realized Sam couldn't hear a nod. She walkied again.

"Yeah," she said. "Only it was so awful this time. I could actually feel warm blood gushing onto my hands."

"*Your* hands?"

"I'm always her in my dreams," Adria reminded Sam. "You know that."

"Yeah, I know," Sam said. "And you know what *I* say."

Adria said nothing. She only sighed again and shook her head.

The girls reached their destination. They both pulled into the parking lot of Seaside High School and got out, walking together. Sam looked at Adria with trepidation.

"Are you mad at me?"

"No," Adria said. "But you have to understand."

"I'm trying," she said. "I'm trying to help you."

"You're not a doctor," Adria said. "Your theory's not even relevant in the actual world of psychology. My mom wants me to see her therapist again."

"Emphasis on again," Sam said.

She wasn't going to back off. Not when she cared this much for her best friend. They were walking through the front doors of the school now, and heading down the hallway. They went to Adria's locker first.

"But, I've done the research," Sam led, continuing. "I've confirmed facts."

"But, it's bullshit, it's impossible. First off, it makes no sense, and secondly, did I mention it's not possible?"

"You dreamed something from history," Sam said.

"So?" she shot back. "I sit in history class every day, listening to that shit. So, I incorporated it into my dream, so what?"

"So, it gave me something to go on," Sam pressed.

She reached into her bag and pulled out a sheet of paper. She looked at Adria with trepidation again.

"Just try and keep an open mind, okay? I didn't want to show you this here."

"Show me what?"

"Look, in one of your dreams, you said there was a newspaper stand, right? And on the front page of the paper was a headline."

"So?"

"So, you told me the headline read, 'St. Valentine's Day Massacre,' remember?"

"Again, so?"

"Nice attitude," Sam said. "You also told me the scene clearly looked to you like New York, with all the buildings, only kind of old-looking, with the cars, remember?"

"So what?" Adria was frustrated now.

"So, it's called research," Sam said. "I did some. I looked up the St. Valentine's Day Massacre. It took place on February 14, 1929, in Chicago. Nine gangsters were shot, but, that doesn't matter. What does matter is, I looked up all the news reports from New York City on both February 14th and February 15th, 1929, and guess what I found? It took a while, but, here it is."

Sam handed the paper to Adria. It was a print out of a news article from the New York Chronicle. Adria read it, her eyes looking fearful. She shook her head.

"Their names were William Fenmore and Elizabeth Harris. And get this, they were both twenty-three."

"So?"

"So, I did some research on them as well, trying to find out where they came from. I traced them both back, thanks to Google. Found out where each of them was born. They were born in different places, but that doesn't matter. What does matter is that they were both born on the same day."

"So what?" Adria handed the paper back to Sam.

"Are you joking me?" she said. "They were born on the same day, that doesn't strike you as being odd?"

"It's a coincidence," Adria shrugged. "We're going to be late for class."

"Adria, you dreamed about these people. You saw how they died."

"No, that's just a coincidence as well."

"I'm trying to help you," Sam said. "Your dreams, they're *hurting* you. Look what they're doing to you."

Sam reached out and stroked Adria's hair, looking at the newest strands of dark to infiltrate her once light-blonde locks. She looked at her best friend with affection.

"I don't know about any of your other recurring dreams," she continued, gently. "But I can tell you that at least one of them appears to be something that really happened. And for whatever reason, you're dreaming about it. And there's definitely something weird about this couple."

"It doesn't matter," Adria said. "Even if it were true, how would knowing help? I'll still have the dreams anyway. Can you stop the bad dreams?"

"No," Sam said, defeated.

"Then I don't want to talk about this anymore."

She sighed, looking at herself in her locker mirror and finally began gathering her books for all her morning classes. She turned to look at Sam.

"I don't mean to sound ungrateful. It's just, these dreams already have me feeling like I've lost my mind. You spin all this freaky-weird bullshit at me, when I can already hardly think straight, and it isn't good. I'm not in a position to deal with this right now. You know it takes a few days to get over it, each time."

"I know," Sam said. "I'm just trying to tell you, I think you have a connection to the other side. I really do."

Adria laughed, rolling her eyes. Sam wouldn't let it go.

"It has to start somehow, doesn't it? It all started after your aunt died, right? When you went to the cemetery? I seriously think you're a medium or something. I think these are ghosts reaching out to you, trying to communicate. You're fucking Allison DuBois, or something."

"I don't give a shit who I am," Adria said. "I care that I look like shit."

"No you don't. You're hot."

"No I'm not. I look like death."

"Yeah, a little," Sam said. "But it's kinda cool. It goes along with your whole musician-chic singing thing. You're dark and mysterious. Guys dig that shit."

"I'm not dark on purpose, I can't help it."

"I know."

Sam looked at Adria with concern again. It was not unlike the look from Adria's mother earlier that morning.

She'd seen a shadow come over Adria's face, and she recognized it.

The darkness came and went, but lately, it had been much worse. Sam was afraid she was losing her best friend and she was actually terrified.

"I hate to see you like this. I wish I knew what to do. You don't smile, you know that? You don't ever look happy anymore – except when you're playing or hearing music." She paused, thinking. "You know, I'm always here for you, Adria. No matter what. Whatever's wrong, I will always have your back, you know that, right?"

Adria nodded, looking down at the floor. Sam pushed her hair away from her face with both of her hands. Two boys walking by smirked.

"Lesbies," one of them said, and then both boys laughed, walking away.

"Hey, fuck you, assholes!" Sam yelled after them. She looked at Adria again, smiling.

"They wish."

A man's voice from behind them could be heard clearing his throat. Sam turned to see a teacher peering around his door at the two girls, his eyebrows raised.

"Sorry, Mr. Leeds," Sam shrugged.

Mr. Leeds walked up to the girls, sighing and shaking his head.

"Girls, you know I can't allow that kind of language in the halls," he said. "Office."

"But, I didn't," Adria said, but Mr. Leeds cut her off.

"I don't care, you two are always in cahoots."

"In cahoots?" Sam said.

"Hey, I don't like the attitude, Samantha," Mr. Leeds said. "And by the way, nice hair. Both of you. Now go. I'm getting on my intercom, and if you two aren't in the office in the next three minutes, your bottoms belong to Mr. Prince."

"Fine," Sam said. "Thanks a lot."

She pulled on Adria's sleeve, walking away.

"Way to start our day," Adria said, but her voice was soft.

"I'm sorry," Sam shrugged. "I'll take the heat with Prince, okay?"

"No, then you'll be in detention without me."

"So?"

"So, if you have my back, then I have yours," Adria said.

"Thanks, babe."

3. October 21, 2009 –Micah

In the office, the two girls looked at the assistant, Ms. Willis, who only sighed and motioned for them to sit. They both plopped down into their seats and Sam sighed.

"Look at it this way, you got out of first period."

At the counter, to the right of the girls, a middle-aged man with dark hair stood in front of the registrar. A teenage boy, presumably the man's son, stood on his left.

His hair was substantially dark, almost black, and was slightly waved. It was long and shaggy, covering his ears. He had a thick scud of long bangs swept across his forehead.

Adria sized him up, feeling bored. He was medium height, she figured. She was five-six; he looked to be about five-ten, perhaps a bit taller. His skin was as pale as hers, she noticed. She was practically a ghost.

Sam looked at the boy, taking him in from behind. He glanced over his shoulder at the two girls and turned back toward the counter. Then he looked back at the girls, again, and his eyes locked on Adria.

He stared at her for several long moments, and she stared back at him, neither one blinking. This went on for over a minute. Sam looked back and forth between the two of them, taking in the scene with bemused surprise.

"Hello," Sam said under her breath.

Adria looked at the boy and felt her heart skip up into a faster rhythm. Her breath caught in her throat. It felt as if the entire world had stopped; as if the very planet had ceased to rotate. She was dizzy, and felt a sensation of falling. She stared at the boy in wonderment.

Meanwhile, Sam watched the scene unfolding, in continued surprise. The boy frowned and blinked several times, as if trying to clear his head. He continued staring at Adria, and she stared back at him. The boy's father was talking to the registrar clerk, completely oblivious.

The young man walked over to Adria, passing Sam, ignoring her completely. Adria stood to meet him and the couple came to rest, looking at each other.

He looked down into her face, peering at her with affection and wonder. When he spoke, his voice was soft and gentle.

"Hello."

"Hi," Adria said.

"Micah," his father called. "Get over here."

Micah turned, sighing and walked back over to his father. He glanced back and shrugged at Adria, giving her a crooked grin.

She smiled and sat back down, feeling breathless. Sam saw her friend's smile and her mouth fell open. Meanwhile, the registrar clerk was handing a paper to the father, explaining Micah's schedule and classes.

Ms. Willis bellowed out then, causing both girls to jump. Sam let out a yelp-laugh of shocked surprise.

"Girls! Mr. Prince is ready to talk to you in his office."

Sam and Adria stood together and walked past Micah and his father, as they headed out the office door.

Micah turned back to look at Adria and she returned his gaze. Both of them smiled, acting shy. They both blushed.

Micah walked out of the office. Adria stood staring after him.

"Holy shit-on-a-shingle," Sam said, pulling on Adria's sleeve.

Ms. Willis gasped at Sam's exclamation of profanity. She gave the girls a reproachful look, shaking her head.

****

In the hallway, after their meeting with the principal, Sam turned to Adria, smiling. They both had detention after school.

"What the hell was that?"

"What?" Adria frowned.

"That thing, with the guy," Sam said. "*Micah.*"

Sam's tone was playful enough, but Adria looked serious. She eyed her friend.

"It was like, instant attraction," Sam said. "You should have seen the looks on both your faces."

"I don't know what you mean."

"Oh, come on," Sam said. "You guys were drooling all over each other. You wanna have sex with him."

"What?"

"He's hot," Sam said. "He's got that dark, troubled-boy look going."

"Whatever," Adria said, but she was smiling now.

"Hey, fine. Forget it. But maybe a hot-ass lay is what you need to brighten things up."

"You are such a slutty cunt, you know that?" Adria laughed.

"And you love it," Sam said. "Besides. He made you smile, Adria. I haven't seen that in a while. If he can make you smile, he's good in my book."

Adria shrugged again. Sam threw in one more try.

"Maybe this is what you need, to take your mind off things? A nice distraction. What song did you hear?"

Adria sighed, her eyes dreamy and far off. She glanced over at Sam, blushing and looking shy.

"Can't Let Go by Landon Pigg."

"Nice. Appropriate? Not so sure."

"The music's never appropriate. It's just what pops into my head."

"Sometimes it's appropriate," Sam said, smiling. "But I don't know that a breakup song is quite in order just yet."

****

The girls parted ways, each going to their separate classrooms. Adria reported to her first period English class.

In second period history, she sat down in her seat at the back of the classroom. As students filed in, she felt her heart skip a beat again, as she saw Micah enter the classroom.

He walked up to the teacher, Mr. Sutterton, at his desk. They spoke briefly. Adria watched, craning her neck around the boy in front of her to get a better view.

Mr. Sutterton pointed to a desk in the row next to Adria. She sighed as she watched Micah sit down in his seat two desks back from the front.

He wasn't right next to her, he was still two desks ahead of her, and she felt disappointed. As the bell rang to start class, everyone took out their books and unloaded their materials. Adria reached into her bag and pulled out a spiral notebook and a pen.

When she looked up, she caught Micah's eyes. He had turned and was now looking at her. She blushed. He turned back around to face the front again, as Mr. Sutterton called everyone's attention.

"We have a new student today, class. Micah Foster... from Ohio?"

Micah nodded, remaining in his seat. He was hunched down in his chair. Adria smiled. Micah seemed shy.

"And what made you move out here?" Mr. Sutterton asked.

"Uh, my dad's a hotel manager," Micah said. "He works for Wyndham Hotels and Resorts. He got transferred out here, to Cannon Beach."

"Are you living there?" the teacher asked.

Micah nodded. Mr. Sutterton nodded back.

"Ah, another commuter. We have several district-transfer students from Cannon Beach here."

Micah nodded again. The teacher then removed any further attention from him by instructing the class to open their books to chapter four.

As the period unfolded, Adria found she couldn't pay much attention to the lecture in class. Her eyes kept going to Micah's back.

She took in as much of him as she could, starting with his black Doc Martin's, which made her smile, for he kept shaking his right foot back and forth, energetically, his feet crossed over one another.

She pulled her eyes up to his dark blue jeans, and his button down black shirt. His hair was medium long, ending at the nape of his neck, and was definitely wavy, she noted. His skin was ivory.

Micah intermittently looked over his shoulder at Adria, and gave her a sideways smile that made her heart melt. He did this several times over the next hour. Finally, the bell rang, ending the period.

As everyone stood, Adria gathered her things into her bag and walked up her row, past Micah. He stood and waited for her.

She paused when she reached him, and they walked together, side-by-side in their two rows, until they reached the end, smiling and laughing shyly as they did so.

Adria felt so strange with Micah, as if she knew him already. She was nervous and comfortable at the same time. This confused her. Micah seemed equally as shy, albeit a bit more comfortable.

They walked out into the hall together, and it was as if the other students were not even there. Despite all the noisy conversations, slamming of lockers and general laughter from the teens around them, the only sound Adria could hear was Micah's voice.

"What's your name?"

"Adria," she said. She found herself mindlessly blabbering. "I used to have a nickname though. November. My best friend gave it to me back in middle school, but she doesn't call me that anymore." She felt stupid.

"November?" Micah frowned.

"Well, no, it's Adria," she said. "November was just my nickname, once."

"Why?"

Adria shrugged feeling like an idiot. Why had she even brought that stupid tidbit up? Her mind was reeling. Micah didn't seem fazed at all.

"Who's your best friend?" he asked.

"Her name is Sam."

"Why did she nickname you that? Were you born in November?" Micah said, but his voice sounded strange.

He asked the question in a tone that seemed to belie that he already knew what her answer would be. She nodded. He nodded back.

"So was I."

Adria thought he sounded sad. He wasn't looking at her now, he was looking away and she felt confused.

"November 12," he finished.

"Really?" Adria said. "Me, too. How funny."

Adria frowned, remembering what Sam had told her that morning, about the couple in New York. She shook it off, however.

Micah nodded again. He didn't seem surprised at all to find out they shared the same birthday. He looked down at the floor, then around at the hallway and all the people around them. He seemed sad.

"Are you okay?"

"Can I call you Adria?" he asked.

"Of course," she said.

Adria frowned. Micah smiled at her and she felt even more confused. He sighed.

"I'll see you around," he said, and walked away.

"Wait."

Micah turned to look at her. He smiled, and again, she melted, hating herself for it.

"We have time," he said.

Then he walked away, leaving Adria to stand in the hallway, as confused as ever.

****

At lunchtime, Adria sat with Sam at a table in the corner of the cafeteria. Sam peered out the window.

"Oh good, it's raining," she said. "Winter, thou arriveth."

Adria picked at her food. Sam watched her, sighing.

"If you don't want to look like death, you should eat more. Put a little meat on your bones." She paused. "Besides, you want to keep up your health. Someone's interested in you."

"Huh?"

"Staring, three O'clock. A certain dark-edgy dream we saw in the office this morning?"

Adria frowned, looking to her left. Sam snickered.

"Three O'clock would be to your right," she said. "Over there, in the far right corner."

Adria looked where Sam had indicated and saw Micah watching her. When she caught his eyes, she smiled, blushing. He waved at her, and she waved back. Sam watched this and rolled her eyes, amazed.

"So, what's the deal?" Sam said. "What are we listening to now?"

"Shriekback; The Only Thing That Shines." Her eyes were still locked on Micah.

"Oh, God," Sam said. "That's the nail in the coffin."

"What do you mean?" She finally turned her attention back to Sam.

"Did you talk to him yet?"

Adria nodded. She looked down at her hands.

"He's in my second period history class. We talked."

"What did he say?"

"He said, '*we have time,*'" Adria said.

"What?"

"Yeah," she said, nodding and sounding perturbed.

"What does that mean?"

"I don't know."

"Huh," Sam said. "He's certainly playing mysterious, isn't he?"

Micah stood and walked across the cafeteria, toward Adria's table, but as he got closer, he suddenly turned and exited the room.

"Huh," Sam frowned. "That's weird."

Adria stared after Micah, feeling confused.

****

She didn't see him for the rest of the school day. At the start of each period, she eagerly watched and waited for him to appear, but he never did, nor did she even so much as catch sight of him in the hallways.

She spent the entire rest of her day walking around in a fog, lost in a reverie starring Micah's face and his crooked smile. As the final bell rang, Adria felt extremely disappointed. She met up with Sam, waiting for her at her locker.

"Ah, poor honey," Sam said, seeing her friend's disappointment. "What song?"

"Walking After You," Adria said, looking pained.

"Foo Fighters, Jesus," Sam said, looking at Adria with pity. "Well, at least you know you'll see him tomorrow, in second period, right?"

"Yeah, I guess."

A loud commotion broke out behind them, further down the hallway. Several students shouted.

"Fight-fight-fight-fight!"

People were whooping and yelling, calling and whistling. Sam rolled her eyes, smiling.

"Another teenage-hormone, testosterone explosion, I presume," she said. "Come on, let's go gawk. An hour of complete boredom awaits us."

The girls skipped down the hallway to stand on the outer edge of a circle of students who had formed a ring around the two fighters. They shoved their way closer to the front to get a view. As Adria made her way to the second row of students, she was able to see who was fighting.

Micah was in the ring, along with Westley Kane, the school's star jock baseball fanatic. Kane easily outweighed Micah by a good fifty pounds, as well as stood at least two inches taller.

Despite these facts, Micah was holding his own. He threw punches with such force, his fists whistled through the air. Kane had trouble keeping up with Micah's speed.

Adria caught sight of Micah's face as he fought, and something inside her mind felt oddly drawn to the anger that resided in his expression. It was a look of slight madness, she thought.

Micah's eyes shone with life and excitement, as if the fight were pure amusement and utter enjoyment for him. To Adria, it seemed as if a wellspring of anger and emotion were bottled up inside of him, and she was watching a geyser explode.

Music danced alive inside her head, and she broke out in a smile, in response to the mad grin she saw on Micah's lips. She was awestruck.

Adria looked around in a daze, at all the faces in the chanting crowd, feeling shocked and bewildered. She felt like she was watching everyone rant and cheer in slow motion.

They were all so caught up in the excitement. She looked to the spectators closest to the two fighting boys, and watched as droplets of blood landed on a few of their faces. They seemed to have no reaction to the gore, or perhaps, had not noticed. Then one spectator wiped the blood from his cheek, looked at his hand, and laughed.

Micah had an insane fire in his eyes of sick enjoyment, but Adria felt connected to the emotions emanating from him, as if he were feeding them directly into her. She felt alive, revived.

Then, everything sped up to real time again, as she continued to watch Micah's madness present itself. It was infectious and seemed to be affecting everyone around him, she mused. He had a power.

Micah threw himself into Westley then, with such force, the jock was thrown backwards into a line of lockers with a loud bang. Micah's fists kept flying. Droplets of blood landed on the lockers, and Kane's blonde hair gained several strawberry streaks as blood from his own nose flew, landed and smeared.

"Holy shit!" Sam said. "That guy's a maniac!"

Adria stood and stared with her mouth hanging open. Several teachers made their way through the thronging crowd of students and ran at the two boys, pulling Micah off Westley.

Micah did not attempt to fight any further, or resist in any way. He didn't seem angry at all, but rather, calm and amused, as if the fight had been merely an entertainment.

He smiled and he didn't see Adria. Micah was dragged off by a teacher, toward the front office. Westley received help from another teacher, who led him to the nurse's station. His nose was bleeding profusely. The crowd began to disperse.

"Jesus," Sam said. "Your buddy, Micah, is a poster-child for steroid don'ts. What a psycho."

"He's not a child."

She sounded breathless. Something about the fire she'd seen in Micah's eyes connected to her. She felt as if she understood it, somehow.

There was a darkness living within her, and she did not know why, or what it even was. She thought there was something violent and dark, perhaps, living inside Micah, as well.

"Jesus!" Sam said again. "You still like him? After seeing that?"

Adria shrugged. Sam stared at her friend in confused shock, as they made their way to the detention room.

"I know you're into broody and shit, but still. He's cute, but obviously, he's mental. Look at how aggressive he is. He gets you out on a date in his car, for example, and you'll be prime target, rape-meat."

"What?!"

"You'd better be careful, Adria," Sam said. "He's trouble. Dark, brooding, bottled-up-anger. Not cool and mysterious, just trouble. He's cute as hell, I'll give you that, but, still."

Sam looked at Adria and saw the look in her friend's eyes. Adria liked Micah.

It had already happened, and there was no stopping it. Sam felt it. She saw it.

She got the distinct impression that something was happening beyond her understanding. It was as if events had already been put into motion and it would be a futile attempt to do anything to try and stop it. Sam frowned, feeling confused.

"Come on," she said, pulling on Adria's sleeve. "What song did you hear?"

"Walcott," Adria said. "Vampire Weekend."

"Nice."

****

In detention, Adria pulled out her history book to read the chapter she'd missed in class, as unable to pay attention as she'd been. After about ten minutes, the door opened and Mr. Prince, himself, delivered Micah to the room.

Sam sighed, watching as Micah took a seat in the far left corner of the room, and proceeded to intermittently stare at the desk, then Adria. Eventually, he took out his history book as well, and began to read.

He still kept glancing over at Adria, however. Adria did not look back, but continued to read her text.

Sam tossed a note to Adria when the teacher was not looking. Adria unfolded it.

Psycho is eye-stalking you.

She smiled, and Sam huffed in surprise. She couldn't believe Adria wasn't freaked out by this guy's behavior.

Adria looked over at Sam and shrugged. Her cheeks were high with color. It was the healthiest she'd looked in several, long weeks.

Sam sighed again. She sent another note that simply read, **song?** Adria wrote back, **It's You, Balance.** Sam sighed again, rolling her eyes.

Detention ended. In the hallway, Micah approached Adria and Sam.

He stood, staring at the redhead for several long moments, with a look. Sam shrugged and walked a few feet away, eyeing him warily.

Adria hugged her history book in her arms. Micah smiled, but he looked sad. There was a serious edge in his eyes, and an intensity that confounded her. He seemed sad and resigned, somehow.

"How many lives have you learned about?"

Adria frowned at Micah and he smiled again, but she thought she saw tears in his eyes. She felt heat spread throughout her entire body.

"Your history book," Micah indicated to her arms.

"Oh," Adria said. "I was just re-reading the chapter from class this morning."

He nodded.

"So, you live in Cannon Beach?" she asked.

"Yeah, we moved into this little house on Spruce Court."

"Oh, yeah," she said. "I live on Haskell Lane. Well… when I'm with my mom, anyway. When I'm with my dad, I'm way over on Washington. Not that it's so far."

"Your parents are divorced?"

Adria nodded. Micah spoke to her with such intensity in his eyes, with such gentleness in his voice, it made her heart ache. She couldn't believe this person had been beating the living hell out of someone only an hour ago. He seemed concerned about her. She frowned.

"What about your parents? I saw your dad."

"Yeah, it's just me and him," Micah waved the question off.

"What about your mom?"

He looked at her, his eyes suddenly sketchy and worried. Adria smiled, trying to put him at ease.

"She's in prison."

"Oh," Adria said. "I'm sorry."

"Yeah, it's been tough."

It was clear to her that Micah didn't want to talk about his family anymore. She quickly changed the subject.

"Well, if you're new to Cannon Beach, you don't really know your way around, huh?"

"I drove here. My dad followed."

"No, that's not what I meant. You're from Ohio, right?"

"Yeah?"

"Well, Cannon Beach is a whole different world. You need a tour guide, to help you acclimate."

Adria smiled at Micah, suddenly feeling completely comfortable. He smiled back. They exchanged phone numbers and addresses and parted ways.

Sam came back over and looked at Adria in both shock and relief. She took in the look on her friend's face, and relaxed.

"Don't say it," Adria said.

"I'm not," Sam said, feeling resigned.

"But you want to."

"I love you. You've been my best friend since second grade. I don't know how I could have lived in this shitty, touristy-trap hell of ours without you to keep me sane all these years. You know that.

"I've watched you go through hell this last year, and I don't know why. Nothing has helped. Until now. I don't know what the deal was with Micah today and his fists. I guess I don't care, as long as he treats you right. And I see the way he looks at you. Whatever pent up hostility he may have, it doesn't seem to exist when he's with you."

"Thank you," Adria said.

"No problem."

****

As the girls walked to their cars, Sam saw Micah getting into an old black Volkswagen van. Adria didn't see him.

Sam waited for Adria to get into her car, and then she ran up to Micah's van, knocking on his driver's side window. He rolled the window down and smiled at her.

His crooked grin was somehow endearing. She began to understand why Adria was so taken by him. Micah definitely had a dark charm about him. Sam sighed, frowning at his ride.

"Nice rape-mobile," she said.

He frowned at her, smiling in confused amusement. Sam pushed on.

"Adria is my best friend, you got that steroid-freak?"

"Steroid freak?"

"Yeah, you heard me," Sam said. "Your little fight today? You're a psycho."

"No, I'm not," Micah said. He sighed. "I just get angry sometimes, that's all."

"Why?"

Micah only looked at Sam, his face sending her a stern warning to drop the subject. She returned his look with equal warning.

"You hurt her, I will fuck you up the ass, you got me?"

"Jesus," Micah said, frowning and smiling. He shook his head.

"I'm not going to hurt Adria. I had to do something to land myself in detention, didn't I?"

"Wait, what? Are you telling me you beat up the baseball jock, just so you could get detention?"

Micah nodded. Sam looked at him in disbelief.

"You saw us in the office, and you knew we'd be in detention today, didn't you?"

She looked at Micah, giving him a shrewd stare. He only smiled, looking away.

"You're nuts, you know that? You could have gotten suspended."

"I have a way of charming people," Micah said.

"Don't be arrogant. Adria is special."

"I know." He looked at Sam with an intense stare, and she finally abated.

"Fine," she said. "But, I'm watching you."

"Good to know," Micah smiled, shaking his head again. "You're a good friend, Sam. I see why Adria hangs with you."

He delivered another crooked grin, his statement landing on Sam's ears with such overwhelming, genuine honesty, she deflated. Micah was right; he did have a way of charming people.

"Get the fuck outta here," she said, completely relenting. "You fucking charm-freak."

Sam walked away and got into her own car. She shook her head and sighed. She feared that Adria was already lost.

4. October 22-November 6, 2009 –Adria

Over the next few weeks, Micah and Adria spent almost every day together, after school, back in town in Cannon Beach. Sam was a bit perturbed by this, for she was now unable to spend any time with her best friend. Sam saw the effect Micah was having on Adria, however. The two girls still talked at school and on the drive there in the mornings.

As Adria spent more and more time with Micah, she felt ecstatically happy. Her hair was still darker, but the nightmares seemed to vanish, almost over night. Sam noticed this as well, which only confirmed her decision that Micah was good for Adria.

Micah seemed unendingly interested in Adria. They spent long hours together talking. He asked her a million questions about her life, as if he were trying to catch up on everything he'd missed from the moment she was born. His stare was so intense as she talked, it unnerved Adria to no end, but as she continued spending time with him, she felt more relaxed, and she opened up to him in a way she never had with anyone before.

One afternoon, Adria took Micah down to Ecola State Park. They hiked the trails in the drizzly-gray afternoon gloom. They stopped at the head of the trail, after a good two-mile trek, and Adria pointed out a lighthouse on a rock, far out into the ocean.

"You see that? It's Terrible Tilly. That poor lighthouse has been battered by a thousand storms, probably. But it's still there."

"They don't light it anymore?" Micah asked.

"No, they stopped at some point. I can't remember when. Long before we were born. Some guy bought it, and turned it into a moratorium."

"What?" Micah laughed.

"Yeah, people pay to have their urns stored in there."

"Why?"

"Beats the shit out of me. I guess some people want to be buried in a lighthouse. Their ashes, anyway."

"Seriously?"

"Yeah, but several years back, there was this huge storm, when I was baby. My dad told me this. And the windows got broken in. Water went flooding through the whole lighthouse. Destroyed most of the urns, soaked the ashes. Urns were swept out to sea, never to be seen again."

"That sucks."

"Yeah," Adria laughed. "And now, the guy who owns the lighthouse? Anyone who wants to still have their ashes stored inside, has to sign a waiver saying they understand there's a good possibility that they'll end up being buried at sea."

"Shit," Micah shook his head. "How do you know all this stuff?"

"I read," Adria said. "There's nothing else to do around this place. It rains half the year, and then you're stuck inside. You have to find something to do, to pass the time. People come here in the summer, from Portland, from all over, really. It's nice for those three months or so. They think we live in this seaside paradise. They don't see the winter."

"It's not so bad," Micah said. "It lends to the atmosphere. I like it dark. I can hide."

"What are you hiding from?"

Adria looked at Micah in concern and curiosity. He shrugged.

"The inevitability of my life."

The drizzle fell all around Micah. His hair was wet, hanging in thick rat-tails all around his face, droplets of water falling from the ends. His face was pale-white, but his cheeks had pink color pulled up by the chill in the air. Almost imperceptible puffs of steam spouted from his nostrils as he breathed out warm air into the cold. He was beautiful.

He looked at Adria and she radiated life. Her own breaths came out in warm clouds of steam, her green eyes bright in the dimpled light of the sun, as it played peek-a-boo with the clouds. Her cheeks were also high with color from the cold, her face equally as pale as his. Her heart raced. She longed for him, and she still could not comprehend why.

Micah saw her look, and his face filled with sadness. His dark brown eyes shone with wetness. He looked disappointed, and he turned away. Adria frowned. Shouldn't he have attempted to kiss her?

They made their way back up the trail and he drove her in his van, dropping her off at her father's house. She invited him in. He looked at her, unsure.

"My dad's cool. You should really meet him."

She begged him with her eyes. He nodded, wanting to please her.

Inside, Adria introduced Micah to her dad. He was still in his uniform, as he'd just gotten off his shift. He had short, salt and peppered, brown hair. He shook Micah's hand.

"The name's Richard, but you can call me Mr. Allan. You want to stay for supper?"

Micah nodded.

"You need to call your folks, run it by them?"

Micah nodded and used the phone. At the dinner table, Mr. Allan launched into a tale about his work the night before.

"Jayzus H. Key-rist, last night was a hullaballoo. Damn great night, too, let me tell you. Micah, you see this uniform? I am a proud Oregon State Trooper, Fish and Wildlife. So is Adria's mom, did she tell you that?"

Micah nodded. Mr. Allan continued.

"Well, it didn't work out betwixt us, but we still work pretty well together. Today, at least. Always crossing paths. Like last night. I'm an OSP pilot, see. I'm up in my Cessna 206, with my infrared. You go at night, and they can't see your plane, see? Don't even know you're there. That's how we catch 'em. Always go at night, 'cause the stupid fuckers, sorry, excuse my mouth, the stupid shits, think they're invisible. But not to me. Eyes in the sky, that's what they call me. Eyes in the sky."

Mr. Allan took a long drag off his beer bottle and smiled, shaking his head. He set the bottle back down and belched. Adria smiled. Micah smiled as well. He liked Adria's dad already. He was cool.

"Anyway," he belched while talking. "I got a whiff of them, got my spotlight on. I'm one mile up, night vision goggles. And Adria's mom is part of the ground support team I call in. They're my hands, see? Five thousand feet up in the air, I'm eyes in the sky, they're my hands on the ground. I spot the shits, and tell ground OSP where to go. They track these fuckers down, and I land, and when I get there, it's all over with.

"Know what they found? A god damned uncle and nephew, illegally huntin' at night. In their vehicle, they've got rifles with rounds in the chambers, alcohol, marijuana, and ecstasy. In the flatbed of the truck, we find 2 does. A doe and a young faun, in fact. They god damned shot bambie and her mother. Fuckers.

"You wouldn't believe what we find, when we catch these shitters. Everything you can think of. Black bears, eagles, fish, bucks, all off-season, of course. Cougars. It pisses me off. That's why they need us. We help preserve nature, keep a balance going. I take what I do very seriously. I love my job."

There was silence at the table for several moments. Then Mr. Allan belched again and looked at Micah.

"So, what does your dad do?"

"He runs a resort hotel," Micah said.

"Oh," Mr. Allan said, and then grew quiet. "Okay, then."

****

After dinner, Adria took Micah up to her room. Mr. Allan didn't seem to mind at all. The only thing he said, as the couple headed upstairs was, "I trust you, Adria."

"Thanks, dad," she said.

In her room, Micah looked around, intensely interested in all her things. She watched him, marveling. He looked at the photos on her wall.

"Those are from when I was little, when my parents were still together."

Micah looked at the rows and rows of CD's lining the shelves of the wall closest by her door. Then he glanced at a full keyboard in the far-left corner of her room, next to her desk. His eyes traveled to her guitar, sitting in its stand, in the other left corner of her room, near her bed. He looked at Adria, his face questioning. She blushed.

"You play guitar?"

"Yeah, my dad taught me. Even had me in lessons for several years. I stopped about a year ago."

"Why?"

"I just got busy," she said. "I play keyboard, too. But I just taught myself. I have a good ear," she said, attempting to change the subject.

Micah walked over and stood in front of Adria, looking down at her intensely. She thought he was finally going to kiss her, and she waited, breathless. He only kept looking at her, however, his eyes shining and wondrous.

"Why did you stop playing?"

"I didn't stop playing, I just stopped taking lessons," Adria said.

She was confused by Micah's behavior. He continued looking at her, making her feel flushed and claustrophobic. With the anticipation of his kiss fast removed, his close proximity only made her feel panicked; crowded. She took a step back, flustered.

"Why did you stop taking lessons?" he pressed.

"Because we couldn't afford them," Adria said, sounding annoyed and angry.

"Why?" Micah's voice was so gentle and understanding, Adria wanted to slap him. She didn't answer him.

"Why," he asked again.

"Because," she said, her voice low. "Because I had to go into therapy."

"What for?"

"Bad dreams."

"What kind of bad dreams?"

Adria looked at Micah and frowned. He looked at her with sympathy. She looked away, at her guitar and sighed.

"Music makes me feel better," she said, changing the subject again. "It's my passion."

"Your passion?" Micah seemed very interested.

"Yeah," Adria said. "I guess it's sort of, my defining characteristic. You know? It's who I am."

"Tell me," Micah said, leaning against her desk.

"Okay."

It was much easier for her to talk about her music than her bad dreams. She was not afraid of having an audience. She walked over to her guitar and picked it up, carrying it over to her bed, where she sat on the edge and strummed a few chords to check the tuning. Micah smiled.

"You heard what my dad said, right? About being an OSP pilot? Eyes in the sky, and all that?"

She played all the while, and Micah's smile widened. He felt as if he was watching an unplugged concert. He nodded. Adria nodded back.

"Well, there's this song, Eye in the Sky, by Alan Parson's Project?"

Micah shrugged. Adria's eyes widened. She continued to strum.

"We need to educate you, then. Anyway, my dad loves that song, because of his job. So I heard it all the time. But I like to slow things down, you know? Take fast rock songs, and slow them down a bit, make them more, earthy. This is my version of Eye in the Sky."

Micah listened as Adria began to play. It was lyrical and beautiful, and as she began to sing, he was surprised and impressed by the emotion in her voice. She was in her own world, he saw. She was in love, enraptured.

When she was done, he stared at her. She frowned, setting her guitar down next to her, leaning it up against the bed.

"You didn't like it?"

Micah surprised her then. He stood and walked over to Adria, who immediately stood from her bed to meet him, her heart racing. He kissed her with passion and her whole world melted away. They kissed for several moments. Then Micah pulled away, attempting to restrain himself.

"It's okay," she said.

"No, it isn't," he said, looking sad and disappointed.

Adria frowned, her own disappointment filling her. Then she softened, smiling. It was Micah's turn to frown.

"You know what song I'm hearing now? Sailed On."

Micah continued frowning. Adria looked at him in wonderment.

"You've never heard Landon Pigg?"

Micah shook his head. Adria passed him and sat down at her computer, turning it on.

"Sit down, 'cause it's gonna be a long night."

Micah sat on Adria's bed and smiled. He loved her. He always had. As she booted up her computer, she continued talking, in an animated fashion, excited; on fire.

"I always have music playing in my head. Always. It's kind of this weird thing about me. Sam knows about it. She thinks it's cool. Anyway, I'm going to go to state for college, probably at Eugene. They have a decent music program there. I'm gonna major in music. Become a teacher, I guess. But I like to write songs, and I'm saving up my money for some decent recording equipment. To help finance my way through school, and make some money on the side, you know? I'll release some MP3's, try and sell my songs."

"Wow," Micah said, sounding sad. "You like, have your whole future planned out."

"Don't you?" Adria said, looking over her shoulder.

"What?"

"Have your future planned?"

"Not so much, lately," Micah said, his voice soft, sad.

"Well, it's right around the corner."

"What?" he asked.

"Graduation," Adria said. "Next year."

"Yeah…"

"The end is fast approaching," Adria said, sounding dramatic.

Micah smiled at Adria's humor, but it quickly faded as he took in her statement fully. She looked at him, frowning again. Then she turned around and pulled up a song, sighing.

"Music is timeless," she said.

"So are we," Micah's voice was sad. Adria frowned, again ignoring his statement.

"Okay, listen up, 'cause you're about to get educated, Adria-style."

For the rest of the night, which was several hours, Adria played music for Micah, from all different eras. It was overwhelming and eclectic, and wonderful. Adria's love for music was contagious. Some of the songs, he recognized, although Adria could not have guessed how deep the recognition ran. At times, Micah's face would cloud over, and she would find herself looking at him, attempting to discern what floated just behind his eyes.

Much of the music, however, was from modern bands and self-published songwriters that Micah had never heard before. They were all wonderful, however, and with Adria's relentless onslaught of tutorage, over the next few weeks, it wasn't long before Micah found himself walking around with music constantly playing inside his head all the time, as well.

****

Over the next several days, Micah and Adria walked together, talked, laughed, and listened to music. They took long drives in Micah's black van up and down the Sunset Highway, through the drizzle and almost constant rain. Their skin was always damp, their hair, matted.

They drove on the two-lane highway, which rolled over hill after hill of thick forest, dense with foliage. They felt swallowed up by the forest on certain stretches of the road. Always, as they reached Cannon Beach junction, and parted ways with Highway 26 and the 101, they both smiled at the first glimpse of the ocean as it came into view. Micah pointed to a tall rock outcropping on the beach, in the distance, one day.

"What is that?"

"That rock?"

"Yeah."

"That's Haystack Rock," Adria said. "Shit, I need to take you down there. But, you'll need boots, especially this time of year."

"What song are you hearing now?" Micah smiled.

"Sentimental Lady," Adria smiled. "Bob Welch?"

Micah shook his head, his smile broad. He loved how Adria always had a song playing in her head.

"Well, let's put that one down on the list, then," Adria said.

****

The next day, Adria showed up at Micah's door holding a pair of rubber, knee-high boots. She held them out for him to take. It was the weekend.

"I borrowed them from my dad," she said.

They drove down to Cannon Beach and walked along the sand. The sun was peaking out intermittently from behind the clouds. There was no rain today, but the air was crisp and cool. A slight breeze blew Micah's thick scud of dark bangs into his eyes.

"You ever thought of cutting your hair?" Adria teased.

"Hell, no," Micah said. "That's *my* trademark."

"Bangs in your face, that's your trademark," Adria said, sounding amused.

"Yep," Micah said. "It's not much, so you have to give it to me," he laughed.

"Fine."

They reached Haystack Rock and walked around the far side. It was low tide. The water on the far side of the rock, facing the ocean, was still about two feet deep, however. Adria waded in, unperturbed. Micah held back, watching her. Then he looked at the ocean with trepidation.

"What's wrong?" Adria said, turning to look at him.

"Are you sure this is safe? What if the tide comes back in?"

"It's dead low tide right now, Micah. Water won't be coming back in for another thirty minutes. Come on."

Micah reluctantly followed her around the rock, continuing to cast cursory glances out at the ocean. On the far side, to right of center, the sheer rock face opened up, into a cave.

"Whoa," Micah said.

They ventured into the maw. The sun filtered in through cracks in the rock, emitting slats of light that illuminated the cavern within. Streams of seawater drifted past their boots, in small channels, headed out to sea.

The air smelled of salt and seaweed. Micah closed his eyes, breathing it in. Adria waded over to a crop of various colored sea anemones and hunkered down to look at them. She poked one with the tip of her finger and its soft, waving tendrils closed up. Micah hunkered down next to her to watch. She touched the small, feathery fans of a rock barnacle scavenging for particles, and it pulled its fan inside and closed itself up. She smiled, and Micah sighed his own pleasure, smiling as well.

"You see?" Adria said, turning her face to look at him. "It's a whole different world out here."

"Yeah," he said, looking at her with intense affection.

Adria had no expectations of any kind today. She did not expect Micah to kiss her. He hadn't kissed again, not since the first night in her room, when she'd played for him. She'd given up hoping. In a strange way, she did not mind, however. She was simply overwhelmed, already, by his company. She'd grown so used to him, so fast, she couldn't even remember what her life had been like before Micah arrived.

He surprised her now, by kissing her and gently placing his hand on her jaw and caressing her face. She kissed him back, but not nearly as eagerly as before. She held back quite a bit. He pulled away and looked at her, concerned.

"Are you okay?"

"Yeah," she said, looking down at the water pool at the edge of her boots. "You're just, really confusing me, you know?"

"I'm sorry," he said. "I just, don't know how to proceed with this."

"Do you like me?" she asked.

He looked at her intensely, and she blushed. He never gave her any verbal answer.

"Then, I don't understand," Adria said. "Why are you so hesitant?"

"It's hard to explain," Micah said. "I don't think you would understand, or even believe me."

"You could try giving me the benefit of the doubt," Adria said, feeling hurt.

"Not with this," he said. His voice was so soft, she wanted to throw herself into his arms and bury herself there.

His eyes were sad and pleading. She knew he was hiding something. He'd told her once this was what he wanted – to hide.

"Try me," she said.

He did not speak again, he only took her face in his hands and kissed her, once more. This time, she relented, reciprocating. Micah was so overcome with the act of kissing her, he leaned forward. His knee splashed down into the cold water, as he forgot where he was, and shifted his weight off his feet, attempting to sit. His pants were soaked in freezing water.

"Shit!"

Adria laughed, standing and putting her hand out to help him up.

"Come on," she said, pulling him up. "You can dry off at my house, and I'll educate you on Bob Welch."

****

In Micah's van, Adria smiled. She felt radiant and alive. Micah looked at her, smiling himself, despite being extremely damp and cold.

"Song?"

"One Fine day," she responded, needing no further cue. "David Byrne and Brian Eno."

She looked at Micah and he shook his head. She scoffed.

"What the fuck do you listen to, Micah?"

"You."

"Jesus," she said, lost in his face, his voice, his eyes.

****

In her room, she played Micah her music, putting on the songs they'd discussed. Then she took her guitar out and played a slow, lyrical version of Chicago's, 'If You Leave Me Now,' that was so different from the original, Micah didn't even recognize it at first.

"Please tell me you've heard that song before," Adria said, setting her guitar down.

"Of course," Micah said. "But I like your version ten times better," his voice was sad, his face shadowed.

"Thanks," she said. "I love music. I heard a quote once that said, 'music is the soundtrack of our lives,' or something like that. I always have something playing in my head. There's never silence. Never."

Micah smiled, listening. Adria sighed, pressing on.

"I like to play with music, change it around. You know, reinvent it? Take songs people know and make them mine."

"Like sampling," Micah said.

"No," Adria said, frowning. "You mean, like, techno?"

Micah nodded.

"Yeah, that's what they do," he said. "They take a song, and change it around. Add a beat. Take a slow song and turn it into a rave fest." Micah smiled.

"No," Adria said. "That's not what I do. Techno is crap. Is that what you listen to?"

"Sometimes," he said.

"Well, shit," Adria said. "I wish you had told me that before you ever kissed me."

Micah frowned, but Adria smiled.

"Techno is not cool. You can't just take a cool song, like, 'Eye in the Sky,' for example, and just stick it to a fast beat. That's crap."

"No, it's fun," Micah said. "Haven't you ever been to a rave?"

"No," Adria frowned. "Why, have you?"

"All the time, back in Ohio," Micah said. "Akron's got a slammin' rave scene goin' on."

"Really," Adria said, eyeing Micah. "You're a rave boy? Huh."

"What's wrong with that?"

"Nothing," Adria said.

She stood up from her bed and walked over to Micah, who was leaning on her desk. She was aggressive for the first time in the relationship. She approached him and kissed him, and he kissed her back. He moved his hands to place them on her back, but they hovered in the air, inches from her body, shaking. He was attempting to hold himself at bay, but his lips continued kissing her, for several more moments. Then he regained his composure, and he pulled his face away from hers, looking down and away. This time, Adria had taken enough.

"What," she said, her jaw set, her voice angry.

"Nothing," Micah said.

"Bullshit," Adria spat, backing away. "This is bullshit."

"No," he said, his voice soft. She wanted to beat the shit out of him.

"What!" she yelled.

Micah stood fully upright, an angry fire dancing alive inside his eyes. Adria saw the heat flash and she recognized it from the day he'd fought with Westley Kane. She backed away from him, afraid. Micah saw her look and grew even more angry, yet he pulled back at the same time, controlling himself.

"You think I'm going to hurt you, Adria?" he said, sounding both angry and sad.

"I don't know," she said.

"I'm not gonna hurt you," Micah said. "Don't you see? That's what this is all about. I shouldn't even be here."

"What are you talking about?" Adria yelled.

"I'm talking about this. I'm talking about us. We just keep doing this over and over, and it always ends the same."

"What always ends the same?" Adria screamed.

"Nothing," Micah said, "never mind, I have to go."

"No!"

Adria walked to her bedroom door, cutting Micah off from leaving. He had tears in his eyes and he looked up at her from a downward glare. Her heart broke for him, and she felt all the air rush from her lungs – deflated. She couldn't breathe. Micah looked broken.

"Please, let me leave," Micah said.

"Why?" Adria said. Her voice was shaking. She was on the verge of tears, her confusion, anger and longing were so great.

"Why are you being like this?" she said.

"Because, if I don't leave now, it will all happen, again," Micah said. "If you love me, you'll let me go."

Adria looked at Micah in surprise. Was he acknowledging the obvious fact that she was in love with him? Tears welled up in her eyes and spilled down her cheeks. Micah looked at her with the utmost concern and sadness. He rushed forward and embraced her. Then he spun her around, away from the door, released his hold on her body and left her room. Adria stood, in total shock, as he went.

5. November 7-11, 2009

As the week of Adria's seventeenth birthday rolled around, Sam found herself having to console her best friend. It had only taken two weeks for Adria to fall head-over-heels in love with a young man, who was now ignoring her. Sam was pissed.

In the hallways at school, whenever Sam saw Micah, she glared at him as he passed her. He would walk by Adria's locker, glancing and attempting to coax a smile, but she always looked away, not meeting his gaze.

"What the fuck is he trying to do?" Sam exclaimed one day. "Still be friends? Idiot. You're better off."

Sam looked at Adria in concern. Her friend was not fairing well with the breakup. Adria shrugged at Sam's comment and walked away.

In second period history, Micah would often turn around to look at Adria, but she would look down, pretending to read her textbook. Micah looked miserable after the first several days of this dance between them. He never smiled, and his countenance and complexion looked not much better than Adria's.

Meanwhile, Adria's nightmares made a sudden, unexpected return. This time, Sam was ready. She came to Adria's house two days before Adria's birthday, on November 10, and handed her a present wrapped in blue paper.

"What's this?"

"An early birthday present," Sam said.

Adria opened it and held a journal in her hands, as if it were a foreign object. She looked at Sam, her eyes sad and empty.

"Forget about psycho-hunk," Sam said. "It's a journal. For your dreams."

Adria looked down at the floor. They were in her room. Sam sat down next to Adria on the edge of her bed.

"I know you're having bad dreams again. Your hair has gotten darker."

"They started right after Micah left me," Adria began to cry.

"He didn't leave you, Adria. He was never here. The guy's a jerk, obviously. He just likes playing with you."

Sam hugged Adria as she sobbed. She closed her eyes, feeling her friend's pain. Sam had hoped Micah was the solution to Adria's ailments, as her composure seemed to brighten the moment Adria first saw him. Now, Adria was worse off than ever, and Sam was beside herself, not knowing what to do. She spoke to Adria over her shoulder, as her friend continued sobbing. As she held Adria, her eyes drifted first to her guitar in the corner, then to the keyboard.

"Adria, you still have your music. It's gotten you through this in the past. You can use it now, to help."

"I already have," Adria said. "I wrote a song."

"You did?"

Adria nodded, pulling away to look at Sam in trepidation.

"But, you won't like it. It will upset you."

"Why?" Sam frowned.

"It's just what came out," Adria shrugged. "It doesn't mean anything."

"I want to hear it," Sam said.

Adria looked at Sam for a moment, and then sighed. She got up and sat down at her keyboard.

"Piano seemed more fitting for this one," she said over her shoulder.

Adria turned her keyboard on and set it to piano, adjusting the volume. She began, playing lyrical, soft chords. Sam smiled. What was so bad about this? Then Adria began to sing. As the lyrics continued on, Sam's smile quickly faded.

"I, I woke up this morning late,
made myself some toast, that I never ate.
I went into, my living room,

sat on the couch, and thought of you.
My best friend, said that this would happen,
but I didn't believe her, now you're gone.
You said, that you would be in love,
with me forever, you were wrong.
And I,
I don't want to feel like this for another minute, 'cause
you and I,
aren't coming back and I'm really sick of it.
I wrote a note, and put it by my bed,
with your name on it, I can't remember what it said.
I went into, my bathroom,
closed the door, and locked it, too.
Turned on the water, then I brushed my hair,
turned it up a little hotter, it's almost there.
For one last time, I took off all my clothes,
this moment's mine, I'm all exposed.
And I,
I don't want to feel like this for another minute, 'cause
you and I,
aren't coming back, and I'm really sick of it.
It doesn't hurt, well maybe a little bit,
but that doesn't matter now, I'm sick of all this shit. It's
other things, I mean it's not just you,
this little girl, just wants it through.
To mom and dad, it wasn't either of you,
so please try not to be sad,
there was nothing you could do.
It's almost time, it's almost here,
I feel a little sad, but I have no fear.
'Cause I,
I don't want to feel like this for another minute. There's
too much time,
to feel like shit, and I'm really sick of it.
It's all been said, I'm slipping away,
the water's red, nothing left to say.
I'm tired now, like I'm going to bed,

and in a moment now, I'll be.... "

Adria stopped singing and ended the song with a few last, slow piano chords that echoed in the small room. Sam sat, frozen, staring at Adria's back for several, long, shocked moments. She swallowed audibly. Adria turned her head around and looked at Sam with fear.

"Okay, listen to me, Adria," Sam's voice was shaking. "Don't argue with me, because this is too far gone for arguing, now. I want you to start keeping a journal of your dreams. Got it? Every time you have one. I want you to get up, and write it down. As much detail as you can remember, okay? I want you to do this, for me."

Sam looked Adria in the eyes. Her chin was quivering. Adria stood and sat back down next to her on the edge of the bed.

"It's just a song," Adria said. "I would never really do that. It's just what came out. It helps to deal with the dreams. You know how they all end."

"Promise me," Sam said, unflinching. "I believe it will help. You have to try. Please?"

Adria nodded her agreement and Sam sighed in relief. She would never lie to her. It was one thing Sam was certain of. If she made Sam a promise, Adria would keep it.

"Adria?" Sam said.

"Yeah."

Silence. Then Adria spoke again.

"He said if I really loved him, I'd let him go."

Adria crumbled. "I don't want to be without him."

"Oh, babe," Sam said. Another beat of silence. "Song?"

"Exit Music, by Radiohead," Adria said, and she seemed to calm down a bit. Sam, however, was not relieved by the choice of music in Adria's head.

****

November 11, 2009

At school the next day, Sam marched up to Micah's locker and slammed it shut in his face, almost taking his fingers off. He jumped back, looking at her in shock.

"What the fuck?"

"Exactly. What the fuck?" Sam yelled. "What the fuck is wrong with you, huh? You remember what I told you before? I told you if you ever hurt Adria, I'd fuck you up the ass, you fucking cunt."

"Jesus," a boy said as he walked by the two teens.

"Take it easy, Sam," Micah said, trying to calm her down. He kept his voice low, but she continued yelling.

"No, you have royally fucked her up," Sam said. "Do you have any idea what she was going through before you came here? No, you don't. I bet you never even bothered asking, did you?"

"As a matter of fact, I did," Micah said, growing angry.

"You have no clue," Sam said, challenging him.

"Are you talking about the dreams?" Micah said.

"Wh…" Sam stammered, but she couldn't finish.

Micah looked at Sam, the fire leaving his eyes. She looked at him with suspicion.

"What do you think you're talking about?" she asked, her voice shaking.

"She told me she had bad dreams," Micah said. "I can only imagine. I can only imagine they were fairly similar to mine."

"What are you talking about?" Sam stared.

"Look, I didn't come here to hurt Adria," Micah said. "Don't you see; that's what this is all about? I can't. I can't be near her anymore. If I am, things will happen. Very bad things. She can't be around me. I should never have even spoken to her. I just couldn't help myself."

"She's in love with you," Sam said, crying now.

"I know," Micah said, lowering his eyes.

"Song?" Sam asked, looking hopeful.

"Distance, by Editors." Micah looked infinitely sad.

Sam watched in disbelief as tears fell from Micah's eyes. Her eyes widened. He'd answered her question without hesitation, and suddenly Sam knew something very powerful was happening.

"You're in love with her," Sam said.

Micah looked away. She looked at him, pleading.

"Then why?"

He shook his head.

"Please, she is my best friend," Sam said. "I am *losing* her."

"If I do what you want me to, you *will* lose her," Micah said. Without further warning, he turned and walked away.

Sam looked after Micah, watching him go. There were tears in her eyes, a frown on her face. She was beginning to understand the level of insanity that went hand-in-hand with Adria's confusion. Sam felt half-mad herself.

****

In the cafeteria that day, the old Micah presented itself like a hurricane blowing in. He sat in the far right corner, on the end of a table, away from everyone. Sam looked at him, rolling her eyes. She looked at Adria, who only looked down, her face buried in a book. She was not eating.

"Fucker," Sam whispered under her breath. Adria didn't even notice.

Micah stood then and quickly headed towards the cafeteria's exit. As he passed the table where Westley Kane sat, the jock stuck his foot out and tripped him. Micah went flying, but was up in a flash, quickly turning on Westley like a wild wolverine.

It had been almost a month since Micah fought with Westley. The fire that had started the brawl, quickly died inside Micah as he spent all his time with Adria. Westley Kane, however, had been brooding. He'd been made into a fool, beaten by a strange new boy, who, in Westley's eyes, was much smaller and weaker. He'd been humiliated. After all, a considerable amount of blood had been shed during that fight and none of it had belonged to Micah.

To make matters worse, Micah had somehow managed to get off without a suspension. He'd gotten detention for one day. Westley was not sure how Micah had pulled this off, but he wasn't about to let things go. He'd been biding his time, deciding how to handle things. Today, he'd had enough. It was time to redeem himself.

Micah launched himself over the table Westley sat at. He was no longer spending long hours with Adria. His heart was broken, the old rage and fire that lived inside him, wide-awake. Westley Kane had no idea who he was dealing with, or what he was attempting to play at. He'd mistakenly thought that if he picked the fight this time, he'd be ready for it. He was not, however, ready for the level of insanity that resided inside Micah.

First off, Westley didn't expect Micah to get up as quickly as he did. He also expected Micah to stand, inviting the fight. This is what he'd done the first time. Westley did not expect to trip the young man, and within moments, have Micah on top of the table, pummeling him. He had highly underestimated Micah, and he immediately knew it.

The cafeteria erupted in loud cheers and yells, as people rushed from their seats to surround the two boys. Adria looked up from her book, dazed. Sam only rolled her eyes.

"This is a fucking circus," Sam said. "Ridiculous. Look at these blood whores."

The two girls could not see anything from where they sat, however. Inside the ring, Westley toppled off his table seat, with Micah right on top of him. Westley's head was slammed to the floor and he felt dazed. His face felt like a punching bag. His nose was broken, his cheeks immediately swollen in large, bruised lumps, his eyes already darkening and swelling as well.

The cheers of "fight-fight-fight-fight," quickly faded, as the students watched in horror while Micah continued beating Kane to a complete pulp.

"He's killing him!" one girl exclaimed.

The room was deadly silent now. The only sound was the sickening, meat-thud of Micah's fists, continuing to hit Kane's face. The crowd watching felt a uniform, shocked nausea begin to wave through them, as if they were all psychically linked, if only for those few, short moments. Several students looked at one another, their eyes wide and scared.

A group of boys standing together looked at one another, and without saying a word, four of them nodded, then together, in unison, they stepped forward and grabbed Micah's arms, two boys to an arm, and pulled him off.

Shocked students stood around, their faces and mouths covered by their hands, taking in the gruesome scene. Several more boys stepped forward to aid the four that now struggled with Micah. It took six boys, in the end, to overpower Micah completely. His entire body shook with rage.

Westley Kane lay on the floor, his face an unrecognizable, raw, bloody mess. His breathing came in small gurgles from the back of his blood-filled throat. Several girls ran from the cafeteria, sobbing.

"Jesus," Sam whispered. "This is bad."

Adria sat, her book now limp in her hands, watching the entire scene unfold. Micah was dragged off, out of the cafeteria. An ambulance was called to take Kane away.

"Micah's out of this school, now, for sure," Sam said, her voice low and sad. "Jesus, what a fucking psycho."

Adria said nothing. She stood and walked out of the cafeteria.

6. November 12-December 1, 2009

Adria's seventeenth birthday came and went. She celebrated it quietly with her mother and Sam. Her father dropped by and left a present for her, hugging her. Then he left. She would be at his place the following week.

When Adria opened the small box, she found a necklace inside, with a heart-shaped pendant. It was a mood pendant. She read the small card inside the box. It read, 'for the changing mood of your beautiful heart,' and Adria cried.

Her nightmares continued unabated for the next two weeks, almost nightly. They were attacking with a vengeance now, and Sam watched with growing dread and concern, as Adria's hair turned from dark blonde, to light brown. The darker hair was no longer streaked in sparsely, but seemed to be taking over. Adria's eyes were dark and sunken, once more.

She kept her promise to Sam, however. Every morning that she awoke from her nightmares, she grabbed her journal from the nightstand next to her bed, and scribbled as quickly as she could, in as much detail as she could remember, her dreams. She wrote madly, filling page after page. By the end of the second week of doing this, the journal was already almost full. She wrote the same dreams down, over and over again, sometimes recalling new details here and there, many times, simply repeating the same descriptions again and again. When the journal was nearly full, Adria grew weary of writing things down.

She handed her journal to Sam one morning at her locker. Sam looked at Adria's pallid face and her eyes filled with tears.

"You're not thinking about doing anything stupid, are you?"

"Like what," Adria asked. Her eyes looked empty.

"You know what I mean."

"I wouldn't do that," Adria said. "I have too much to live for."

But Adria's voice sounded devoid of any real emotion. She looked at Sam, and it was as if she were looking straight through her. Sam opened up the journal and frowned at the yellow sticky note with scribbling inside. It read, 'Something I Can Never Have, NIN.' Sam looked at Adria with fear and the utmost concern.

"It's just a song," Adria shrugged, and walked away.

****

Sam poured over Adria's journal for the next several days. She rushed through it, desperately looking for an answer, any answer she could possibly find. The entries were graphic and disturbing. Sam spent hours upon hours in her own room, closing her eyes, trying to see the images the way Adria did. She pulled out small details here and there, and kept her own notes in a separate journal. She went online and researched information. She drove into Seaside and did further research at the public library there.

Then Sam went to the Cannon Beach Cemetery and visited the grave of Lynn Allan, who had died almost two years ago by this point. It was only after her aunt's death, that Adria began having her nightmares. She'd been to therapy, along with her mother, who had lost her only sister when Lynn died. Adria's mother, however, had faired much better after several sessions, than Adria had.

Sam stared at the tombstone of Lynn Allan and sighed. She couldn't understand what had kicked this all off. After several minutes, she left the grave and wandered among the other tombstones. She looked at the various names and wondered who the people had been, when they were alive. She wondered about their stories. Then she smiled.

They were all locals, some of the graves dating back to the mid-eighteen hundreds. Chances were, that Adria would already know about some of them, with how much she'd read about their hometown and its history. Adria had wandered among the graves herself, the day of Lynn's funeral.

Sam frowned then, thinking hard. She'd come across some fairly disturbing facts in her research lately. She'd already formulated some very odd hypotheses on Adria's condition, that were so out there, Sam was more willing to dismiss them, than even attempt to truly entertain them. Now, she began to have a sinking suspicion that her theories might not be so crazy after all.

"Everything started here," Sam whispered. "She saw something that sparked her memories."

She took out her notebook and a pen and began scribbling madly, the various names on several of the tombstones. Her pen flew with desperation and urgency.

"Before 1906," she whispered.

If anyone had been there to witness her statement, or the look on her face as she dashed through the cemetery, recording names, they would have thought that Sam Keegan had lost her mind.

Her research continued after she left the graveyard. Sam went to the Cannon Beach Historical House and looked up information on several of the names she'd recorded. She went back home and lay down in her bed, closing her eyes. Sam played several of the dreams out in her head, using the descriptions in Adria's journal.

****

February 15, 1929 –New York City, New York

Rain gently fell on the pavement. Crowds lined the sidewalks. Faces streamed by, strangers who never made eye contact. A large crowd of theatregoers began streaming out into the vestibule, many remaining to stand around, discussing the live performance with their friends or family.

A young couple, in their early twenties, walked out of the theatre, hand-in-hand. They walked down the sidewalk, past the milling crowds. On the corner they stopped, waiting to cross the street. Behind them, a newspaper stand exclaimed out in bold, black letters the latest news.

St. Valentine's Day Massacre

This was all the young woman had time to read, before she heard her fiancé calling her. The light had changed, and he was already standing just off the sidewalk. He was holding his hand out for her to take, to help her across the street.

He smiled at her, his eyes full of love. She smiled back, her heart bursting with joy. She looked down at her left-hand ring finger, and watched the small diamonds of her new ring twinkle in the street lights of the mid-evening, feeling enraptured. She looked up at the man, her smile widening. He saw her smile and his own smile broadened. His hand was no longer held out to hers. His arms now lay limp at his sides, as he gazed at his new fiancée in wonder, awe and total love. It had just begun to rain, lightly, but neither of them noticed.

She frowned then, as she heard a car's horn. She looked to her right, and saw a model ford speeding toward the corner, the inhabitants inside all laughing. The driver was looking at a pretty lady standing by a wastebasket at the newsstand, several feet back down the sidewalk.

As she looked on, she saw the car collide with her fiancé, and everything became an instant blur. Her heart stopped. She ran into the street, where he had been thrown several feet. As she passed the ford, she glanced at its windshield. He must have collided with the glass, flying up on the hood, she had time to think sickly to herself. The glass was broken into triangular shards, and she could see smears of red on some.

She ran to his side, as he lay in the street, bleeding. Most of the blood was being washed away by the rain, which was now coming down much harder. She looked at his face, beginning to cry. The glass had cut him badly about the neck and face. Blood was pouring from the side of his neck, just under his jaw. He looked at her, gasping. She could see that he was trying to tell her something. She leaned down, closer, her own tears blending with his blood and the rain.

"Follow me," he whispered, the blood gurgling in his throat.

She looked into his eyes and he saw a promise there. He smiled at her, and she smiled back, tears streaming down her face.

"I'll find you," she whispered.

His eyes shone with joy, just for another moment. Then they grew dull and lifeless. There was a large crowd around the couple now. Several people were screaming at the gruesome sight of the dead man now lying in the street. All traffic at the intersection had come to a halt.

The woman looked around, desperate. She knew she was running out of time. She didn't know exactly how she knew this, but she was aware of this fact, nonetheless. She looked down at the pavement and spied a shard of glass, near his body. She wondered if this was the very shard that had pierced his neck. It didn't matter.

She picked the glass up in her hands, and before anyone could stop her, or even realize what her intentions were, she fearlessly plunged the jagged-triangle end deep into her own neck. She buried it in her own flesh. Then she pulled it downward, roughly, ripping open a huge crevice in her throat. Blood spurted and poured out, and several onlookers fainted. A few turned and vomited into the street gutters.

She could feel the warm blood flowing down her front shoulder, soaking her bosom and torso, and it comforted her. She was floating quickly away, finding peace. Even as she took her final breath, she could feel his presence, near. She smiled, knowing she was flying to meet him.

****

Sam sat up in bed, feeling ill. She still needed more information. She was missing the key, she knew she was. She had almost everything she needed to convince Adria, but there was one key element she still had to track down. She went online again and did research on the Tillamook Indian tribe, specifically their myths and legends. She printed out articles, stories, and translations. Her head began to spin, as she went back to her notebook, reading over her information again. Finally, in complete exhaustion, she lay down to sleep, but she had troubling dreams of her own.

****

October 7, 1976 –Southern Methodist University, Dallas, Texas

The wind was light and cool on her face. She looked on in horror, however, as her boyfriend swung his fists at the frat guy. A circle of young men stood around, cheering and jeering. She was the only one rooting for him. He was winning, however. Despite the frat guy being much bigger, her boyfriend was winning. He was, after all, defending her honor.

They'd been kissing under a tree, and he had dared, in what they both thought was a place of complete privacy, to reach his hand under her skirt, drawing his fingers up her outer thigh, giving her the shivers. She sighed in delight, pressing her body even tighter against his, feeling his lips, his warmth. She was enraptured. The entire world had fallen away, and the last thing on her mind had been that someone might see them.

His hand had gone from her outer thigh, to her inner thigh, caressing her, making her sigh harder. He kissed her neck, and he gently inserted his hand into the top of her panties, now caressing her with his bare fingers. She moaned. Then the snickering could be heard, from behind the nearby bushes. A few loud, raucous laughs drifted to the couple, and the moment of eroticism quickly died.

He turned to look, as several frat brothers came out from behind the bushes. He gently pulled her skirt back down over her legs, covering her. She closed her eyes, embarrassed.

"Hey, man," one of the men said, "don't stop on our account. Go ahead. Fuck the cunt. We're just enjoying the show."

"Watch your mouth," he said. "That's my girlfriend you're talking about."

"Yeah? Well your girlfriend's a whore, friend. What kind of lady lets her nethers hang out for the whole world to see, huh?"

"Shut the fuck up!" he yelled, launching himself at the other man.

She watched in horror as the two began fighting. The rest of the peepers quickly formed a circle around the two fighters, and began chanting for their brother. She looked on, wishing this horrible event would be over soon.

He was winning. Despite the frat guy being much bigger, her boyfriend was winning. He was, after all, defending her honor. She could see the rage on his face. He had the other guy on the ground and he was on top of him, pummeling him. The frat guy's face was horribly bloodied by this point, and her boyfriend didn't look so much worse for the wear.

One of the cheer members stepped forward then, and kicked her boyfriend in the shoulder, sending him flying off the other guy, who stumbled to his feet, dazed and beaten to a pulp. From somewhere, she wasn't sure where it came from, a baseball bat was produced, and then, the bloody frat guy was back, wielding the stick in his hands.

She was bent down on the ground, trying to help him up when the frat guy came at the two of them, his face contorted in both humiliation and rage. She screamed, but at the same time, she threw herself over her boyfriend, to protect him from the blow. He was on his knees with his back to the guy, and hadn't even seen him coming. Someone grabbed her by the shoulders, however, and pulled her away.

As she struggled to pull her shoulders loose from the gripping hands, she watched as the bat swung downward, like an axe chopping wood on a block. It made contact with his skull with a sickening thud. There was a cracking sound, and she wasn't sure if it was the bat breaking, or his head. One blow was all it took.

She was released, and there was silence. Everyone stared down at the lifeless body of the young man. As she stumbled towards him, her stomach flip-flopped, taking in the now distorted shape of his skull. Blood ran down the sides of his down-turned face, onto his cheeks, and into the grass.

She looked up, dazed, and frowned at a large paper banner on the far building across the quad. Even from here, she could read the large, black painted letters.

'Congrats frats of Sigma Chi '76. Welcome to 3100 Binkley'

Then she vomited into the grass, turning to look at the frat brothers who'd just committed murder. They looked at her, then him, their eyes wide and disbelieving.

She went to his lifeless body, and knelt down, turning him over, looking at his face. His eyes were open, but empty and vacant. He was already gone. She hadn't even gotten to say goodbye. She bent down, kissed his lips, then stood and walked through the grass, across the quad, and entered the far building. No one tried to stop her.

She made her way up the side stairwell, to the top floor, to the roof access. She opened the door and burst out into the cool night, feeling the soft breeze blowing against her skin. She didn't have much time. Somehow she knew this, deep inside her heart and mind.

She was quick. She walked to the building's edge, stepped up and simply let herself fall, throwing her arms out to her sides, as if she were a bird taking flight. The wind rushed all around her, and she never felt the pain of her sudden landing. Her spirit was already flying to meet him, somewhere off in the ether.

7. December 2, 2009

It turned out that Sam didn't have to try and convince Adria of her crazy theories. On December 2, 2009, Adria's dreams took on a new life. She awoke from another nightmare, sweating and panting, shaking all over. When she went into the bathroom, she gasped at her image in the mirror. Her hair was light brown now, but there were several even darker strips of color running throughout, since the night before. Adria stared into her own eyes and didn't recognize herself.

"Celia?" she whispered.

She knew things – things that weren't in her dreams. She knew details upon waking that morning that she'd never been aware of before. She sat in her bathroom, frozen, frowning, thinking hard.

"John," she whispered, sucking in her breath.

She dressed and ran downstairs. Her mother was sitting at the dining room table with a mug of coffee. She hadn't made Adria breakfast. Adria had stopped eating any breakfast a few weeks before. She sat down at the table and looked at her mother with weary eyes.

"Mom?"

Emily Allan stared at her daughter, her eyes resigned and defeated. Adria attempted to coax a smile out of her and failed.

"You have an eating disorder, don't you?" Emily asked.

"What?"

"That's why your hair keeps changing. Anorexia causes hormone imbalances, especially in teenage girls who are still developing. Their hair tends to thin out, sometimes fall out, even. And sometimes it can change color," Emily said.

"Mom, that's silly."

"Is it?"

"Look, I'll eat if you want me to, okay?"

"You need help, Adria."

"Mom, I'm okay."

"No, you're not!" Emily yelled. "Look at you, Adria. You're thin, you're pale. You look like you haven't slept in days. I can hear you moaning and screaming in your sleep. These nightmares of yours, they're only getting worse."

"No, it's okay, mom," Adria said. "I think everything's going to be okay. Really."

"Why? How?" Emily looked at her daughter with pleading eyes. "Baby, I'm losing you. I can't lose you, honey. Please."

"Mom, I'm okay. Trust me, everything's going to be okay," Adria said.

She stood up and fixed herself a bowl of cereal. Then she sat back down and ate it, while Emily stared at her in surprise. Adria seemed cheerful. Emily was completely baffled.

"You're okay?" she blinked.

"Mm-hm," Adria said, slurping her milk with her spoon.

She finished eating, then put her bowl in the sink and kissed her mother's cheek. She smiled at Emily and this time, her mother smiled back, looking relieved.

"I'm gonna go wait outside for Sam, okay?"

"Okay, honey," Emily said. "I love you."

"I love you too, mom."

****

When Sam pulled up to Adria's house in her Prius, she was surprised to see Adria smiling. She rolled down her window as Adria walked up.

"Song?"

"Skyway, The Replacements," Adria said. "We need to talk."

"Yeah, we do," Sam said.

They drove to school in silence. As usual, they went to Adria's locker first. Sam had a notebook overflowing with loose papers stacked inside it. She opened it and handed another online printout of an old newspaper article to Adria, and waited. Adria read it. This time, she said nothing, only stared at the floor when she was done. Finally, Sam couldn't take the silence anymore.

"Devon Rogers and Sophie Prescott," she said. "They were college sweethearts at SMU in '76. Rogers got in a fight one night with this frat guy, and the guy hit him in the head with a baseball bat and killed him. Sophie Prescott was so overcome with grief, she immediately climbed to the roof of the frat house across the quad and swan dived. She killed herself, Adria. Right after her boyfriend died. Just like that couple in New York, in 1929, remember? They're real people, Adria. You're dreaming about real people, from the past, who've died."

"I know," Adria said.

"You know?" Sam frowned.

"I had another dream last night," Adria whispered. "And I woke up today, and I just knew things. I remembered."

"Adria, I don't think you're hearing me," Sam said. "Look I did a ton of research, on all your dreams. The ones with enough detail to track anything. I don't know about the Mexican couple, or the couple in Chicago. You didn't give me enough to track those ones down. Or the black couple, either. But these two other dreams? They're real people, Adria. You've seen the news articles.

"And I tracked down the birth dates of Devon Rogers and Sophie Prescott, by the way. And guess what? They were both born on the same day. Just like William Fenmore and Elizabeth Harris, from 1929."

"I know," Adria said. "I had a dream last night, Sam. The one about the black couple."

"And?" Sam asked, looking anxious.

"And I know her name," Adria said, pausing to take a deep breath. "*My* name. It was Celia. And his name was John. We lived on a farm in Virginia. I just know it now. Our families were slaves on different farms, before the emancipation. They stayed after, to work the fields anyway, for pay.

"We were kids. Then when I got old enough, I looked for work, on his farm, two miles away. We were only two miles away from each other, and never knew it, not until I went there.

"I was eighteen when I met him. He died two years later, before we ever got married. A farmer shot him – said he was poaching on his land. But the fence was down from a storm, and he just went a little too far over, chasing a rabbit that got freed from a trap, for our supper.

"I heard the shot, and went runnin'. When I got to 'im, he was layin' on the ground in the field. I held 'im, and the bullet'd gone clean through. I hugged 'im, and I could feel all his life running out of 'im, warm and sticky 'tween my fingers.

"I knew he was goin'. And then, suddenly, I knew I needed to go with 'im, if I ever wanted to see 'im agin. I haid to go quick, before the distance got too far.

"That farmer was just standin' there, lookin' down at me, at us. He never said nothin'. He never 'pologized. He wadn't sorry none. I stood up and walked right up t'im, spat in his face. I told 'im to shoot me."

"Adria," Sam whispered. She was scared. The longer Adria spoke, the more her voice became unrecognizable. She'd slowly begun to talk more and more with an emphasis of a southern drawl that did not fit Adria at all.

Her voice was high and reedy, and Sam thought of those ventriloquists that throw their voices while making the puppets talk on their laps. Adria went right on, not even hearing Sam, not even seeing her. Her eyes had a far off look in them.

"I told 'im to shoot me, go on. But he wouldn't. I grabbed that gun, pulled it right up t'ma chest. I told 'im to pull the trigger, but he just stood there, lookin' at me like I's crazy. So I reached my arm out, reached as far's I could, and leaned in good. I put m'thumb on that trigger, and I pulled. That's awl."

"Adria, you're scaring me," Sam said. "Who are you?"

Adria stood for several moments staring off into nothing. Then she blinked several times and looked at Sam in bewilderment. She smiled, and Sam was certain Adria had lost her mind.

"I remember," Adria said. Her voice was hers again. "I remember, Sam. It was 1899."

"We need to meet after school," Sam said. "I have to show you a lot of things. Okay?"

"Sure," Adria said. "I'll meet you at my car."

Adria gathered her books up and closed her locker, walking away. She left Sam to stand in the hallway alone, feeling lost and confused.

****

Sam went to find Micah. She was desperate. Micah had been gone, after the fight with Westley Kane, for two weeks. He showed up again, after Thanksgiving break, on November 29. When he reappeared in the hallways, everyone was shocked.

Somehow, Micah had managed to charm his way out of being expelled. Sam had no idea how this incredible feat had been pulled off. On the day Micah came back to school, Westley Kane still walked around with faded, yellow bruises on his face, vague signs still lingering from the humiliating beating he'd taken.

Today, Sam found Micah at his locker and she marched straight up to him. He looked at her with resignation, waiting for the yelling to begin.

"I need to talk to you at lunch time. Meet me in the art room, it will be empty."

Micah stared at Sam for several moments, unblinking.

"Don't be a no-show, or I'll kick your ass."

Micah looked at Sam for several more, long moments then nodded his consent.

****

At lunch, Micah showed up in the art room to find Sam pacing, waiting for him. When she saw him, she motioned for him to sit down at a table. She looked at him, shaking her head.

"How are you even here?" she asked. "You should be in juvy, after what you did to Kane's face."

"The family didn't press charges," Micah said, sounding ashamed. "My dad pulled the sympathy card, with my mother. That and a fair amount of money was exchanged."

"To the school, or Kane's family?" Sam frowned.

"Both," Micah met Sam's gaze, his eyes shiny with tears. "Let's just say, the first year of Kane's college tuition is covered."

"Minus yours," Sam's voice questioned.

"I'm not going to college," Micah said, looking down at the table.

Sam sighed and sat down across from him, launching into her speech without any further hesitation.

"I know what's going on here, Micah. I figured it all out. I started by doing research on some of Adria's dreams, the ones with enough details for me to track. She's dreaming about real people. Only now, she's flipped out, talking about them as if she *is* them."

"Wait, what?" Micah looked concerned.

"Just shut up and listen. This is all your fault. Well, not entirely, but, pretty much. Look, Adria started having her nightmares right after her aunt died, almost two years ago by this point. She was barely fifteen.

"I finally figured it out. She saw something, something when she was at the cemetery – something that triggered a series of memories inside of her, or maybe awakened them somehow.

"And I already figured out that the couple she dreamed about in New York were both born in 1906, on the same day. Later, I found out that the couple from 1976 was also born on the same day.

"Just like you and Adria."

Sam did not pause here, or wait to see if Micah was following her explanation. She continued on.

"Anyway, I reasoned, that whatever Adria saw in the cemetery, whoever's grave she saw, it had to be someone who died prior to 1906. I looked at all the graves, and wrote down all the names of people who died before that year.

Then, I found two graves that made my blood freeze. I found these graves, of this man and woman, who both died on the same day. Then it hit me. If all the couples Adria dreams about were born on the same day, and they all died on the same day, then this couple must have been what triggered her memories."

Sam looked at Micah, waiting for a response. He looked back at her, defeat on his face. His eyes were sunken, and he looked like he hadn't washed his hair in over a week. He was deathly pale and emaciated. Sam had failed to notice these things when she approached him at his locker, or even in the past several days when seeing him in the halls. Micah looked just as bad as Adria did. He looked at Sam with empty eyes.

"You know all this already, don't you?"

Micah nodded, which surprised her. She expected him to deny everything.

"What do you know?" Sam asked.

"I know I've lived more lives than I care to remember," Micah said. "And now I know why. I started having bad dreams when I was fifteen. Probably at the same time as Adria... because she remembered, and we're connected. It's what draws us together, every time. Even if we're born in different places, somehow, we always find each other. And every time, something goes horribly wrong. It's a curse, I figure. I don't know how, but it is. I don't know why."

"I know why," Sam said.

Micah looked at Sam in shock. She looked back at him with sympathy. She opened her notebook and pulled out several articles and research papers.

"I think it all began in 1879. That's when the couple from the Cannon Beach Cemetery died. They died on August 29, 1879, on the same day, but unlike all the other couples, they weren't born on the same day. They weren't the same age."

Sam pulled an article out from her notebook to show to Micah. He took it and read it, while she talked.

"Master mason Justin S. Tremaine was twenty-four. His fiancée and assistant, Charlotte Felice Williams was twenty-two. In 1879, Tremaine came to Cannon Beach to survey Tillamook Head, the rock where the lighthouse now stands.

"He was a lighthouse engineer. He was hired to survey the rock to determine if a lighthouse there would be feasible. Even though the seas were rough, however, on August 29, he and Charlotte boated out to the rock, to get a closer look, but when Tremaine attempted a landing, he slipped from the boat and was swept into the sea.

"Charlotte dove in after her fiancé, and both of them disappeared in the waves. Neither of their bodies was ever found. They disappeared – their bodies carried out to sea. There's nothing of them buried in the cemetery. It's just tombstones, to keep their memory."

"How does this explain what's happening to me and Adria?" Micah said, his voice low and soft.

"Well," Sam took a deep breath. "If that was the beginning of all these lives, then I figured; something about the way that couple died must have caused this cycle to come about.

"Something in the way you and Adria were killed, caused the curse. So, I researched anything and everything I could think of. The lighthouse, the rock, the waves, the land the waves rise to, the cliffs. Then I researched the Indian tribes, specifically the Tillamook.

"In one accounting of Tremaine and Williams' deaths, I came across an odd quote about the sea surrounding Tillamook rock. I mean it is, after all, named after the Indian tribe. They named it Tillamook Rock because the Tillamook thought it looked like a giant sea monster, rising up out of the ocean.

"Legend says that rock is where Eastern storms go to die. The Tillamook believed that surrounding that rock, there are under ocean tunnels where spirits lived, and they came to the surface to swallow the last life of the storms. That's why the storms end, in Tillamook legend. The tunnel spirits take their life."

"I still don't understand," Micah said. "How does this help us with this curse? Do you have any idea what this is doing to both of us?"

"Yes," Sam said. "I do. I've watched Adria spiral down. And I've watched you pulverize a guy's face. Adria is miserable, and you're the only thing that ever brought her even close to being her old self. You made her happy, Micah."

"I can't be around her, I told you that," Micah said. "She'll die if we're together. That's how the curse works."

"Explain it to me," Sam said.

"I don't know why, but in every life we've had together, something always happens. It's almost like, if we get too close to one another, it awakens the curse. But we never remembered before. I never remembered. At least, not until death arrived.

"Every life, we're drawn together. We fall in love. We're happy for a short while. Then something always happens to me," Micah stopped talking then, clearly upset.

"You die," Sam said, her voice soft. Micah nodded.

"Different ways, but it always happens. And then I know, if Adria ever wants to see me again, she has to follow me. She has to go when I do, or we'll be separated, forever. And I've always asked her to go with me. And she always has."

"If you die, she has to kill herself, or you'll both be separated," Sam nodded. "So she kills herself, to follow you, and you both get reborn again, on the same day, because you always die on the same day. And this has been happening since August 29, 1879. For one hundred and thirty-one years," Sam said.

"And if I let myself be around Adria again, if we fall in love…" Micah stopped.

"You already are in love," Sam said. "The curse is set in motion."

"No, not yet," Micah said. "She can still live a full life, if I leave her alone."

"What do you mean?" Sam said, "You've already met each other, you've already fallen in love. What else does it take to set it off?"

"We haven't been together," Micah said.

"You spent days together, weeks. You kissed."

"It takes more than that," Micah said.

"I'm confused."

Micah took a deep breath.

"The curse, as far as my memory serves, begins the moment we're…*together*," he said, emphasizing the word.

"Together?" Sam frowned, thinking about Micah's statement. "Oh," she said, suddenly understanding his meaning. "Well, if that's what it takes, then you can still be around her," she said, sounding hopeful. "You can hang out, like before. You can even kiss and hold hands."

"It's not that simple," Micah said.

"Sure it is," Sam shrugged. "Just be friends, don't have sex. Abstinence is all the rage, right?"

"We're star-crossed lovers, cursed to live again and again, because our souls can't stand to be apart," Micah said. "We're drawn to each other like magnets, no matter how far apart we're born. We're destined to find each other. If we're together, we'll only be able to resist each other for so long. *If* we're together."

"But…" Sam said, trailing off. "You can be friends."

"And live our whole lives never being able to touch each other, get married, have children? I mean, marrying other people is out of the question."

"Of course," Sam said. "You're meant for each other."

"No, we're just cursed," Micah said. "This isn't Romeo & Juliet. This is just completely fucked up. And if I go near Adria, it will happen all over again. I'll die, and she'll follow me. She'll die, and she has her whole life planned out ahead of her."

"Not anymore," Sam said. "Micah, she's going insane. Her dreams are getting way worse. She's beginning to remember her past lives. I don't even recognize her anymore. She's miserable away from you. You don't look much better yourself.

"You're telling me you think she can somehow be happy living a long life, but without you? That's crazy. What has the last hundred and thirty years even been for, if you're just going to give up now?"

"Give up?" Micah said. "What other option is there, Sam? We can't be together. We'll both just die, and it will all start all over again. If Adria's beginning to remember, like I did, then she must understand by now, why I left. If she remembers, then she knows.

"This is our chance, Sam. Maybe next time we won't remember. I only remembered because Adria did. She only remembered from seeing our graves. It was bound to happen sooner or later, with how many lives we've lived, that one of us would see something that triggered it, but what if it never happens again? Or, what if we don't remember again, for another ten lives?

"Don't you see? We *both* remember. We *know* about the curse. We *know* what will happen if we're together. For the first time since this whole thing began, we have the ability to choose. We never had that before. We can choose to end the curse, simply by not being together."

"But then you're not together!" Sam yelled.

"Do you want Adria to die?" Micah looked at Sam in disbelief.

"No, of course not," Sam said. "But I don't know that being without you, like this, isn't killing her anyhow. She's scary-thin, and freaky-pale. She's not eating. Her body, it's almost like, it's failing her. Micah, being without you is killing her. It's killing both of you."

"We just need some time to get over it," Micah said.

"Get over it?" Sam looked at Micah again, in disbelief. "Can you get over it, Micah?"

Micah sat with tears in his eyes, looking deflated. Sam huffed.

"Just, please, talk to her," Sam said. "Hang out with her. You can fix this. Bring her back to me, Micah. You're the only one who can. She needs you. You need her, too. Just be friends, resist the urge to touch her. If you try hard enough, I'm sure you can do that."

"Have you ever been in love?" Micah asked.

"Sure," Sam said. "Maybe. Sort of."

"It's not quite that simple. Yes, I can be around Adria, and I can resist, but only if she does, too. Before, she...Look, it wasn't her fault, she didn't know any better. She didn't remember. She had no idea that she was playing with fire."

"Micah, Adria is remembering watching you die over and over again. You say you remember, too? You remember *you* dying. Only you. She has to carry the burden of remembering your death, *and* of killing herself. She's dealing with this all alone. You can't leave her all alone with this, Micah. If you love her, you'll be there for her. You can love her without it hurting her, if you try hard enough."

"You said you were trying to figure out how all this started, didn't you?" Micah frowned at Sam.

"Yeah, I've had to track down some books on Tillamook legend. There aren't that many. None of them have helped.

There is one more hope. I found a text in the Salem public library catalogues.

"You see, the Tillamook kept all their history orally, passing it down from generation to generation. But as they were driven from their lands and put on reservations, many of them died."

Sam pulled some more pages from her notes.

"In 1856 the Tillamook were placed on the Siletz reservation, along with twenty other tribes. The last speaker of their language, died in 1970, so the Tillamook language has been extinct for almost forty years. But, I found a book that was written in the early seventies. It's been out of print since 1981, but this group of researchers in the Polynesian Islands actually interviewed the last few remaining Tillamook between 1965 and 1970, trying to preserve the language before it was completely destroyed.

"They wrote a one-hundred-and-twenty page book, filled with the Tillamook's oral legends and myths, translations, and definitions, spanning back to the first ancestors to settle in the Cannon Beach area, back in the 1400s. I have the book on order to be sent to the public library in Seaside. I'm just waiting for it. I think if there will be any clues to what happened when you died in 1879, it might be found in that book."

"That's a real long shot," Micah said. "You don't even know if the Tillamook have anything to do with this curse."

"I'm not saying they do have anything to do with it," Sam said. "I'm saying, their myths might actually contain some information that will help explain why you and Adria drowning off Tillamook rock over a hundred years ago, has caused you to reincarnate over and over again, and seemingly be cursed to never be together."

"I really don't see why you think some Indian tribe would know what happened off those waters," Micah said. "Because of some legend about, what? Sea tunnel spirits?"

"That," Sam said. "And the fact that the word Tillamook is translated as 'land of many waters.'"

"So?" Micah said. Sam pulled more papers out of her notebook.

"So, the name Tillamook is a Chinook term. It means 'people of the Nekelim.' Also referred to as 'Nehalem.' Now, there are various spellings of the word, including Calamox, Gillamook, and Killamook. Tillamook itself, is translated as 'land of many waters,' but the word Nekelim is translated as 'people of many waters. The word Nehalem, is translated as 'water of many lives.'"

Micah stared at Sam for several moments, taking in her statements. She looked back, unflinching and unblinking.

"The river that lets out into the ocean by those cliffs overlooking the lighthouse and Tillamook Rock? It's the Nehalem River. The 'water of many lives,' intersects with the very cliffs and seabed that the Tillamook tribe believed held tunnel spirits who take life away.

"So, use your imagination, Micah. What do you get when you mix spirits who take life away, with water that grants many lives?"

"That's crazy," Micah said. "That makes no sense. You're telling me you believe that people who drown off Tillamook Rock, will be cursed to live again and again? That's stupid. And if it were true, there would be other people like us. I mean, that guy died trying to get on that rock, right? To see if they could even build the lighthouse? How many people died building the thing?"

"None," Sam said, her eyes twinkling. "I thought of that. If the very first surveyor they sent out died, then tons of builders must have been killed before the lighthouse was finished, right? Wrong.

"Amazingly, Tremaine and Williams were the only deaths to ever happen in regards to the lighthouse. It wasn't easy, and it was definitely dangerous, but they managed to finish building the lighthouse with no other deaths. None of the subsequent lighthouse keepers to run Terrible Tilly were ever killed either. As far as I can tell, it looks as if you and Adria are the only people to ever drown in that exact spot."

8. December 2, 2009

Adria waited by her car after school, expecting Sam to show up. She never did. As she waited by her car, she opened her umbrella, for the rain was beginning to fall. A storm was quickly moving in.

Adria hid under her umbrella, staring at the dark, wet concrete, wondering why Sam was making her wait so long. She also wondered what Sam could possibly want to talk to her about. There was nothing to talk about, in her opinion. Adria knew who she was now. Perhaps not entirely, but her nightmares were no longer a mystery, nor was Micah's standoffish behavior.

Adria continued staring at the pavement. Her eyes suddenly took in Micah's black Doc Martins, slick with rain, and she raised her umbrella to look at him. She hadn't been this close to him for several weeks. She immediately felt drawn to him, feeling the almost overwhelming urge to throw herself into his arms and shower him with kisses. She felt sick to her stomach.

She stood staring at Micah for several moments. He had no umbrella. He was completely soaked within moments. He looked like a ghost, dressed in black. He looked sick. Adria immediately became concerned about him, as she took in the dark circles underneath his eyes, and the fact that his lips were so pale, they were no longer pink, but light beige.

Micah was also taking in Adria's appearance. Seeing her up close this way, he became fully aware of what Sam had been trying to tell him.

Adria was thinner than ever, and her skin was so pale it was almost translucent. She looked like a frail flower, whose stem might break in the slightest hint of a breeze. Her hair was now almost as dark as his.

His heart broke for her and he longed, almost uncontrollably, to take her into his arms and never let go. He resisted this urge, but with incredible difficulty. Finally, he spoke to her, but his voice was weak and strangled, in his effort to resist any physical contact.

"I'm sorry," he said.

He looked down at the ground, away from her pained eyes. She only watched him, confused. When he looked up at her again, tears were standing in his eyes.

"I wanted to tell you. Tell you what I remembered. But you would have thought I was crazy."

"No, I wouldn't," Adria said.

"Yes," Micah shook his head. "You didn't remember who you are. They were only bad dreams."

"You should have told me."

"How? Tell you what, Adria? That if we keep seeing each other, I'll die, and then you'll kill yourself?"

"No," Adria said, looking away. "I don't know. But you should have said something."

"I did," Micah said. "I told you if you really love me, you'll let me go."

"Like you let me go?" Adria's eyes accused. "Wasn't it you, who asked me to come here? Every time?"

"I didn't realize," Micah was crying now. "I didn't realize what I was asking you to do. I was selfish, Adria. I didn't want to live without you."

"But you're making me do so now," she said. "Why?"

"Because I love you," Micah said.

Adria stared at Micah, her eyes filled with pain. He was drenched now. His clothes stuck to his body, plastered to his thin frame. He was shivering madly, but did not even seem to notice.

"Micah, you're going to make yourself sick," Adria said, her voice warm.

"No, I don't care," he said. "If we're together, I know bad things will happen."

"That's not what I meant. You're going to catch pneumonia, if you don't get out of the rain and cold."

"Oh," Micah looked at Adria, embarrassed.

"Come on," Adria said.

She took Micah's arm and led him over to his van, placing the umbrella over both of them. He was shaking so badly now, his arm was too numb to register her touch. She was so overcome by the urgency to simply get Micah out of the rain, her own hand on his forearm did not fully register on her, either. But contact had been made, again, for the first time in weeks, and neither of them realized it had kicked off a growing urge that would be impossible to resist for long.

Micah climbed into his van, and Adria instinctively went with him, going around and opening the passenger side door and getting in. He engaged the ignition and blasted the heater, trying to get warm. Adria looked at him with sympathy.

"Two months in Cannon Beach, and you still don't own a winter coat?" she asked. "Or a rain slicker?"

"It would cramp my style," Micah gave her a crooked grin. He was still shivering, but less now.

"What style is that, death warmed over?" Adria said.

Micah looked at her, his eyes suddenly haunted. She looked back, her slight smile fading.

"You still don't remember fully, do you?" he asked. "How much do you remember, Adria?"

"I know you were John, and I was Celia. In 1899," she said.

"That's all?" Micah asked, looking shocked.

"I remember all my dreams," Adria said, sounding defensive.

"No, that's not the same thing," Micah shook his head. He was disappointed. "It's not the same thing at all."

"Look, I know they're not dreams now, okay?" Adria said.

"You don't remember me?" Micah was almost yelling now. "You don't remember my names? Other than John, I mean?"

"No, what names?"

"¿Cómo puedes sentarte allí y decirme que entiendes, cuando ni siquiera te acuerdas?" (How can you sit there and tell me you understand, when you don't remember?)

Micah's voice was soft and low as he said this, different, somehow.

"What?" Adria stared at Micah, completely confused.

"Amaya," Micah said. "Tu moriste en 1993. Y cuando eras Camila Flores, moriste en 1954." (You died in 1993. And when you were Camila Flores, you died in 1954.)

"What the fuck are you saying?" Adria yelled.

"If you remembered, you would know," Micah said.

There was a fire in his eyes now. He turned the ignition fully, to start the engine. The tires of his van screeched on the wet asphalt as he quickly backed out of the parking lot and sped away.

"What are you doing? Where are we going?" Adria yelled.

"You have to remember, Adria. I can't do this with you, if you don't remember as much as I do."

"How are you going to do that?" she asked.

"I don't know," Micah sighed. "Sam seems to think that seeing our graves when your aunt died, is what first made you remember, and start dreaming. When you remembered, so did I. We're connected, Adria."

"But if I'm the one who remembered first and I made you remember, then how come you know more than I do?"

"I don't know," Micah said. "Maybe because it was me who came to you? Because I was the one who had to find you."

"What?"

"It wasn't an accident that my dad moved here, Adria. He could have picked one of about half-a-dozen other places. It was me. I chose for us to move here."

"Why?"

"I don't know," Micah said. "My dad wanted to get us out of Akron, away from Ohio. Away from my mom, away from the prison. I was in trouble, getting into fights.

"He wanted to move us somewhere quiet. His company could have transferred him anywhere. Florida was on the table. So was North Carolina, and Southern California. And Cannon Beach.

"He laid everything out on the table one night. All the different hotels, all our choices. He asked me to look them all over, and tell him where I thought I might be happy. He just didn't want me fighting anymore. He didn't want me to be angry. As if we could just run away from everything," Micah shook his head.

"Why is your mom in prison, Micah?" Adria's voice was soft and cautious.

"She was a meth addict," Micah sighed. "She cooked in a friend's house. My dad had no clue. Neither did I. He was always busy at work, at night. I was gone a lot, at clubs, raves, wherever. My family's not exactly a poster for the happy unit."

"I'm sorry."

"I know," Micah said. "It doesn't matter. My dad's a decent guy. He just married the wrong woman, that's all. I love her, because she's my mom, but she never gave a crap about me. How could she, to do what she did?"

"How did she end up in prison?"

"The kitchen blew up in her friend's house. He died. She was in the bathroom. She got lucky. But she got caught. Ten years. First offense, but they don't take lightly to drug traffickers. The courts go heavy on that shit. Even for a first offense. Especially a lab explosion, where someone dies. I was sixteen. I'd already been having the dreams for a year, when she went away. It was a lot to deal with."

"I'm sorry," Adria said again.

"Fine," Micah said. "But when it came time to choose, and I looked at all the destinations laid out on the table in front of me, I saw Cannon Beach, and I just knew. I knew I had to be there. Here.

"I closed my eyes, and I could hear the waves, even though I'd never seen the ocean before. I could smell the water, the seaweed. I could feel the rain. I could sense you, Adria. I knew I had to come here. I knew I had to find you."

"And now that you have, you want to walk away," Adria accused.

"I didn't remember then," Micah said. "The dreams were still only dreams, like they are for you."

"When did you remember?"

"About a month before we moved here," Micah said. "The closer the move got, the more I began to dream, and not just of how I died. I started dreaming about our lives, before that day. How we met, who we were. And when I woke up, each time, I found I knew things. Impossible things. I knew another language, one morning."

"The Mexican couple," Adria whispered. "You got stabbed. I used the knife to cut my own wrists."

"I didn't see that happen," Micah sounded sick.

"No, you were already gone," Adria spoke softly.

"But I remember everything, Adria. Our names, how we met, who we were. I remember you. Loving you. Making love with you. Touching you. And I remember dying. All you remember is the death. You don't remember our lives."

"And yet, I'm the one who wants to be with you," Adria said. "All I have are visions, memories of death. And I want to be near you, Micah. If you remember our lives, how can you stand to be apart?"

"Because I know what touching you means, for both of us," he said. "It's a curse, Adria. If you remembered all of our lives, you'd see. It just keeps happening over and over again. You'd understand why. If you truly knew."

"Then tell me," Adria said.

"I can't," Micah said. "You have to learn for yourself."

They were in Cannon Beach now. Micah had turned down Elk Creek Road, and he slowly pulled his van into the front parking lot of the Cannon Beach Cemetery. He turned the van off and looked at Adria with heavy concern.

"I don't know any other way to make you understand the gravity of what's happening," Micah said. "To be near me, you have no idea what you're letting in."

"Why are we here," Adria whispered.

"Because this is where it all started," Micah said. "This is where you first began to remember. I don't know any other way to make you see."

Micah got out of the van and went around to Adria's door, opening it. He stood back, motioning for her to get out. She did, opening her umbrella. He walked with her, this time making a conscious choice to remain a few inches behind her, despite the rain falling on his back this way.

The cemetery rested on a slight hillside. It was a peaceful place, overlooking the vast expanse of ocean. On a clear day, the sky would be blue, the ocean steel gray. Today, however, the horizon was nothing but black-gray clouds, and the tombstones, themselves, fought to be seen, competing with the mist and fog. It was an ever-changing vista, as with all of the Oregon coastline.

The cemetery was further shrouded by heavy stands of alder and hemlock trees, which lined the entire outer fencing of the graveyard. As Micah opened the front gate, the black wrought-iron fencing creaked on its hinge. They walked, together, down the muddy pathways, to Lynn Allan's grave. As they walked, stands of alder trees dripped rain onto the umbrella. They reached her aunt's grave, and Adria looked down at the tombstone.

"How did she die?" Micah asked.

"Breast cancer," Adria said. "She fought hard."

"I'm sorry," Micah said. Adria nodded, shrugging.

Micah looked around, reading the names on the surrounding tombstones. He wandered away from Adria, who remained at her aunt's grave for several more moments, before following after him.

He'd left on a direct course, feeling a sudden pull. As Adria came up behind him, her eyes fell on the two graves he'd come to rest standing in front of. She looked down, following his gaze and took in the names.

M.M. Justin Stephen Tremaine
b. July 17, 1855
d. August 29, 1879
Lost At Sea

Charlotte Felice Williams
b. June 11, 1857
d. August 29, 1879
Lost At Sea

"Lost at sea," Adria whispered. "Like all those urns."

"But urns aren't cursed to live again and again," Micah said. "They were *us*, Adria. This is when it all began. Something about the way we drowned, caused all this."

"How do you know?"

Adria was still looking at the graves. She was not looking at Micah. She was transfixed, her eyes wide. He watched her, hope filling his heart.

"Sam thinks she has it half-figured out. She's done a lot of research."

"Sam?" But Adria's voice was far-off, drifting away.

"Remember, Adria," Micah said.

He dared to lean closer and whispered in her ear, "Please remember."

His warm breath on her face, in her ear, made her whole body tingle. She closed her eyes, enraptured. A sudden vision of herself flooded her mind, her senses. She heard music, and it was old, echoing in her head, some kind of band music. She caught a brief glimpse of a dance floor, and saw his face, but it was not Micah. He was handsome, and smiling. He twirled her around the floor and she laughed. Adria smiled, sighing through her nose. Micah watched her, waiting. Then Adria's eyes flew open and she turned to look at Micah, feeling panicked.

"It's okay, Adria," he said. In his haste to comfort her, he grabbed her shoulders.

She felt the warmth of his hands, and her entire body was electrified from within. He felt it as well. She stepped forward and gently kissed his lips, once. He did not resist. Her eyes were closed.

"William," she whispered.

"You're remembering," Micah said. "You have to go further. You have to remember everything. I can't be alone with this. I can't be alone with these lives."

He spun her around to look at the graves again. Then he backed away from her, removing the temptation of his presence.

"Look at them, Adria," he said. "Don't back off. Remember. Close your eyes and let it all in. Do it for me."

Adria looked at the graves. She closed her eyes, and she could hear sounds drifting to her ears from far away. Images blurred through her mind. She felt her sanity slipping away. Then, all at once, a crystalline image appeared in her mind, and she knew who she was – who she had been, once. She remembered a new name, besides Celia from 1899.

****

Chicago, Illinois. May 14, 1953.

She met him when her car got a flat tire. Luckily, she'd been on side streets. She walked to the corner, and there was an auto shop, attached to the gas station. As she walked towards the garage, she smiled, hearing the radio blare. Fats Domino was begging his love, saying 'please don't leave me.'

In the garage, she walked over to the coverall clad legs sticking out from under the green Oldsmobile, and gently tapped her heel.

He turned his head and saw heels and legs, quickly sliding out from under the car to gaze up at the most beautiful woman he'd ever seen. She was wearing a yellow print sundress, her dark hair pulled back in a ponytail. Her lips were cherry red, her skin lightest olive. He was instantly in love.

Camila looked down at the tan, young man, and thought, surely he could be no older than twenty-five. He turned out to be twenty-three, just like her, even sharing the same birthday, but she would not learn this for another few days. She took in his shiny, oil-stained skin, the hint of scruffy stubble lining his chin and cheeks, and his dark brown eyes, and she was instantly in love.

"Puedo ayudarle?" he asked. (Can I help you?)

"Mi neumático se pinchó, cerca," she said. (My tire went flat, nearby.)

"Bueno. Puedo llevarte un neumático nuevo, si estas cerca," he said. (Okay. I can bring a new tire, if you're so close.)

"What's your name?" she asked.

"Rafael," he said. "Rafael Acosta. And yours?"

"Camila Flores," she said, smiling. "But, I don't have a lot of money. How much does a tire cost?"

"Sin costo," he said. (No cost.)

"Sin costo?" she asked. "but…" she trailed off.

"Nothing, if you'll have dinner with me tonight," he said.

He looked at her face with worry. Had he gone too far? Was he attempting to bribe her into going on a date with him? It wasn't his style. She looked at him for a moment, her smile fading, and he knew he'd blown his chance. He did not know that she was already in love.

"¿Es habitual aprovecharse de automovilistas varados?" She smiled at him. (Is it usual to take advantage of stranded motorists?)

"Sólo tú," he said, and her heart melted. (Only you.)

His voice was so gentle, his eyes so kind. She immediately consented to the date.

Her father's family was from Puerto Rico, and it turned out, so was his. Both their families had moved to Chicago, at different times, but Camila and Rafael discovered that they'd been living within miles of each other for the last few years. At dinner, they eagerly drank up the facts of each other's lives, swimming in each other's eyes all the while.

"Without your flat tire, we would never have met," Rafael said.

"Not the tire," Camila said. "I decided to turn right, instead of left, and there was your shop."

"It's not my shop, it belongs to my older brothers," he said. "I just work for them. What do you do?"

"I wanted to go to school," she said, "but we didn't have the money. Now, I apprentice at a salon. Mostly I sweep up and make the appointments, but my friend is teaching me to cut hair. I made a man bald, using the wrong sheer setting."

Rafael laughed. Camila looked down, embarrassed.

"Well, maybe he can join the army?" He smiled. She laughed.

They were together from that night on. Their families initially approved. After all, they were both Puerto Rican. But Camila was only half, her mother was white, and when Rafael's brothers learned that their little brother's girlfriend was actually half-Caucasian, they gave him a hard time.

"Mitad y mitad, crema para el café," they called her. (Half and half, cream for coffee.)

Camila was hurt. She spoke their language. What did it matter?

She and Rafael had to keep their intimacy under wraps. It was not considered appropriate for them to sleep together before marriage. But they both could not help themselves, it seemed. They resisted as long as possible, but as the months rolled by, and New Year's Eve, 1954, arrived, neither of them could help it any longer. They were madly in love, and already, they both knew they wanted to be together forever.

On the roof of the auto shop, on an old, beat-up mattress, just before midnight, Rafael slipped a ring onto Camila's finger as she gazed up at the crisp night sky and the stars. It was unusually clear for a winter night in Chicago. Clear and fairly calm, the wind barely blowing.

They huddled under warm blankets anyhow, and he fumbled around beneath them, just to find her hand. She smiled as she felt his fingers touch hers. This was the only place they could be alone. Then she frowned as she felt something constricting slide down her ring finger. She pulled her hand out to look at the ring and gasped.

"It's not much," Rafael said, "but it's forever. If you'll have me."

She threw her arms around him, whispering yes over and over again. This was the night they could no longer resist their love for one another.

He'd asked her if she would have him, and she did. It felt natural, right. It was wonderful. It was not his first time, but it was hers. He could tell. He worried he was hurting her, but she only wrapped herself around him, panting and sighing in pleasure and complete rapture. When they were done, they lay in each other's arms, smiling up at the stars. 1954 had arrived, while they were making love.

Then they heard the rooftop door open and raucous laughter flooded their ears. Rafael's brothers were there, with a bottle of cheap wine in one hand, each, and a date on the other arm. The four drunkards stood staring down at the couple on the mattress, taking in the scene. Then Rafael's oldest brother, Ricardo, flew into a sudden rage, fueled by his inebriation. He glared down at Camila with hatred.

"Facilona. Puta barata. Basura sucia blanca!" (Slut. Cheap whore. Dirty white, trash!)

Rafael stood, zipping up his pants. Ricardo watched this, his eyes flying wide, ever more shocked and disgusted.

"Y tu eres basura, para estar con ella." (And you are garbage, to be with her.)

"We're engaged!" Rafael screamed.

"So?! She ain't your wife, yet, hermano." (brother.)

"And what were you planning on doing with her?" Rafael motioned to Ricardo's drunken date, wearing a much-too-short skirt. "Up here, on the roof, eh?"

"Fuck you!" Ricardo yelled.

Camila stood, smoothing down the hem of her dress, looking ashamed. Ricardo looked her up and down, and Rafael felt white-hot rage building within him. Ricardo suddenly smiled.

"I get it, li'l bro, I really do. She's a hot piece of *puta*. But *puta*, still. And she laid down with you, after how long? A few months? You want to marry a girl like that? How many guys has she lain down with, huh?"

"Ningún otro hombre!" (No other man!) Camila cried, her own rage boiling up to the surface. "Lo hice porque lo amo." (I did it because I love him.)

"Yeah, I'll bet," Ricardo spat. "I'll bet you loved it. Hey, Rafael? ¿Ella sangro? Huh?" (Did she bleed?) Ricardo sneered a sick smile at his little brother.

Rafael flew into a rage, launching himself at Ricardo, throwing him to the ground. The dates screamed. Hernesto, the other brother, only looked on, too drunk to react quickly enough. He swayed on his feet. Meanwhile, Rafael's fists flew, and Ricardo did his best to shield his face, but to no avail. His nose was broken immediately.

"Para! Por favor para!" Camila cried. (Stop! Please, stop!)

Ricardo managed to shove Rafael off of him, and kicked him with his feet. Rafael stumbled backwards and fell to the ground. Ricardo stood then, and pulled a switchblade from his pocket.

"Ella? La escogiste a ella por encima de tu propio hermano? Tu propia sangre?" Ricardo said. (Her? You choose her over your own brother? Your own blood?)

"You chose, brother," Rafael said.

"No," Ricardo shook his head. "Tu elegiste." (You chose.)

Ricardo ran at his brother, as Rafael stood, attempting to get out of the way. They came to stand together, face-to-face, body-to-body. There was no space between them.

Then Ricardo backed away, and looked at Rafael's stomach. The knife was buried up to the hilt. It was a small blade, but the damage was enough. The knife had punctured deep into Rafael's liver. It was a precise wound, although, this was not Ricardo's intention. He was simply drunk and angry, and everything was an incredible blur.

Camila stood on air, floating, making her way to stand in front of Rafael, tears in her eyes. No one else moved. Rafael instinctively pulled the knife out, and suddenly, the entire midsection of his white dress shirt was drenched with blood. Camila screamed, covering her mouth with both her hands. She turned to the four onlookers, her eyes desperate.

"Call someone!"

Hernesto ran. His date left with him. Ricardo's date turned away, crying and sat down on her own knees, tucking her legs under her, her back to the gruesome scene. Ricardo only sat down, dazed, on his butt, and looked on in disbelief.

Rafael collapsed, too dizzy and weak to remain on his feet. He looked up at Camila, who sat down with him. She put her hands over his wound, in a useless attempt to stop the blood, but it only flowed out around her fingers, in warm, gushing streamlets. Something was happening. They could both feel it.

Rafael knew he was dying, and in an instant, he knew that they could still be together. This didn't have to be the end. But he knew she would need to follow him, if they ever wanted to see each other again. His eyes held a wisdom inside that he'd never possessed until that moment; until the moment of his death. She would need to follow quickly.

"Camila," he whispered. His strength was fading fast. "Sígueme. Tienes que estar cerca."(Follow me. You have to be close.)

"Lo sé," (I know) she cried. "Voy a estar justo detrás de ti." (I'll be right behind you.)

"Lo prometes?" He looked at her, desperate. (You promise?)

"Prometo," (I promise) Camila said. "Voy a encontrar una manera." (I will find a way.)

He died in her arms. The knife lay next to his lifeless body. She felt him go. She knew the moment the life left his body. She immediately felt the pull, as their souls were separated, and it pained her so.

She was not afraid. Physical pain ceased to be any kind of worry, compared to the pain she now felt inside. Her very soul ached. She looked down at the knife and picked it up with one hand, while still holding Rafael's body with her other arm.

Her back was facing Ricardo. He still looked on in complete and utter shock. He did not realize, yet, that his brother was dead.

Camila stabbed the knife into her wrist, sinking it deep into her flesh there. Then she twisted the blade parallel to her forearm and pulled upward, slicing her arm open from wrist to elbow. Blood spurted out in large jets, but Camila was numb to the physical pain.

Her heart ached. Her mind was desperate to catch up to Rafael, before he drifted too far from reach. She knew they must remain on the same plane of time. Somehow, she just knew.

She repeated the dark deed to her other arm, then took up Rafael's body, once more, holding him tight. It took less than a minute for her mind to fade; and her soul drifted free of its bodily confinement, to fly towards love.

****

Adria opened her eyes. She was standing in the rain. The umbrella was at her feet, her arms lowered to her sides in her revelations, her sudden slam of memories. The floodgates were open, however, and more was flowing in all the while.

She breathed heavily, overwhelmed by the memories that streamed into her waking consciousness, even now. She was hearing music, voices. Images flashed across her mind, simultaneous movies playing out parallel lives all at once. Every life she'd lived suddenly downloaded into her, in a mad rush of recollection, and Adria gasped.

Micah watched from behind her. He closed his eyes, forced by the images now playing through his own head. He was connected to Adria all the more, with her sudden, full return of memory. He saw what she saw. He learned what she learned. He relived not only every one of his own deaths, but witnessed Adria's deaths as well.

He saw every desperate taking of life, every sad drawing of blood, every forced injury. Micah watched Adria kill herself again and again. His entire body shook with the morbid images that flooded his own mind, his own senses. He tasted bitter metal-blood in his mouth, as he bit his own tongue in shock. Bits and pieces of joy drifted in and out as well, as he continued to share in all of Adria's memories.

****

–1976

On the common. His sophomore year, and Devon sat on the grass, soaking up the late afternoon sun, just before sunset. Twilight in early August, as the heat of the day finally simmered down to something manageable.

Girls laughed under trees, a football flew between two Sigma Chi's, and someone had a radio blaring out their dorm window. Maxine Nightingale crooned about how 'love is good.' Right back where we started from, Devon thought, and frowned.

He had an odd feeling of déjà vu. The song ended, and then he saw her. Sophie Prescott. In less than two days, she would be his girlfriend, but he did not know that then. He did not even know her name. All he knew was that she was the prettiest girl he'd ever seen. She wore a bright yellow t-shirt and bell-bottom jeans. Her hair was blonde, long and straight. She had brown freckles speckled across her nose and cheeks. She was breathtaking.

She sat on the grass, and threw her head back, basking in the last remnants of the day, smiling. Then she looked over, and their eyes locked, even from so far away. She was on the other side of the common, but he may as well have had eagle eyes, for he could read every detail of her features, despite the distance. It was as if he already knew her, somehow. He instantly had every detail of her face memorized, etched into his brain.

She stood and walked over to him, as the radio blared 'Still the One,' by The Orleans. Neither of them noticed the song, or realized the odd implications of the words. It was as if the entire universe had stopped, and the world only existed for the two of them…

****

Micah blinked, even as The Orleans song echoed and slowly faded from his mind. He looked at Adria's back and waited, still feeling her memories flooding in.

****

–Hermosa Beach, California. September 3, 1992.

Smells Like Teen Spirit blared along the beach walk. Eduardo Olivas sat, looking out at the ocean. English drifted to him in foreign waves. He'd only been over the border for four days. He was completely out of sorts. He only chose to come to Hermosa because when he saw the word, it called to him. Beautiful. Now, here he was, on 'beautiful beach,' and he had no idea where to go, or what to do.

He was supposed to meet a contact here that would give him a place to stay, until he could get settled. He'd already been warned it would most likely be a small apartment, where several men would sleep to a room, but he did not mind. He'd dealt with much worse in Metlatonoc. No matter what happened to him here, in the U.S., nothing could be worse than where he'd come from, what he'd already survived. It was a minor miracle he was still breathing. He looked at the ocean in wonder.

"Eduardo? Eduardo Olivas?"

Eduardo turned to rest his eyes on a teenage girl, who looked to be about his age. His eyes were fearful, but hers were friendly.

"Si?"

"Soy Amaya. Me enviaron a mostrar dónde alojarse." (I'm Amaya. They sent me to show you where to stay.)

"¿Va a estar allí también?" he asked. (Will you be there, too?)

"Si," she frowned. "¿Por qué?" (Why?)

"Sin razón," he said, gazing at her. (No reason.)

She smiled at him, amused. He was handsome. She felt oddly drawn to him. He was also, instantly drawn to her.

"De dónde eres?" he asked. (Where are you from?)

"Oaxaca," she said. He nodded.

"Tienes novio?" he asked. (Do you have a boyfriend?)

She shook her head, blushing. She looked at him, shy.

"Tu si?" she asked. (Do you?)

"Un novio? No seas tonto," he smiled, teasing her. (A boyfriend? Don't be silly.)

"No, no. Una novia?" She waited. (A girlfriend?)

"Si," he said.

"Quién? Dónde está ella?" Amaya looked troubled. (Who? Where is she?)

"Ella está parada justo en frente de mí. Su nombre es Amaya," he looked at her, waiting. (She's standing right in front of me. Her name is Amaya.)

"Crees que es tan fácil, ¿verdad?" she said, but she was smiling now. (So, you think it's that easy, do you?)

"No, pero espero que sí," he looked at her longingly. (No, but I hope so.)

"Lo es. Me siento como si te conociera." She gazed at him. (It is. I feel like I know you.)

"Espero conocerte por siempre," he said. (I hope I know you for forever.)

"Bueno, se supone que debes seguirme, ¿recuerdas?" (Well, you're supposed to follow me, remember?)

He nodded. She put her hand out, and he took it. They were together from that moment on.

****

Micah smiled, remembering. Then he felt sudden panic. No new images flashed through his mind. Whatever had just taken place, it had ended. He stood looking at Adria's back, watching her shiver in the pouring rain. She had dropped her umbrella. She was now drenched as badly as he was. She shook violently. He rushed up to her and looked at her face, worried.

Adria's stare was far off and vacant. Micah realized that he'd had several weeks, if not months, for his memories to slowly stream in. Adria had just remembered all of their lives together, all at once, in a matter of sheer minutes. He saw her blank face, and he felt horrible for what he'd done, for what he'd forced into her mind. It was simply too much for her, he realized.

"Adria?" his voice shook. "Adria?"

He looked at her, his heart filled with fear. He did not dare to touch her, however, for after reliving his own memories, he realized the danger, all too well.

"Adria!" he screamed.

She turned to look at him, blinking. Her whole body shook from the shock and the cold. Steamy breaths issued from her mouth in a stream of vapor clouds. Her respiration was labored and quick, her face deathly pale.

"We have to get you inside," Micah said.

At that moment, Adria lost consciousness and collapsed. Micah caught her, and he was no longer worried about whether or not it was safe to touch her. He carried her in his arms and placed her in the back of his van. Then he drove away from the cemetery as fast as he could.

9. Micah and Adria

Micah placed Adria's body in his bed. She'd never been in his room before. He'd never brought her there, and she'd never even met his father. He'd never shown her anything of his life, other than the inside of his van. He'd refused, even when she asked in the past, to elaborate on his mother, until that day.

He simply felt it was better to keep her at a distance from him, despite drinking up as many details about Adria and her life as he could. He could have listened to her talk for days, listened to a thousand of her favorite songs. He could have lived inside her eyes, her smile, forever.

He watched her now, as she slept, and felt his heart ache. He had always loved her. He had always wanted to be with her. In every life, he'd found her, even when she came to him first.

In some lives, he'd been with others, before meeting her, but always, he never loved anyone but her. Physical intimacy never registered as love to him, until her. Always, with anyone else, it was empty and wholly unsatisfying, as if his body somehow felt something was wrong.

He knew it was the same for her, even in lives where she'd been with other men before meeting him. Neither of them knew true physical longing, until each other. Then, both their bodies ached, and they felt drawn, compelled to love one another.

Always, they resisted, even before knowing the true cost, but the longing became so great, each time, it grew to be physically painful, and the emotional anguish of not allowing themselves to touch one another was simply too immense to withstand forever. In some lives, they'd been too young to be with anyone else, before each other, as was the case with Eduardo Olivas and Amaya Rios.

Micah looked at Adria, and he longed for her, already. He could feel his body aching, his emotions and desires rising to the surface, threatening madness. Along with this, came the urgent need to share all of himself with her. Everything he thought, everything he knew and loved. Everything that made him who he was. He wanted to share it all with her and there was no more holding back for him. He knew that now.

There wasn't much to share, however, Micah thought now, as he continued looking at Adria. He glanced at the brown walls, which he'd painted dark the day he and his father moved in. With the few lamps lit in the corners, the room had a warm, inviting, chocolate-rich glow.

Micah felt more comforted in his room now, than he ever had. Perhaps the warm comfort simply lay in the fact of Adria's presence in a place so personal to Micah, it felt like a relief to finally let her in.

She knew. She knew, now. Adria was aware of as much as Micah was. The simple relief of such a burden was immense. Carrying all that knowledge on his shoulders alone, had created so much tension inside Micah, he'd grown to be an angry young man, with nowhere to put his frustrations; with no relief to be found, anywhere.

His walls were bare, save for a few, sparse items that had brought him a small modicum of comfort over the last few years. A Donnie Darko movie poster was plastered to the back of his door. Another poster of an Italian techno band, TRIM, was on the far wall, next to his bed, across from the closet. A small desk and computer sat in front of his window, with the shades drawn.

A few books lined a tiny shelf on the wall next to his monitor. There was a copy of Catcher in the Rye, as well as Tuck Everlasting, Stephen King's Different Seasons, and the collected short stories of Roia Marin Williams. On the right side of his room, between his bed and his closet, stood the boots Adria had brought him the day they hiked to Haystack Rock. The day he'd first kissed her. This was all.

Micah stood and went to his computer, turning it on. He pulled up his own music, and turned his speakers on. He chose something soft, gentle. He wanted Adria to wake up. He wanted to see her eyes. He needed to talk to her, now that she remembered everything.

They'd never been in this position before. They'd never been able to remember, to talk about it. They'd never had the chance, before, to try and figure anything out. He needed to talk to her about everything.

There had to be a solution to this problem, something they could both live with. He needed to be with her, to be close to her, but he couldn't lose her. He refused. No matter how great the longing was, he would resist it, he had decided. He couldn't do this without her, however. She must agree. He set the song to repeat.

The music began to play, and he went back to the chair he'd placed next to his bed, and sat, watching her. Waiting. He studied her face. He felt so much for her. All the darkness that resided inside him seemed to drift away when he was with her.

He regretted ever trying to be without her. The last several weeks had been hell on him. The worst pain for him, however, was seeing the toll it had taken on Adria. She looked so pale and weak, his heart broke over her.

He gazed at Adria, and he felt complete and utter peace inside his soul. This was how everything was supposed to be. Micah knew now, he could never be without Adria again. He could only hope that when she awoke, she would feel the same. That she would forgive him for the pain he'd put her through the last several weeks. But, perhaps, knowing what she must know now, she would pull away? If knowing that being near him might cost her life?

He intended to make her a promise, if she would let him; a promise never to hurt her again. He would never touch her; never allow the curse to take effect.

His heart rate increased, as Adria stirred. He smiled. He knew the music would bring her around. He thought awaking from her shock in this way, would be the most comfort he could offer her. He knew her so well. He knew who she was in this life, and in half-a-dozen others.

He'd loved her for so long, he knew exactly how to make her smile, and it did not take any words. He knew her soul. He knew giving her music to come around to, would be like dropping her into a warm pool of liquid tranquility. He would never hurt her again, but only strive to bring her joy.

Adria opened her green eyes, and they smiled and danced with light and happiness. Micah did not know it, but her happiness ran so deep, already, simply because her soul felt the proximity of his, and she was immediately comforted.

She knew where she was, and this told her all that she needed to know. He'd never brought her to his home before. She'd never asked him, but he'd never freely given her that kind of access to him. She'd longed for it, but had to settle for giving him everything of herself, first. He'd drunk up every detail she'd shared, and this had sufficed.

Now, Adria looked around Micah's room, and although in his mind it was bare, Adria saw traces of Micah everywhere. She felt him. The color he'd chosen to paint his walls revealed parts of him that he was not even aware of. The walls were dark, but not cold, nor uninviting; quite the contrary.

Adria did, indeed, feel warm, chocolaty comfort in the ambient lamplight that fell on the rich, brown walls. She thought, briefly, that if every soul had a color, than, surely, these walls were the color of Micah's soul. Perhaps it was simply the music, however.

Adria smiled. She'd never heard this song before, but she loved it. It was sad, yet beautiful; tragic, yet inviting. Again, it told her everything she needed to know. It told her everything had changed between she and Micah. He was ready to let her in. He was finally ready to share himself with her.

She turned her head to look at him, afraid of what she would see, frightened of the intensity of her emotions. She'd known he was sitting next to her all along, but hadn't dared to look at him until now. When she did, her eyes came to rest, locked on his. Her eyes welled up with tears of immense happiness, love and relief. Micah smiled at her, tears standing in his own eyes.

"¿Qué canción?" she asked, her voice barely a whisper. (What song?)

Micah's smile widened. She remembered. She remembered everything now. Her eyes were both happy and pained.

"Fever Dream," he said. "Iron and Wine."

"I like it," she said.

"I knew you would."

"John," she looked at him and cried.

"Celia, it all be okay," Micah said, his own voice deeper, southern. "I ain't chasin' no mo' rabbits 'yond th' fence, no mo'," Micah said.

Adria looked at Micah, and her mind saw John. She remembered every feature of his face. A thousand memories played through her mind, and they changed her.

"I never even got my dress hemmed," she said.

"Betty," Micah said, and his mind was back in 1929.

"Te extrañé," she said, still crying. (I missed you.)

"Lo siento, yo nunca quería irme. Nunca quise hacerte daño," Micah said. (I'm sorry, I never wanted to leave. I never meant to hurt you.)

"I know," Adria said.

She smiled. Then her smile faded, and she looked sad. Micah's heart broke.

"We're mad, now, aren't we?" she said.

"No," Micah said. "Not if we stay together."

"I look at you, and I see other faces."

"I know."

"I'm not as pretty as I was when I was Sophie," Adria said.

"Yes, you are."

He leaned forward and touched her cheek with one finger. She closed her eyes.

"I'm not as handsome as John," Micah said. "Or Devon."

"You're beautiful," Adria said. "You've always been beautiful. All of you. In every color."

He nodded. A tear slipped down his cheek.

"So have you."

"What name should I call you?" she frowned.

"Micah," he answered immediately. "It's who I am now, in this life. If we stay focused, we can handle this – if we stay focused on this life, and who we are, now."

Adria shook her head. She closed her eyes, seeing Eduardo, seeing Rafael. She cried again.

"Adria," Micah said, his voice soft and strangled. "Everything's going to be okay. It will get easier. Trust me, I know. You just need some time. The memories are too fresh, that's all. You're still reeling in them. It will wear off. Eventually, you'll stop seeing other faces. Then you'll only see mine."

"I've watched you die so many times, Micah," Adria said.

"I'm sorry," he whispered.

He could offer her no comfort with this. The memories were plastered to both their souls, haunting them, constantly reminding them of their impending fate.

"I can't watch you die again."

"You won't have to," Micah said.

"How?" she cried.

"We can be around each other, and the curse won't set in," he said. He was cautious in his delivery. "The curse won't take hold, unless we make love."

She looked at him, her eyes full of longing. Even now, amidst all the pain, his statement, the very words he'd spoken, caused a great aching in her soul. She looked away, embarrassed. She looked back when she felt the warmth of his hand as he took hers and held it.

"I can't make love to you," he said. "But I can touch you."

"No," she said, pulling her hand out of his. "The temptation is too great."

"Then I won't touch you at all," Micah said. His voice was sad, pained. "We'll be friends. We'll talk. We'll know each other. We can live our lives, together, for the first time."

"For how long?"

"Forever," he said.

"We can't live like this forever," Adria said. "It's not possible. We both know that."

"What do you want me to do, Adria?" Micah asked, but his voice was gentle, kind. "Do you want me to leave you alone?"

"No," she said, looking at him with fear and desperation.

"I won't ever leave you alone again, Adria," Micah said. "I promise. But I also promise I'll never touch you. Not like that. Not when I know what it means for you."

"For me?" Adria said. "You're the one who will die."

"I don't care about me," Micah said. "I care about you, Adria. If I die, I know you'll follow me."

"No quiero que te mueras," Adria said. (I don't want you to die.)

"I won't," Micah said. "I won't ever put you through that again. I swear."

"You can't stop it, Micah," Adria said. "After all this time, don't you know that?"

"No, I won't give up," Micah said. "Not when we both remember. We can choose now. We can choose not to let the curse in."

"I love you," Adria said, crying again.

"I love you, too," Micah said. "We can be together, Adria. For years and years. We can make this work."

Adria lay in his bed, still crying. Micah got up and pulled the few books on his shelf into his hands. He brought them back to Adria and set them next to her, on the bed cover. She sat up then, for the first time and frowned, looking down at her still damp clothes.

"I didn't dare undress you," Micah said. "Sorry."

She looked at the books on the bed, picking them up and reading the covers of each. She looked at Micah, a small tinge of hope in her eyes.

"What are these?"

"Books," Micah said.

"I know that, *tonto*. (silly) Why did you give them to me?"

"I like them," Micah shrugged.

Adria looked at his face, curious and amused. Then she looked at each of the books again, with more interest.

"So, this is it? You're going to let me in, now?" Her voice was soft, hopeful.

Micah nodded.

"What's this one?" Adria held one of the books up.

"This writer I found online. She's self-published. Her stories are good, though."

"And this?" Adria held up another book.

"You've never read Stephen King?" Micah asked.

"No," Adria said. "I don't like scary stories."

"Sorry," Micah shrugged. "I listened to all your songs."

"I'll read them," Adria quickly said, feeling awful. "If you like them, I want to read them."

"If you really want me to share myself with you, you have to promise to keep an open mind."

"Why?" Adria squinted her eyes.

Micah's eyes went to the poster on the wall next to his bed. Adria looked over and studied it.

"Oh, no," she said. "No way."

"You want me to share myself with you, don't you? Everything I'm into?"

"I don't dance," Adria said. "And I don't listen to techno. And I certainly don't dance while listening to techno."

Micah only smiled, his old, crooked grin reappearing. Adria melted.

"Well, there's a rave in Portland next Friday night. If you tell your mom you're sleeping over at Sam's, we can go."

"You want me to lie to my mom?" Adria said, but there was a twinkle in her eye.

"I want you to go with me," Micah said.

"I guess love is worth lying for," Adria teased.

"Is it worth dying for?"

"We're not going to die," Adria said. "Apparently we're going to dance."

Micah looked at Adria and smiled. For the time being, they were both at peace, just being near each other. For a short while, they were both only seventeen again.

10. December 3-10, 2009

Sam went to Adria's house after school the next day. She told Adria everything she'd already discussed with Micah. Adria, in turn, told Sam everything she remembered in the cemetery the day before. She also told her about waking up in Micah's room, in his bed. Sam grew visibly upset by this.

"He put you in his bed?" she said. "That was not smart, Adria."

"I was soaked. He didn't want me to get sick," Adria sounded defensive.

"Adria, this is a very dangerous game you guys are playing. I told Micah to be your friend. But you guys cannot touch each other. If you do, it will only open the door to temptation."

"I don't see how anyone can even know that," Adria said. "Just because we had sex in all our other lives, before Micah died, doesn't mean that's what caused the curse to awaken. For all we know, it's already been set into motion, just by us seeing each other."

"That's what I said," Sam said. "But Micah's adamant. He says you'll be safe, as long as you guys don't do that one thing."

"So, we can do other things?" Adria looked hopeful. "We can kiss, hold hands, go on dates."

"No," Sam shook her head. "Every time you touch each other, it will get harder and harder to resist going further. Micah seems to know what he's talking about."

"Look, how hard can it be to not have sex? We'll just monitor ourselves, and if things start to get too hot and heavy, we'll pull back."

"Adria," Sam said. "You can't even risk it. Not with the way the two of you are drawn to each other."

"Well, then what do you suggest? I mean, according to the theories I'm hearing, if we're so drawn to each other, then, eventually, we'll end up doing it, no matter how hard we try not to. If we're cursed, it will happen."

"That's what I'm afraid of," Sam said. "The two of you obviously can't be apart. Look how miserable you were when you both tried. You both looked near death. And you were writing songs about girls slitting their wrists."

"It's just a song," Adria said. "I'm writing a new one. It's not as bad."

"Good, it better not be. Can I hear it?"

"It's not done yet," Adria said. "I started writing it last night, after I came back from Micah's. It practically wrote itself. It'll be done in another day or so."

"Well, I'm still waiting for that damn book to be shipped in from Salem," Sam said. "Can you believe someone has it checked out? I'm sitting here waiting for them to return it, so the library can send it here. Luckily, we have time. Provided you and Micah can behave."

"Um, about that," Adria said.

"Oh, God. Please tell me you didn't have sex?"

"What? No!" Adria said. "But, I need you to do me a favor next Friday. Micah wants to take me to a rave. It goes 'til three or four in the morning."

"A rave?" Sam said.

"Don't make fun," Adria said. "I wanted Micah to share who he is with me. He really wants me to go."

"But, it's dancing, Adria. In a huge crowd. It gets all hot and sweaty. People start taking all their clothes off. They dance in their underwear."

"They do?" Adria looked shocked. "He didn't say anything about being in my underwear."

"You don't have to," Sam said. "But, you'll be dancing with each other, up close. You'll be touching. I don't think it's a very good idea."

"Well, we're certainly not going to have sex right there on the dance floor," Adria said. "Come on. He asked me. I promised. All you have to do is, if my mom calls, just say I'm on the toilet. I'll tell my mom I'm sleeping at your place. You come to my house to pick me up, she'll have no idea."

"Where are you going to sleep at four in the morning?" Sam asked.

"I don't know," Adria frowned. "I didn't think about that."

"Have you thought about anything?"

"Of course," Adria said. She grew quiet for several moments. "I've replayed Micah dying in my head, over and over again. It's him now, in every dream I ever had. Even if it's a different face. They're all him. And they're all me, too."

"This is so fucked up. That actually made sense to me," Sam said.

"Look, I'm not stupid. And I'm not selfish. Don't you know that? If I gave in to my urges, if I made love with Micah, I might as well stab a knife through his heart. You really think I could do that? Why? Because I'm horny? If I make love with Micah, I'm murdering him. That's plenty enough to stop me, every time."

"Fine. But we're not talking about being horny here, Adria. This goes way beyond that. We're talking about a bond you and Micah share. A bond so strong, your souls find each other, over and over again, in every life. A connection so intense, he knew where to find you, even though he didn't know who you were. He was drawn to Cannon Beach. We're not dealing with normal forces, here."

"You make it sound like we have no choice."

"No, you have a choice," Sam said. "Adria, listen to me, 'cause you're not going to like what I have to say right now. I know you think you can withstand being with Micah. But if you can't, if something happens, then…" Sam trailed off.

"Then what?" Adria said. Sam took a deep breath.

"If, for some reason, the unthinkable happens, and the two of you hook up. If the curse gets set into motion, you still have a choice."

"What choice, what are you talking about?" Adria was visibly upset now. "It's not going to happen."

"But if it does, you can still choose to live," Sam said.

"Choose to live?"

"You don't have to follow Micah, if he gets killed," Sam said. "You can choose to live."

"What are you talking about?" Adria stood, pacing the floor of her room.

"Adria, you don't have to kill yourself. You don't have to follow him," Sam said.

"If we make love, which won't happen, then it'll be my fault that he dies," Adria said. "You think I'm going to let him die, and just leave him all alone?"

"No, Adria," Sam said. "I think if you really love him, you'll let him go."

"Let him go?" Adria looked at Sam in disbelief.

"If you don't follow him, he'll be reborn, and live a normal life. He'll never meet you, and he'll never have any idea you exist. He could live a full life, meet someone. Maybe even fall in love and get married. Have a regular, actual life."

"With someone else?!" Adria screamed.

"At least he'd live," Sam yelled back. "And so would you!"

"You saw what being away from him for just a few weeks did to me, Sam," Adria shook her head. "There's no way I could let him go, and not follow him. I would never do that to him."

"You'd be doing him a favor!" Sam yelled.

"No, I'd be abandoning him!" Adria yelled back. "I'm not going to talk about this anymore. It's not gonna happen, anyway. Micah's not going to die."

****

But Adria couldn't help bringing it up with Micah the next day. They walked along the Tillamook Head Trail, connected with Indian Point, and hiked to the view of Terrible Tilly. Along the way, Adria mentioned her argument with Sam. She told Micah everything Sam had said, and then waited for his response. When he finally spoke, he surprised her.

"Sam's right."

"What?"

Adria stopped walking. They were still a good quarter mile away from the view of the lighthouse. The sky was overcast and dark gray, but there was no rain. It had rained all morning, but now it was done. A moderate breeze blew, however.

Both their noses were red from the cold. Adria had her hands stuffed deep into her coat pockets, and her fur-trimmed hood obscured much of her face. Micah also wore a heavy, hooded, navy blue sweat jacket. His scud of black bangs could still be seen, pushed down by his hood, covering part of his eyes.

"Sam's right," Micah repeated. "If the unthinkable happens, you should let me go."

"Are you crazy!" Adria was livid. "After everything we've been through?"

"If you follow me, it will just happen all over again," Micah said, trying to remain calm. "Then we'll only suffer through more lives, and more deaths. Remember, Adria, next time we probably won't remember. Then we'll be forced to replay everything again and again. Next time we won't even know to control ourselves. We won't even practice self-control. We'll have no clue."

"But you asked me to follow you," Adria began to cry. "You made me promise."

"I know," Micah said, his voice lower now.

He couldn't help himself. He came to her and hugged her. He held her tight as she cried. He felt awful. He didn't want to let her go.

"Don't you realize what you're asking of me, Adria?" he whispered. "You're asking me to ask you to take your own life. How can I ever be that selfish? When I know…I know what it all means. Beyond being blinded by love? If I really love you, I could never ask you to hurt yourself. Not even to be with me."

"But I'll never see you again," Adria said, pulling away to look at him. "Don't you care about what I want?"

"You want to die?"

Micah looked at Adria with heavy concern. His eyes were pained, but so were hers.

"I don't want to live without you," Adria said. "Do you want to live without me?"

"No," Micah said, pulling her into his arms again. "I don't. But how can I hurt you this way?"

"It's not your fault," Adria said.

She pulled herself out of his arms again, and looked at him. Her cheeks were aflame from his touch, from being in his arms. Her body was on fire, but her mind was elsewhere, for the time being. Micah raked in heavy breaths, also highly aroused. His whole body was also on fire, but it soon cooled, when Adria spoke.

"We have to decide what we're going to do," she said. "If the worst happens. If something happens to you. We have to agree, now, what we're willing to live with, and what we're willing to do. What we want."

"Adria," Micah sighed.

"No, if something happens to you, I need to know what you want from me."

"What I want?"

"Do you want me, Micah?" Adria asked. "Do you want to be with me?"

"Of course," Micah sighed, closing his eyes.

"Then you want me to follow you," Adria said.

"Adria," Micah shook his head.

"Then you don't want me," Adria yelled.

She walked past him, stomping up the trailhead. Micah remained where he was standing, feeling stunned. His thoughts swirled. They were arguing? When they should have simply been astounded and overwhelmed with happiness at being together, they were actually fighting?

Micah's anger, a hibernating beast, quickly rose to the surface, and he trudged after Adria. The fire burning in his chest fueled his rage to new heights. He reached her and spun her around. She cried out in surprise.

"How can you ask me such things?" he screamed. "How can you ask me for permission to kill yourself? Why don't you just put the knife into my hands, and drive it through your own heart, then?! You're asking me to kill you!"

"No, I'm asking you to love me!" Adria screamed. "If you die, I want to go with you. Do you really want me to stay here, all alone, without you?"

"No!" Micah screamed.

He was too emotional. He walked past Adria and began pacing. Then he turned back, to face her again, as she began to speak. His rage remained, unabated, and his heart felt desperate.

"Then fine," Adria spat. "We do this again. Over and over. This dance. This sick game. Whatever it is, it's all we have. It's all we're ever going to be allowed to have. So just accept it!"

"Accept it," Micah nodded in anger. "Accept that we're both going to die."

"But it won't be the end," Adria said. "If I follow you. We'll find each other, again. We'll meet. We'll fall in love."

Adria looked down at the ground. Her own anger was gone. She didn't know any other way to be at this point. She didn't know any other way to feel.

"So you've accepted it then, is that it?" Micah said. His own anger was not yet under control. "You've just resigned yourself to my death, your suicide?! You're giving up?! What the fuck are we fighting for, then, huh? Hell, what are we even resisting for, then? If you're so sure we're both going to die, then why not just do it and get it over with? Hey, I know, why don't we fuck right here on the trail, then walk up to Terrible Tilly, and throw ourselves off the cliff, huh?!"

"Shut up," Adria said. Her jaw was set, her teeth clenched. Micah wasn't done.

"Why don't we screw right here in the mud, then jump into that cold water down there, huh? Let's hasten to the next life, Adria! Where we can do this all over again! Let's just do it and get it over with!"

"Shut up!"

Adria screamed. Tears of rage slipped down her cheeks. She was livid, but beyond that, she was utterly confused. Neither of them realized that their fight was being fueled by the ridiculous levels of sexual tension that had already built up between them. It wasn't their fault. From the moment they'd touched, the tension began to build, just as their attraction had sparked in an instant, the moment they first laid eyes on each other.

Adria looked at Micah in hurt disbelief at his cold statements. He looked back at her, immediately regretful. He was only frustrated. He only felt infinitely awful and selfish, for wanting Adria to be with him – for wanting her to follow him.

"How do I resolve loving you the way I do, with asking you to die?" Micah said, tears suddenly filling his eyes. The anger had finally drained away. "I want to do right by you, Adria. I want to love you. I want to keep you safe. How does any of that involve me being so selfish, as to ask you to follow me? It's wrong, Adria. If I really loved you, I could never ask you to do such a thing. Don't you understand?"

"If you really love me, you'll understand how much it will hurt me, if you don't ask me to follow you," Adria said, her own tears now falling. "If you tell me to stay, I don't know if I can. You're not the only selfish one, Micah."

"I love you, Adria," Micah choked out. "I love you."

He rushed up to her and kissed her madly. She melted against him, kissing him back. They were a wild tangle of hoods, flying hands and arms, entangling legs. They fell to the ground, to the side of the trail, in the grass, miraculously avoiding the mud.

He was on top of her, and she felt the weight of his body, and electricity flashed through her. She ran her hands along his back, feeling his muscles strain as he pushed himself into her body. Heat flashed through her, and her desire for him was so great, she felt completely overwhelmed. Her hands were suddenly under his jacket, under his shirt, and she felt his warm skin under her palms.

He kissed her all the while, lost in his own reverie of deep desire and lust. His hands attempted to travel under her thick coat, fumbling for purchase. Finally, in desperation, he reached up and unzipped her jacket, his lips never leaving hers.

She went with his movements, neither of them thinking in words any longer. His hands finally made contact with her skin, under her shirt, over her bra, firmly grasping her breast. He buried his tongue in her mouth, and she eagerly returned his actions. Micah's head spun as she reached her hand down, and grasped him, through his jeans. He wanted her so badly. She wanted him as well.

They continued to kiss this way, he caressing her breasts intermittently, with his hands, and running them up and down her torso, over her buttocks, down the length of her thighs. He ran his left hand back up her inner thigh and gently began caressing her, through her own jeans, even as she continued rubbing him. Their tongues wrestled madly, their lips pressed ever more tightly together.

The whole world disappeared, for both of them, their heads spinning with excitement. Neither of them could think at all, but only act. The cold air did not even register on either of them, only the heat between their bodies. Her legs were spread, and he was between them pushing. She moaned, her hands now on his back, once more. He kissed her, then pulled away, his eyes closed, their foreheads against each other. He kissed her again, and she continued making sounds of pleasure, even as his lips pressed against hers.

She couldn't take it any longer. She desperately unbuttoned his pants, pulling the zipper down. She reached in, over his underwear and felt him, caressing gently with her fingers. This time he moaned, kissing her harder. He unbuttoned her pants, pulled down her zipper, and inserted his hand into her underwear. All at once, Adria's mind flared awake, with a memory.

He kissed her neck, and he gently inserted his hand into the top of her panties, now caressing her with his bare fingers. She moaned.

Adria gasped, her eyes flying open. Micah had seen it too, the vision that quickly flitted through her head. They had done this before.

They were both seventeen, and yet, they were not. They were Justin Tremaine and Charlotte Williams, in their early twenties. They were John and Celia, aged twenty. They were William Fenmore and Elizabeth Harris, age twenty-three. They were Rafael Acosta and Camila Flores, age twenty-four. They were Devon Rogers and Sophie Prescott, age twenty. They were Eduardo Olivas and Amaya Rios, age seventeen.

Micah and Adria were all these couples. They had made love before. Although their current bodies had never engaged in the act, their minds had – dozens of times. They had loved each other, body, soul and mind, in one form or another for over one-hundred-and-thirty years.

Scenes of their physical love for one another played out in their heads, and they shared the visions, together. They were intricately linked, in their close proximity, their compromising position.

Both their bodies went rigid, as the scenes of physical intimacy played out, time and time again. Micah fell against Adria, overwhelmed by the visions, and she clasped his back, gasping, for she was remembering Micah making love to her dozens of times, as different people, and the memories were so vivid, so clear, she felt as if they were actually happening. It was the same for Micah.

As quickly as it began, it ended, and Micah and Adria lay in the grass, their breathing rapid, their hearts beating in double time. Then Micah pulled away, up, to look down at Adria in wonder. She smiled at him, and they both laughed.

"I feel like I should be smoking a cigarette now," Adria sighed, her breathing heavy and labored.

Micah laughed again. Then Adria gasped.

"What?" He looked at her in concern.

"Does that count? We didn't actually do it, did we? It doesn't count, does it?" Adria was panicked.

"Shh," Micah smiled, kissing her lips gently. "I don't think that counts. Since our actual bodies didn't…well…connect. We didn't really do it."

"That was way too close, Micah," Adria said. "I don't know what just happened, with those visions, or memories, or whatever, but, if they hadn't happened, we would have. And you'd be dead."

"I don't think it's that instantaneous," Micah said.

"It was in 1954," Adria said.

"But not in other lives. In 1929 we did it for weeks. We got engaged before…" Micah didn't finish.

"And John and Celia. We were together like that for months, too," Adria said.

"But it doesn't matter," Micah said. "Because we didn't. We're safe."

"For how long? This can't happen again, Micah. Ever."

"I know," he said. "It won't. We got lucky. Our memories saved us."

"But we can't expect them to save us the next time."

"There won't be a next time," Micah said.

He stood, buttoning his pants and pulling his sweat jacket back over his jeans, straightening himself up. He put his hand out for Adria to take and she did, quickly dropping it again once she was back on her feet. She buttoned up her own pants, blushing and looking away, embarrassed. Micah smiled.

"You know, it's perfectly natural to do what we did," he said.

"I know," Adria said, but she continued to blush. "But," she didn't finish.

"What?" Micah asked.

"Well, I may have done it before, as other people, but as Adria Allan? I'm, sort of... a virgin."

"So am I," Micah said. "Well, sort of."

"What do you mean, sort of?" Adria looked at Micah now, feeling hot jealousy begin to rise inside her.

Micah put his hand out for her to take again. She looked at him for another long moment, and then took it.

They walked hand-in-hand up the trail, toward the view of Terrible Tilly. The heat of the moment had passed, and they walked holding hands with little temptation, for the time being.

"What do you mean, sort of, Micah?" Adria asked.

"Do we really have to talk about this?" Micah sighed.

"You brought it up."

"I didn't mean to, it just slipped out," Micah said.

"I don't even want to know what that means," Adria said.

Micah looked sideways at her, frowning, not understanding her statement. Then he blushed and shook his head.

"You're crass, you know that? That's not what I meant."

"I know. So, what did you mean?"

"Look, it doesn't matter, Adria, does it?" Micah said, growing frustrated.

"It matters to me."

"Why?" Micah said. "I wasn't in love. I had no idea what I was doing, even. Not really."

"You mean, you've done it before?"

"Adria, please," Micah said. "You won't understand."

"Try me."

They walked in silence for several more minutes. When they reached the vista, they sat down, looking at Tillamook Rock out in the distance.

The lighthouse was shrouded in thick fog. Adria looked out at the dark rock floating in the ghostly white mist and sighed. Micah thought she was still upset about his statements earlier.

"It was right after my mom went to prison," he said. "I was upset, in shock, or whatever. My mom *killed* someone, Adria. I mean, it was an accident, but still. To find out what she'd been doing…" he paused before going on.

"I only went to visit her once. I got really upset. She didn't even seem that happy to see me. It was last year, before I even knew I was moving, before I even knew a place called Cannon Beach existed.

"I was having all those horrible dreams. That was bad enough. Then my mom and the trial… the sentencing. Then my visit with her went so horribly. I was fucked up, Adria. I was barely sixteen. It happened almost right after my birthday.

"My dad was always working the overnight shift, and with my mom gone, I was all alone. No rules, no one looking out for me. I was on the rave scene every weekend, some weeknights, too. I started skipping school. I was getting into fights. Then one night I went to this huge Christmas Eve rave. It was crazy. Kids everywhere, half-naked. Everyone high. I was dancing, I took these pills. I was hyped. I was fucked up, Adria."

"You already said that," her voice was quiet.

"I didn't even know who she was. I'm not even sure how we ended up alone together. We were in this hallway, in the back of the building. Just, right there on the floor. I don't even remember most of it. It was nothing to me. It was awful."

"Awful?" Adria looked at Micah in sympathy.

"I know you won't believe that, but it's true."

"And nothing like that ever happened before then?"

"No, I just went to dance, to chill, to lose myself," he said. "I danced with people, with girls, but nothing like that ever happened."

"Did you do drugs a lot?" she asked.

"No. I don't know why I did that night. After my mom? I would never touch that shit. I just, I was fucked up."

"You've said that enough," Adria said.

She looked at Micah, her eyes discerning. She smiled.

"I guess I shouldn't be too jealous. As I recall, you were the virgin, and I wasn't, back in 1976."

"Yeah," Micah laughed, "that's right. And we both did a few drugs that year. Together."

"It was the culture at the time," Adria reminded him.

They sounded like an old married couple, reminiscing about the good old days. They both smiled. Then Adria grew serious.

"I'm sorry about your life," she said. "This living again and again thing isn't all it's cracked up to be, huh? You never know who you're going to be, or what your family will be like."

"My mom's in prison, and my own brother stabbed me," Micah chuckled. "Also, I grew up in the poorest city in all of Mexico. The average life span is under age eighteen. You're lucky you met me at all, Amaya."

"Me alegro de haberlo hecho," she said, smiling at him. (I'm glad I did).

"Yo también," (Me, too) Micah said. "Te quiero, Adria." (I love you, Adria).

"Yo también Te amo," she said. (I love you, too). "But if you die, I'm sorry, Micah – I'm going to follow you."

"I won't ask you to," Micah said. "It's wrong of me."

"You don't want me?"

"I want you," he said.

He placed his hand on her face and caressed her cheek, staring at her intently. She looked back, smiling.

"It's my choice," she said. "One I'm happy to make. You're everything to me. You always have been. If I have to die, to get another chance with you, I'll take it, every time. For however long it lasts."

"It can last all our lives, if we never take it too far."

"Like just now?" she said. "Can we really do that forever?"

Micah looked away, dropping his hand from her face. He looked out at Tillamook Rock, hidden in the fog. It was just beginning to drizzle again. Micah looked at the waves down below.

"Maybe Sam will figure something out? A way to break the curse."

"I think that's highly unlikely," Adria said.

"It looks so normal out there," Micah said. "Just, normal waves, sea water. What could have caused this, Adria?"

"Me," she said.

"What? Why would you think that?"

"I'm the one that dove in after you," she said. "Maybe my suicide is being punished?"

"Don't think like that," Micah said. "You were trying to save me, Adria. That's not suicide. Besides, if I'd died, and only me, then I'd just be living, again and again, without you. What little life I've had, it's only been worth living because of you."

"And you won't ask me to come with you?" She looked at him, infinitely hurt.

"Not because I don't love you, Adria, but because I do," he said. "I won't ask you to follow me. It doesn't mean I don't hope you will. That's as much as I'm willing to say. If you should choose not to follow me, I would understand."

"Don't say that," she said, her voice wavering. "I would never abandon you that way. Never, Micah. Micah, look at me," she said. "I will never leave you alone."

"Promise?" he asked.

"I promise."

It was the closest he ever came to asking her to follow him, but it was enough. It was enough for Adria. She gazed out at the ocean, smiling. Micah saw her smile and broke out in one of his own.

"You know, we're slightly mad?" he said.

"Yeah," she said, still smiling.

"Song?"

"'Til Kingdom come, Coldplay."

Micah nodded. The two of them looked out at the view. He put his arm around Adria and she rested her head on his shoulder. For the time being, they were in friend mode, simply happy to be in each other's company.

****

The next week went by in a blur of school exams, in preparation for the winter break. Adria actually studied. Micah did not. He passed his exams, but barely. Adria, miraculously, had managed to pull her grades up, since her weeks of depression during the midterm. She drove to school every morning following Sam, and walked with her in the halls.

At lunch, Adria sat with Sam and Micah. They never touched each other at school. For all viewable purposes, they were friends, only.

Every once in a while, Adria would notice Westley Kane glaring over at Micah, from the jock table. She saw Kane brooding one day and brought it up.

"I thought you settled everything with Kane, Micah?"

"No," he said, "My dad settled everything with his dad, and Prince. And my college tuition, in lieu of my being arrested on charges of assault and battery. We paid for his doctor's bills, too. I broke his nose," Micah chuckled.

"It's not funny, Micah," Adria said. "He's looking at you like he wants to kill you."

A chill ran up Adria's spine. She looked at Sam, who looked down at the table. Micah said nothing else. He only looked over his shoulder at Kane, then quickly away again.

"I'd steer clear of him, if I were you," Sam said. "You know?"

"Yeah, well, I'm not planning on getting into anymore fights," Micah said.

His voice was gentle. He looked at Adria lovingly. He'd found peace, now that he was with her – now that they were openly talking about everything.

Adria looked at Sam then, with guilt on her face. Micah frowned. Sam only watched the two of them, curious.

"Micah doesn't know about Westley, does he?" Sam said.

Adria looked at Sam, widening her eyes. Sam looked back at her shrugging, as if to say 'what?'

"Know what about Westley?" Micah asked.

"It's nothing," Adria said. "Nothing, really."

"Then why don't you tell me?" Micah was looking at Adria with great interest now.

"It's a little strange that of all the people you decided to beat the crap out of on your first day here, you chose Westley Kane," Sam said, jumping in for Adria. "Why did you choose him to pick a fight with, Micah?"

"I don't know," Micah shrugged. "I didn't like the way he looked at me. Why? Tell me what about Westley, Adria?"

"It's nothing much," Adria said. "We just, sort of, dated for a few weeks last year. That's all."

"That's all?" Micah looked at Adria in shock and anger. "And you're just now telling me this?"

"Well, you only just told me about that rave girl. And you and her had actual sex! I never had sex with Westley Kane," Adria said, lowering her voice.

"You had sex with a rave girl?" Sam asked.

"I told you that didn't mean anything," Micah said. He was gazing at Adria, and never acknowledged Sam's question.

"Oh sure, that's what guys always say," Sam said.

"Shut up!" Micah and Adria both yelled at the same time.

"Dude, I'm not staying to listen to this. Good luck, you two. Hope you work it out," Sam said.

Sam stood to leave, clearly angry. Adria quickly stood as well. Micah followed her. All the while, Kane watched Micah, glaring.

In the hallway, the fight continued. Sam walked away to her locker down another hallway. Micah grabbed Adria's shoulder, spinning her around.

"Why didn't you tell me you dated Kane?"

"Because it was no big deal," she said. "We only went out a couple of times."

"Why did you stop going out with him?"

"Because," Adria said, growing quiet. "He got sort of… aggressive one night, in his car."

"He tried to rape you?"

"No!" Adria screamed. "He just… got really mad when I told him to stop. That's all. But he did, he stopped. He drove me home. He wouldn't talk to me the whole way. Then he peeled out and drove off. He asked me out again, and I said no. The guy's a steroid-freak, or something. I don't know. He's got a bad temper."

"Yeah, well, he's not so tough. Obviously," Micah said, sneering. "I sure kicked his ass. And now I'm glad. Extra glad."

"Kane's a badass, Micah. The fact that you kicked his ass, is actually pretty amazing. You humiliated him, in front of everyone. Twice. He hates you, Micah. You'd better leave him alone.

"I didn't tell you about him, because after you fought him, twice, I didn't want to give you another excuse to go after him. You can't blame me. If you get into another fight, you'll get kicked out of school. And who knows what your dad will do to you?"

"He won't do anything," Micah said.

"Maybe he'll ground you, and then I won't be able to see you anymore."

"No, he's not so good at setting rules. He's still pretty lenient, even after everything. It's not his fault. He lets me come and go, pretty much. I think he's just waiting for me to turn eighteen, so he can be free of me."

"I'm sorry, Micah."

"I know," he said. "But I wish you'd told me about Kane."

"I just did. Please leave him alone, Micah. You shouldn't mess with him. He could really hurt you, if he decided to."

"I already kicked his ass twice," Micah said. "I'm not worried about Kane."

Micah put his arm around Adria and they walked down the hallway together. Adria, however, had a bad feeling; a feeling of portentous dread that was just beginning to bloom, deep inside her mind, where she hardly knew it was there.

****

Friday night, December 10 arrived, and once home from school, Adria hurriedly packed her overnight things, including a pair of shorts and a white tank top, for the rave. She'd asked Micah about the whole dancing in her underwear thing, but he only shook his head, laughing.

"I'm not sure I want you dancing in your underwear, for other guys to see," he said. "Or that I could handle seeing you writhing almost naked, given our restricted circumstances."

Adria laughed, feeling relieved.

Now she packed the rest of her things, nervous at having to lie to her mother. She went downstairs, where Emily was making herself a bowl of soup.

"Mom? Sam asked me to stay at her house. Okay?"

"Sure, honey," Emily said. "You haven't done that in a while. It's nice to see you looking more happy again."

"I am happy," Adria said, and this was not a lie.

"I can see that," Emily said. "No nightmares?"

"No, not for a few weeks, now," Adria said, again, not lying.

"What a relief," Emily said, stirring her soup. "Maybe that whole business is finally behind us, hmm?"

"Yeah, I hope so," Adria said. "I'll be home in the afternoon tomorrow, okay? Maybe we can hang out."

Adria was feeling guilty about lying. Emily turned and frowned at her daughter.

"Why, what's wrong?"

"Nothing," Adria said. "It's just, we don't really spend that much time together anymore, that's all."

"You're a teenager," Emily laughed, "that's normal."

"Okay," Adria said. "I just didn't want to hurt you, is all. Hurt your feelings, I mean."

"They're not," Emily said. "Is Sam picking you up?"

Adria nodded. Emily poured her soup into a bowl and sat down at the kitchen table. Adria sat down with her.

"Yuck. What is that?"

"It's clam chowder," Emily said.

"It's red," Adria said, wrinkling up her nose.

"It's Manhattan clam chowder."

"Disgusting."

"Don't knock it 'til you try it."

"Um, no. You couldn't pay me to taste that," Adria said.

Emily held a spoonful of the red soup out to Adria and she backed her face away, grimacing. Her mother was playing with her. She laughed.

"No," she said, through her laughter.

Sam honked her horn outside then, and Adria looked at her mother, apologizing with her eyes for cutting their playtime short.

"Go," Emily said. "Have fun."

"Thanks, mom."

She stood, kissed her mother on the cheek and left the kitchen. She grabbed her overnight bag and banged out the door, skipping down the steps of her yard, and hopped into Sam's Prius. Sam was blasting Giving Up the Gun, by

Vampire Weekend. Adria laughed, getting into the passenger seat.

"You'd better enjoy it while you can, honey. 'Cause you're gonna be dancing to shitty techno all night long."

"Don't remind me," Adria laughed. "But I'll be with Micah."

Adria sighed. Sam rolled her eyes.

"Jesus, just don't do anything stupid. I still don't have that book, Adria."

"You really seem to be putting a lot of hope into this one, stupid, little book."

"It's not little," Sam said. "It's a hundred-and-twenty-plus pages of Tillamook legend I've never read before. I'd say chances are pretty damn good that at least a few of the legends will pertain to Tillamook Rock, or the Nehalem River. Or both."

"Well, just don't hold your breath, is all I'm saying," Adria said. "'Cause I doubt the ancient Tillamook tribes found a cure to me and Micah's little ailment."

"Ailment? Is that what we're calling it now?"

"For lack of any better description," Adria said, sighing. "You're dropping me at Micah's. His dad's already left for work."

"I know," Sam said. "Have you ever even met that guy?"

Adria shook her head.

"Huh," Sam said. "It's a wonder Micah's not more maladjusted."

"His dad's not a bad person," Adria said. "He can't help having to work nights."

"Yeah, but how do you know he's not a bad person?" Sam said. "I mean, look at your dad. Your dad rocks, dude."

"Yeah," Adria laughed. "He does."

"Have you thought about that?" Sam said.

"What?"

"What would happen to your dad, if you killed yourself?"

Sam was trying to be gentle, but she wanted to put a scare into Adria, before leaving her in the care of Micah. It wasn't that she didn't trust Micah to do his best to withstand his instincts. After all, giving in to his urges would spell death for himself first, as well as for Adria. But Sam also knew that the couple was madly in love, and that there were also forces at work around them that went beyond normal, rational explanation.

"I'm not going to kill myself," Adria said. "And Micah isn't going to die. Nothing bad is going to happen. Not tonight, anyhow. So don't worry, Sam. Okay?"

"Fine," Sam said. "It's just something to think about. I know you're all madly in love and caught up in this whole, crazy thing. But you might want to stop and think about the people around you, not just Micah. Your mom and dad would be devastated if you died, Adria. And then, there's me."

"I love you, Sam. You know that."

"I know. But if Micah dies, you're going to kill yourself, right?"

Sam pulled up in front of Micah's house, parked, and stared at Adria. Adria only stared back, unblinking.

"Right?" Sam repeated.

"I... I don't know," Adria said, suddenly scared.

"What do you mean, you don't know?" Sam asked. "You don't know if you'd follow him or not?"

"I... I don't know what I would do," Adria said, growing flustered. "I wouldn't know unless I was faced with the situation."

"Well, you've done it every time before," Sam said.

"This time's different, like Micah said."

"How?" Sam asked.

"Because he's right," Adria said, suddenly, fully realizing it, letting it in. "We never had a choice before. This time, we do. Micah doesn't have to die."

"Yeah, if you don't fuck up," Sam said. "I still think going to this thing tonight is a recipe for trouble."

"He wants to share what he loves with me," Adria shrugged. "And I want to know. He said it will be special."

"Jesus," Sam said, rubbing her temple. "I'll bet. To die for."

Sam looked at Adria, her eyes pained. Adria smiled and hugged her friend.

"You're my best friend, Sam," she said. "I love you."

"I love you, too," Sam said. "Now go, before I change my mind, or try to stop you."

Adria got out of the car and walked up to Micah's door, knocking. He answered and Adria disappeared inside. Sam drove off shaking her head. She was smiling, however, despite herself.

11. December 10-11 2009

The drive into Portland took two hours, on the windy, two-lane hwy out of Cannon Beach. They went east on Highway 26, then took the 405 south, then the 5 north. Finally, Micah turned onto I-84 East and they headed into downtown Portland.

They didn't leave Cannon Beach until ten at night. It was after midnight when Micah pulled his black Volkswagen van into the huge, dirt parking lot in front of the large warehouse.

"How did you even find out about this place?" Adria asked, putting on lipstick.

"The Internet," Micah said.

He reached across Adria and opened his glove box, pulling out a silver CD in a clear plastic case. She moved closer to the window, away from his arm.

It had been almost an entire week since their encounter at Indian Point, and Micah had not touched her since that day, nor had she dared to touch him. Just the heat she felt coming off his arm, as he reached across her, aroused her. She breathed out, in controlled breaths, attempting to ignore her feelings, and they passed. She looked at the CD Micah was holding, curious.

"What's that?"

"*Something*," Micah teased, smiling. "You'll see. Come on."

"Wait. Do I look okay?" Adria said. "Like I fit in with the crowd here?"

She was nervous. He smiled his crooked grin at her, and she felt completely at home.

"You look," Micah paused, breathing. "Definitely like you fit in."

They got out of the van and walked to the line that was queued up outside the building. Adria looked at the other patrons who were waiting, feeling uncomfortable again.

Many were pierced about the face. Adria took in the multi-colored Mohawks, tattoos, dog collars and skimpy clothing of the other people and she felt embarrassingly wholesome.

"Micah. I'm fucking Pollyanna over here," she said.

"You are?" Micah said, looking surprised. "I didn't know you leaned that way."

Adria frowned at him for several moments, taking in his joke, before finally getting it. Then she broke out laughing, and Micah touched her for the first time in a week. Before she realized he was even near her, he was kissing her. She kissed him back, fire and electricity igniting inside her stomach, as it flip-flopped with butterflies.

Micah pulled away after a few moments, attempting to restrain himself. Adria could see him struggling. She sighed, trying to recompose herself.

She looked around, and saw several couples throughout the line, also kissing. Many of them were being fairly open in their displays of affection. Adria saw hands groping in places she'd rather not witness, as well as the flashing of multiple tongues up and down the line.

"Ick," she said. "Too much PDA for me."

Micah smiled, relieved that the initial urge had passed in him. He was growing excited for the rave. He hadn't been to one in quite a while. More importantly, he'd never had anyone to share the experience with. He was infinitely happy to be there with Adria. As they waited in line, Adria talked to him.

"You know, we used to dance at night on the porch, 'member?" she said.

"I 'member," Micah said, falling into the personality of John. "Played me a mighty mean banjo, too."

"That's right, ya did," Adria laughed. "This'll be a spot might diff'rent, I 'spect."

"Justa speck," Micah said.

The line began to move and Adria took Micah's hand. He smiled.

"Hope this won't bother y'none," she said.

"So long's y'keep yo' hands in a decent place," Micah sighed. "Not that ah mind when they roam, but," Micah trailed off.

"Where are you from?" The guy in front of Micah turned around. "That accent's a trip, dude."

"Uh, yeah," Micah said, becoming himself again.

"Do they have alcohol inside there?" Adria asked.

"I'm sure you can find some, if you check around," Micah laughed. "Why?"

"'Cause I need me a drank, sore fo' sure," Adria laughed.

Micah laughed back and kissed Adria's cheek, whispering in her ear.

"We're crazy."

Adria laughed again, this time harder, and Micah joined in with her. They were both laughing so hard, by the time they got to the front of the line, they were in tears. The bouncer only looked at them, shaking his head as Micah paid. He stamped their hands with invisible ink, and Micah rushed Adria inside.

"But, the stamp didn't take."

"Yes, it did."

"I can't see it."

"You will," Micah said.

They walked down a long corridor, which opened up onto a huge, open warehouse floor. It was dark, but everyone was illuminated, their clothing and jewelry glowing under black lights that covered the entire length of the immense ceiling. Adria looked down at her hand and saw that her previously invisible stamp was a bright, neon yellow. It was a small dragon image. She laughed.

The music pounded, and so did her ribcage. It was techno, but inside the venue, surrounded by a mass of jumping, writhing youths, the atmosphere was contagious, and Adria broke out in a wide smile. The air was hot and musty, smelling of sweat and gum.

Adria looked at Micah, and saw his own wide grin under the black lights. He was wearing a black shirt, but the white buttons floated to her eyes and she laughed again. Her own white tank top made her painfully visible, as well as her white socks and striped sneaks.

"Aren't you going to be hot?" Adria yelled, to be heard over the music.

Micah shook his head and unbuttoned his shirt. Underneath, he wore a plain white t-shirt. He tied his black shirt around his waste. He looked beautiful. At least now their tops matched, Adria thought.

Micah led her around the outer edge of the massive crowd. He craned his neck, looking for something. He passed the bar and led Adria behind it, into a corner.

In the far back, Micah spotted the person he was looking for. A tall, skinny guy wearing a Dr. Seuss hat, ala Cat in the Hat, stood in the corner, nodding his head to the beat of the music. He was much older than the average rave-goer, Adria noted.

She looked at Micah, her face questioning. He leaned his lips into her ear, and her skin tingled and crawled, her stomach doing another flip. She had it bad, tonight, she realized. She sighed.

"I need your Driver's license," he said.

"Why?"

"No questions," Micah said. "Please?"

"Of course," Adria said, shrugging.

She gave Micah her license, and he took out his own. Micah left Adria standing several feet away, and she watched as he approached Dr. Seuss.

She frowned, as Micah spoke to the guy, and motioned back toward her. Dr. Seuss nodded, glancing over at Adria, then smiled, nodding some more. Adria grew nervous as she watched Micah produce what looked like a decent wad of cash from his back pocket, and handed it to the guy.

Dr. Seuss put the money in his own pocket, not even bothering to count it. Then he clapped Micah on the back and nodded again, whispering something in Micah's ear. Micah nodded and left, returning to Adria's side, smiling.

"What the hell was that all about?"

"Do you trust me?" Micah said.

"With my life," Adria said, looking at Micah with sad eyes.

"Come on," he smiled, pulling her back towards the crowd.

They walked around again, and Micah bobbed to the beat, dancing around Adria playfully. She laughed, shaking her head and rolling her eyes. He was cute. But Adria didn't dance.

Micah led Adria toward the DJ stage, then left her again, this time approaching the DJ and handing him the CD he'd brought from the van. He handed a bill of cash to the DJ, but Adria could not tell what it was. It could have been one dollar, or a hundred, for all she knew. The DJ took the money and the CD, smiling and nodding. He gave Micah a thumb's up, and Micah returned to Adria's side, once more.

"What the hell are you up to, Micah?" Adria laughed.

"You'll see," Micah said. "Now, come on. Let's dance!"

"I don't know how."

"Like this."

Micah began jumping around, shaking his shoulders, teasing her. She laughed, shaking her head. She looked around at the other people dancing, growing shy and embarrassed. People were grinding together. Men stood behind women, so close, there was no space between them, and pumped their groins into female's backsides.

Adria looked away, shocked. It was like watching people have simulated sex, while standing up. Men ran their hands down women's bodies, and women ran their hands over men, reaching behind them.

Many couples were making out, standing in the crowd. Adria looked at Micah, worried. He sidled up to her, looking at her tantalizingly, but he held his crooked smile as well, and there was a twinkle in his eyes. He was only trying to have fun with her. This was what he loved, and he wanted to share it with her.

Micah put his hands on Adria's hips and coaxed her to sway with him. He was gentle about it, and she was grateful.

"This is dangerous," she leaned in and whispered in his ear.

"Not as long as we're in a crowd," he whispered back. "Just touch me, Adria. Let go. Have fun. It's safe, I promise. It's a release, you'll see."

Micah spun Adria around and pulled her body into his. Her stomach flopped again. She breathed as he leaned in and whispered to her some more, closing her eyes.

"Don't close your eyes," he said. "Look at everyone, Adria. They're all so *alive*. They just want to let go of all the shit in their lives, inside their heads, and be free."

He spun her around again, so she was facing him and he threw his arms out, smiling and happy. She laughed.

"This is therapy for the masses!" he yelled.

Several people close to them responded to Micah's exclamation by whooping, screaming and yelling their agreement. Micah got close to Adria again, placing his forehead against hers. This time, he closed his eyes and Adria followed suit. They swayed to the beat, slowly at first, then picking up speed, as Adria began to relax; the energy flowing all around her, becoming contagious, as well as Micah's own excitement.

"Let go, Adria. Dance with me. Be crazy with me. Let it all out," Micah said.

He pulled her close and kissed her, once. Then he ran his hands down her torso and she felt electricity shoot through her. It drove her crazy. She wanted to take Micah right there on the dance floor. She wanted to jump on him, knock him to the floor, straddle him and do unthinkable things. Instead, she took all the energy and anticipation that was building up inside of her and filtered it into her body, moving with Micah as they swayed to the music, faster and faster.

Adria felt so free, so released from all the tension in her life. She was with Micah, and although they weren't making actual love, it was the next closest thing. There was a distinct satisfaction to be had, she found, in moving in time with Micah's body. She found she could touch him now, here, without any fear of bringing a curse upon either of them. It was exhilarating.

They danced to the beat, jumping up and down, writhing against each other, sometimes pulling away, always coming back together again. She was hot and sweaty before the end of the first full song they danced to. One song bled its beat straight into the next.

After about ten minutes, Micah stopped dancing and looked at Adria with a huge smile on his face. She stopped jumping and looked at him, frowning.

"What?"

Micah pointed up at the ceiling, into the air. She frowned again.

"Keep listening," he yelled.

Adria listened. The DJ was just playing another techno song. They all sounded generally the same to her. It was a heavy, thudding beat. Then an echoing voice sounded, underneath the beat, and she heard a few notes that sounded hauntingly familiar.

I am the eye in the sky...

And I can read your mind...

Micah smiled heavily as Adria gasped, her own face breaking out in the biggest smile he'd seen yet. He laughed. The beat continued as the song broke out into its main music. Adria squealed and threw herself into Micah's arms, kissing him madly. He kissed her back. After a few moments, they both pulled away and began dancing to the rhythm.

"Just for you!" Micah yelled.

Any remaining inhibitions residing inside Adria vanished then, and she danced with Micah without reserve. He knew this would happen. He knew Adria so well.

They jumped, they touched, they bobbed, they rubbed one another. Shivers and tingles ran through Adria's body. Micah was alive with energy and excitement. The entire floor writhed with dancing bodies. They all seemed to be connected.

It was heaven, and Adria finally understood why Micah loved doing this, why he felt so free and happy to be there. She also loved him all the more, for wanting to share it with her. It was the most amazing, special thing he had to give to her, she realized.

Her head spun with happiness and love, with euphoria, for she felt she understood Micah more now, than ever before. He was letting her all the way into his heart, by bringing her here. By tailoring the experience to her, attempting to gently soothe her into it, this way – she felt how much he loved her.

****

At four in the morning, the rave ended, and Micah and Adria stumbled out of the warehouse, amidst the last stragglers, to make their way, in the cold, to Micah's van. He'd left her alone only twice during the night, to get them both water to drink.

In the parking lot, Adria shivered. Micah gave her his black shirt to wear and she took it, feeling grateful.

"How many years living on the Oregon coastline, and you still don't have the sense to bring a warm pullover?" he teased her.

"Shut it," Adria laughed.

Micah put his arm around her and they reached the van. When they got there, he opened her door for her, and she could feel his body behind her. He was leaning in, so close she could feel his heat.

The energy was intense between them. She turned and hugged him, throwing her arms around him tight. When she pulled away, he leaned in close, closing his eyes, wincing.

He was trying very hard not to kiss her, but he was failing. It was her fault, for turning around, she knew. But she'd wanted to. She couldn't help herself. She sighed. They came to rest with their foreheads touching, both of them breathing heavily.

"Maybe this wasn't such a good idea," Adria said.

Micah opened his eyes and looked at her with longing. Then he smiled, backing away. He walked around to the driver's side and got in, starting the van. Adria got in, saying nothing else.

They drove for about half an hour, leaving Portland and heading back on Highway 26. The next 72 miles, they were plunged into darkness, along winding roads lined with thick foliage. Rain pattered on the windshield, making Adria feel sleepy.

Every once in a while, a car would pass them. A couple of times, the riders were other motorists heading home from the rave. A few honked at Micah's van and one mohawked girl leaned out her window and gave the rock sign with her hand to Micah, who smiled.

Suddenly, Adria exclaimed out, gasping. Micah slowed down, easing his foot off the gas pedal, and looked at Adria in concern.

"Micah, our driver's licenses! You never got them back!"

"Yes, I did," Micah said, speeding up again. "I have them in my pocket. Plus new ones."

"New ones?" Adria said. "What for?"

"To make us older," Micah said, sounding a bit sad, Adria thought.

She smiled then, laughing. He frowned.

"I see," she said. "Is this because of what I said in the line? About wanting a drink? You got us fake licenses, so we can buy alcohol?" Adria looked at Micah, amused.

"Not exactly."

Micah scanned for a place to pull over. He turned down a one-lane, dirt road and followed it a few yards, where it opened up on a small clearing in the woods. Further up the road, was a farm, but once Micah pulled the van into the clearing, they were hidden among the trees that surrounded them on three sides.

"We're going to get stuck in the mud," Adria said, sounding worried.

"Nah, we'll be okay," Micah said.

He reached into his back pocket and pulled out Adria's original license, plus the new one. He handed them both to her, looking nervous. She took them, and looked at the new, fake ID, frowning.

"November 12, 1991?" She said, sounding alarmed. "Micah, you made a mistake. Or your guy did, anyway. This won't work. You only made me nineteen. I can't buy alcohol with this."

"It's not to buy alcohol with," Micah said.

He handed Adria his own, new, fake license. She looked at it and frowned again.

"But you're only nineteen, too!" she exclaimed. "Why did you change your birthday? It says October 29?"

"I thought it would look suspicious if we both had the same birthday. How ironic is that? The one thing that's not a lie, might have looked suspicious."

"Suspicious to whom?" Adria said. "We don't both need to show our license to get liquor. You didn't need to pay for two fake ID's. You only needed one. You just wasted your money, Micah. Plus, they messed up."

"No," Micah said. He looked at Adria with such intensity, she became nervous.

"I wanted us to be nineteen."

"What for, to vote?" Adria wailed, completely confused. Her heart, however, was beating very fast now.

"No, although eighteen would have sufficed well enough. But barely. I thought nineteen was less conspicuous."

"For what?" Adria's voice was weaker now.

"To apply for a marriage license, in Portland," Micah said. "If we're seventeen, we need parental consent. Now we don't."

Adria stared at Micah, all her breath gone. Her heart continued beating heavily in her chest. She felt dizzy as Micah reached into his front right pocket and pulled out a thin, silver ring. He shrugged.

"I wish I could give you something nicer," he said.

"You're crazy," Adria whispered.

"Well, that's already been established, hasn't it?"

Micah unbuckled his seatbelt and scooted closer to Adria. He took her left hand and slid the ring down her ring finger, his eyes never leaving hers.

"This isn't the first time I've put a ring on your finger," he said, "but it will be the first time I make good on my promise. I'm going to love you forever, Adria. Nothing's gonna stop us this time."

"We can't," Adria said. "We can't be together."

"We can get married," Micah said. "We just can't have sex."

Adria began to cry. Micah wiped her tears away, smiling at her.

"I thought you'd be happy," he said.

"I am," she said, her voice wavering. "I just can't believe this is really going to happen. When?"

"We have to apply for the license in Portland, at the county registrar's office. All we have to do is show our licenses. They should be spot on. I paid through the nose for that. It shouldn't be a problem. Then we fill out the paperwork and pay fifty bucks. Boom, we're done."

"That's it?"

"We have to wait three days, to actually get the license, but yeah. We go back, pick up the paper, then get married."

"Where?"

"Right there, in the county office. We can schedule it when we put in for the paperwork. It's quick, Adria. We bring two witnesses, the county clerk officiates. The whole ceremony only takes five minutes."

"Five minutes?"

"Then we'll be husband and wife," Micah breathed. "For the first time ever."

"We don't have two witnesses," Adria said.

"We can ask Sam," Micah said. "I can find someone to meet us."

"Who?"

"Someone online. A fellow raver? It doesn't matter," Micah said.

"When do we get the license?" Adria asked.

"Next Friday. School will let out for winter break. We can drive back up, get the paperwork done. It takes three business days. Next Friday will be the seventeenth. The license will be ready on Thursday, the twenty-third."

"You want to get married on December twenty-three?" Adria asked.

"We have to. The office is closed the twenty-fourth and twenty-fifth. I don't want to wait that long, do you?"

"Ask me," Adria said. "You never asked me."

Micah took a deep breath, growing nervous. His heart rate increased, despite already knowing what Adria's answer would be.

"Adria Allan, will you marry me? Will you be my wife?"

"Yes," Adria whispered.

The ring was already on her finger. She gazed at Micah in complete love and rapture. He saw her look and moved away, back to his side of the van, behind the steering wheel. He put his hand on the key in the ignition, but Adria was on fire. She scooted to Micah's side and turned his face to hers, gently, but decidedly. She kissed him and Micah was immediately on fire. Adria moved instinctively now, without thought, once more. She straddled Micah, kissing him, and he leaned into her body, taking her torso in his hands, loving her.

Their bodies grinded together and both of them thought they would go mad. Micah's hands were under Adria's tank shirt, as well as his own black shirt, which she still wore. She was ridiculously overheated.

In one, swift motion, Micah had both her shirts off, raking them over her head, and he kissed her bare chest, running his hands over her breasts, caressing them over her white bra. She sighed in pleasure and delight, arching her back. She threw her head back in complete rapture and leaned the weight of her back against the steering wheel, reveling in Micah's hands all over her. The horn blared and both of them laughed.

Then, from the highway, which was only yards away, through the trees, another raver's car passed by. They were loud and raucous. It was obvious they had their windows rolled down. Adria could hear people screaming in uproarious laughter. Then their car backfired and it sounded so shocking in the quite of the empty, narrow highway, Adria heard it as a loud gunshot.

A vision shot through her head, of John on the farm, and the white farmer's gun, flashing in the darkness. She remembered the warm, liquid feel of John's blood, as it gushed over her hands, and Adria instinctively threw her body over Micah, shielding him with her own.

She hugged him fiercely, raking in deep breaths, no longer of ecstasy, but of sheer and utter fear and panic. Micah clung to Adria, his fingers digging into her flesh, turning both his and her skin, deathly white.

Adria pulled away and looked at Micah in shame. They had done it again. They had tempted fate, and, once more, fate had found a way to intervene, saving them both. Adria began to cry.

"I almost killed you," she said.

"No," Micah whispered. "You weren't in it alone, Adria. I was there, too."

Adria returned to her side of the van, hastily putting her shirt back on, and held herself with her own arms, feeling deeply disappointed and ashamed. Micah started the van and got back on the highway. After several minutes, Adria spoke.

"We can't get married," she said.

Micah's heart froze at her statement. He kept driving, not looking at her.

"There would be no point. If we get married, we'll still be stuck with the same situation. It makes no sense to get married, Micah. We can't ever have a life together. Not a real life, anyhow. We can't be together."

"Adria, we can, we have been," Micah said.

"You call this together?" Adria yelled. She was angry now, frustrated beyond belief. "It's been barely a few weeks since we started hanging together again. And already, twice now, we've almost gotten you killed. The curse is laughing at us, Micah. It's just waiting for us to lose control. And if I keep being around you, I will lose control. And you don't seem to be able to control yourself any better than me."

"Me?! *You're* the one who straddled *me*, Adria!"

It was Micah's turn to get upset. He wouldn't look at her.

"*You* were the one who *kissed* me in line," Adria spat back. "And took me to a rave, where everyone writhes against each other. All it did was drive me crazy!"

"You're driving me crazy!" Micah screamed.

"Yeah? Well, then, we can't be together, Micah!" Adria crossed her arms and said nothing else.

They drove the next hour and a half home to Cannon Beach without speaking again. It was after six in the morning when Micah pulled up in front of Adria's house. She stared out the window, brooding.

"Out of sheer curiosity," Micah said, "what song were you listening to this whole drive?"

"I'll Follow You Into The Dark," Adria whispered. Her voice took on a hollow, mocking tone. "Deathcab for Cutie," she said, emphasizing the word death.

The tears came then, slow and hot. Micah wanted to hold her, but he didn't dare. He sat, feeling her pain, feeling completely helpless. Finally he spoke, his voice shaking.

"Adria? Are you really not going to marry me?"

"No," Adria whispered. "I'm not."

She got out of the van and walked away. Micah watched her go, his heart breaking.

12. December 11-15, 2009

"He asked you to *marry* him?"

Sam stared at Adria. Adria had walked, at six-thirty in the morning, to Sam's house. She threw pebbles at her window, until Sam woke up and let her in. In Sam's room, Adria sat on her best friend's bed and silently wept. She'd told Sam everything, including how she and Micah had almost done it, again.

"I told you not to go to that rave," Sam said. "I knew it would get you two all worked up."

"We get worked up just being around each other," Adria said, pulling in hitching gulps of air.

She sat, spinning the ring Micah had given her around on the tip of her finger, the tears still falling. Sam sat down and put her arm around Adria.

"You want some good news? The book is in. Someone finally returned it. It's coming in on Tuesday."

"So?"

"So, maybe it will have an answer to this whole, stupid mess," Sam said. "So, you broke up with him?"

Adria looked at Sam, her face pained with the realization. She nodded, crumbling into tears all over again. Sam held her, rocking her shoulders, like a mother.

"This isn't good," Sam said. "Last time you guys were apart, you got sick, Adria. And that song you wrote," she paused. "Did you finish the new one?"

Adria nodded. She sniffled.

"Can I hear it?"

Sam knew that if she wanted a direct line into Adria's thoughts, hearing the song she had written would be all the information she'd need. Adria nodded.

"Later, at my house," she said.

"It's not about a girl killing herself, is it?"

"No, but I don't think you'll like the lyrics, anyhow."

"Why?"

Adria said nothing else. She laid down in Sam's bed and fell asleep. After all, she'd been up all night. Sam went back to bed as well. They both slept for five hours, and then woke up at twelve-thirty in the afternoon. When the girls made their way downstairs, Sam's mother exclaimed in surprise.

"Oh, hi Adria. I didn't even hear you come in this morning."

"Mom, I'm going over to Adria's house," Sam said. "Can I spend the night?"

"Um, sure, I guess," her mom said.

****

In Adria's room, Sam sat on the bed and listened, as Adria picked up her guitar and sat on the edge of her computer chair. The guitar chords reverberated off the walls, echoing and giving Sam the chills. It was beautiful, strong, and lamenting, all at once. Adria broke into chording solos, intermittently throughout, before leading into each new stanza. It was different from any other song Sam had ever heard her play. It was edgy, a bit country, but still a bit alternative, as well, Sam thought.

Desperately seek the comfort of strangers.
Lie to the sunlight, smile at them all.
Nothing will save her soul,
Once she begins to fall.

Dance in the moonlight,
Hide your face from God.
Everything means nothing,
As the world continues on.

Impervious and strangled,
Lonelier than time is.
Nothing will save her,
From this memory of his.

She says:
He used to kiss me,
Just on my hand.
He said only what he meant,
I could never understand.

And all his crazy notions,
And all his little flaws,
They now live here inside of me,
And scratch me with their claws.

A new Season, a chance to be a human, being,
Living life at last.
Her eyes, they are solemn,
As she fixes her hair.
In the mirror,
They journey into the past.

All the faces, and all the names,
Never mean a thing.
A single tear, I love you dear,
Then she begins to sing.

She says:
He used to hold me,
Never quite enough.
He used to sing to me,
Notes and chords too rough.

And all his words flew by me,
And I never heard his voice.
Never quite on purpose,
An accident of choice.

Now she sits alone,
Humming wordless tunes.

The clock is ticking, slowly licking,
The dirt from her wounds.

And her heart is aching every day,
With every breath she takes.
She remembers all the horrid sounds,
She remembers her mistakes.

As the sun goes down the 'rizon,
The air begins to cool the pain.
She listens to the sound,
Hear the thunder, feel the rain.

Humming a sweet tune,
Of sorrow and love, no hate.
She feels the weight of the world,
Flood through the open gate.

She says:
He whispered in my ear,
The sweetest words.
He used to look at me,
He listened to my world.

And all his crazy notions,
And all his little flaws,
They now live here, inside of me,
And scratch me with their claws.
And scratch me with their claws.

She says:
He used to kiss me,
Just on my hand.
He said only what he meant,
But I could never understand.

And all his crazy notions,

And what I thought were flaws,
They now live here inside of me,
And scratch me with their claws.

And scratch me with their claws...

When Adria was finished, Sam sat and stared at her, feeling bad for her. Her chin trembled.

"Is that what it feels like?" Sam asked. "With Micah? Like claws?"

Adria nodded, setting her guitar down. She looked at Sam, her eyes pained, and haunted.

"Like claws scratching at my soul. It's Micah, Sam. I can't get away from him, no matter how hard I try. I don't know how to be away from him, but we can't be together, either. There is no hope for us."

"Don't say that," Sam said. "I'm going to get that book on Tuesday. I'm going to pour over that thing. There's got to be an answer. There has to be, Adria. They knew, the Tillamook knew. They knew about the waters of life, they knew about the Nehalem. They knew about the sea tunnel spirits, and the deaths of the Nor'easters. There has to be something in their ancient legends about what's happening to you and Micah. I'm counting on it."

"Well, I wouldn't," Adria said, her voice sad and empty.

She crawled into her bed and slept the rest of the afternoon away. Sam used her computer to research on the Internet, but to no avail. In the evening, Adria sat in bed and jotted down song lyrics, humming to herself.

"Another song?" Sam asked. Adria nodded.

Later, Adria read, quietly, while Sam poured over the notes in her notebook. She sighed, at one point pulling out a few papers and jotting down new notes.

Adria was reading one of Micah's books. She still wanted to drink him in, as many parts of him as she could. It was obsessive and unhealthy, but she couldn't help herself. She wondered what Micah was doing at that very moment, and sighed in unison with Sam. Sam looked at her, frowning.

"I doubt we're sighing for the same reason," she said.

"Why, what's wrong?"

"Well, I've been looking at all the dates of you and Micah's past lives, and…" she trailed off.

"And, what?" Adria sat up, looking at Sam attentively.

"It's not anything good," Sam began. "In your first life, after your first life – so really, your second life with Micah," Sam began.

"You've already lost me," Adria said.

"I mean, in your first life being reborn," Sam said, "which would technically be yours and Micah's second life, but the first one being reincarnated, you get me?"

"Sure," Adria said, nodding.

"Okay, well. You and Micah drowned, as Justin Tremaine and Charlotte Williams, in 1879. Something happened, you got cursed, whatever. You and Micah are immediately reborn, in the year 1879, days after your deaths. Later, you meet John, but you guys don't die for two more years. And according to you, you guys had been doing it for several months, right?"

Adria nodded.

"Okay, and you met when you guys were eighteen, but you didn't die until you were twenty. You die in the year 1899, but this time, you aren't immediately reborn. Seven years pass by, and then you and Micah are born in 1906, on the same day. Then in the second life, you and Micah, as William and Elizabeth, meet in 1929. This time, you meet when you're a little older. You were both age twenty-two. You meet in 1928. You guys don't die for over a year, when you're twenty-three, and according to your memories, again, you guys had been doing it for several weeks. You even got engaged. William died two days later."

"All of this, I already know," Adria sighed, lying back down in bed.

"Fine. But then you're born again. You die in 1929, but this time, you're not reborn until 1930, almost a whole year after dying. You and Micah meet again, this time in your third life. This time, you guys are even older. You lived within blocks of each other for half your lives, but didn't meet until you were drawn to him, in 1953, at age twenty-three. You were together for a whole year, but then you got engaged, on New Year's Eve. You guys, ahem, did it, and Micah was killed within hours of your first time. But each life, you guys lived for a while, being together, up until then."

"So?"

"So, again, in your fourth life being reborn, you died in 1954, but this time, two years pass, until you're both born again, in 1956, again, on the same day. You guys meet when you're older than you are now. You meet in your sophomore year of college, at age nineteen, in 1975. You date for over a year, get engaged, and you guys are doing it for months, before Devon is killed and you take a swan dive off the roof."

"What are you trying to say?" Adria sounded hopeful. "That the curse has nothing to do with sex, but with us getting engaged?"

"No," Sam said. "Just listen to me, and shut up. You guys are immediately reborn for the fifth time. This time, in 1976. Within hours of dying, you're both reborn. This time, you meet at a very young age, when you're both sixteen, in 1992. You immediately fall in love, and within months of meeting, you're doing it, you don't get engaged, then Eduardo is mugged and stabbed, and you walk into oncoming traffic, in 1993. On November 12, 1993. That was you and Micah's fifth reincarnation."

"Again, so?"

"So, again, there's no delay. You and Micah are born within hours of Eduardo and Amaya dying. Before your last two lives, there was always a slight delay, of at least one year, sometimes much more. The last two lives have been much more hectic. Eduardo and Amaya met at age sixteen. So did you and Micah. You guys are on your sixth life together."

"So what?" Adria said, sounding annoyed and exasperated.

"So, it seems like, the further along you guys are getting, the quicker the turnaround. You're meeting younger, sooner, getting involved faster. Eduardo and Amaya met at age sixteen, and died at age seventeen. They never got engaged. I doubt you guys even had the chance to. But you and Micah really only met a couple of months ago, again, at age sixteen. And you're already engaged."

"No, we're not. That's been rescinded."

"Okay, well, you don't see the change in pattern? It's almost as if, whatever is happening to you and Micah, the process has been speeding up, hastening quicker and quicker with each life. At least, now that you're up into several lives, now."

"So?"

"I don't know," Sam said, frowning. "I feel like it means something. I feel like I should be seeing something that I'm missing."

"The pattern could be random," Adria said. "There haven't been enough lives to set a pattern. For all you know, if Micah and I died tomorrow, we wouldn't be reborn for twenty years."

"Or, you'd follow the new pattern from your last two lives, and be immediately reborn, within hours of you and Micah's deaths," Sam said.

"Yeah, but, we're not going to be reborn, because neither of us is going to die," Adria said. "You were right all along, Sam. If we're not together, we can both live. No curse."

"Will you be able to stand that?" Sam asked.

"I'll have to, now won't I?"

"If you're anything like you were the last time, you won't be able to. Not without killing yourself, anyhow."

"Fuck that. Fuck this curse. Fuck everything," Adria said.

"See?" Sam said. "You're already going crazy. You're already spiraling down, Adria."

"When I'm with Micah, we just keep spiraling up," Adria said. "And up with Micah leads down anyway, eventually. All roads lead downward, into the abyss."

"You're losing it," Sam said.

"Fuck that, too," Adria said.

****

But Sam was right. Over the next several days, Adria could hardly get out of bed. She didn't eat, she had trouble sleeping. She spent the last two days of school absent.

Sam watched Micah in the hallways, while Adria was gone, and saw that he looked even worse than she did. He was pale, his face drawn and dark. Sam attempted to approach him on Monday, but he saw her walking towards his locker and he walked away. On Thursday, the last day of school before Winter Break, Micah was also a no-show.

Sam had long since given up on trying by that point, however. She picked up her book, The Tillamook Myth Age, on Tuesday, December 14, and by nine at night the following day, she was completely lost in her own miserable revelations. She spent two evenings reading the book from cover to cover, before going back to one specific legend and reading it again and again. Each time she read it, her heart sank deeper and deeper into a dark depression.

Her revelations had fully sunken in by Thursday, but she could not bring herself to tell Adria of what she'd learned. It turned out it wouldn't have helped, anyway. For, what Sam had learned, was that, indeed, a force beyond anyone's control had been at work the past few months. It was a force that would not relent, until its path had been made way for. Something had been building all around them, and they were now caught up in the wheels of motion, of a fateful force, far more powerful than they could ever hope to defeat.

13. December 16, 2009

Micah was out of his mind. He'd been going crazy, ever since Adria left his van, ending their engagement, on the night of December 11. Although only five days had passed, it felt like an eternity for him. He had no way of knowing it, but it was the same in the case of Adria as well. She was wasting away, in her bed. Her hair was now raven black, just as his was.

Micah had poured over his plans for him and Adria. He'd planned the entire night of the 11th, from making certain he could get their ID's, to finding the perfect song for the DJ to play, to help make Adria feel more comfortable. He'd fully believed that they could get married and live a happy life together, resisting the urge to touch one another, if they only tried hard enough.

Micah was as shocked and disappointed in himself, as Adria was in herself, over what happened inside his van. Despite the fact they hadn't gone nearly as far with each other as they had the first time, at Indian Point, Micah still felt that what happened inside his van had been a very close call, indeed.

In fact, he knew it had been. Once it was all over with, and Micah was back at home, he lay down in his own bed and replayed his emotions of that moment. Only then did he fully realize that if the car that had driven by and backfired, had not done so at that moment, he and Adria would have made love. They would have done so without any hesitation, without any true thought as to the consequences.

Micah realized this, and with this realization, came the sad knowledge that, as painful as it was, Adria had been right to do what she did. Breaking things off had destroyed Micah, but he found slight solace in the fact that the distance between them guaranteed that Adria would continue to live. He did not know, then, that Adria's existence had been boiled down to what could barely be called living.

****

Micah did not eat, he did not sleep. He lay in bed every night, tossing and turning, tortured by his own mind. His heart was decimated. His body ached with physical longing for Adria. Not to make love to her, per se, although, those longings were present as well, at times, overwhelming him.

The simple fact was that Micah longed to be near Adria. He needed her. His body ached just to hold her in his arms, his eyes cried out to drink in the view of her face, her smile, her eyes. He heard her voice inside his head – her laughter, her singing. He was lost without her. His soul reached out to feel hers. He longed for her with everything that he was, mind, body and soul.

****

Adria was in similar condition. She also did not eat or sleep. She also tossed and turned at night, her own body aching for Micah. She longed to feel the weight of his body pressing down on her, and, yes, into her. There was a deep, painful throbbing, in her midsection, and she spent hours doubled over in her bed, laboring through these pains. She felt empty. She felt lost and alone.

****

They were both dying. After only a few, short days, Adria was growing ill, and Micah was wasting away. They needed each other. Their fate was already sealed, though neither of them knew it. Their souls felt it, however. They were inexplicably and uncontrollably drawn to one another. The very notion of self-control, when it came to the love between the two of them, was impossible. Their suffering was exponentially growing as each day, each hour passed.

****

Adria stayed home, ill from school, starting on Wednesday. Micah followed suit on Thursday, the last day of school before Winter Break.

Micah went mad. He became obsessed. His body cried out for Adria in such a way, he truly no longer had any control over his actions. His mind was gone, along with any self-control.

****

On Thursday, December 16, Micah left his room, and his father's home, and went to Adria. There was no plan. He simply needed to be with her, near her, to touch her. He would die within days if he did not. So would she.

He knew she was at her father's house that week, so he went there, in the late afternoon, after he knew Mr. Allan had left for work. This much, at least, his mind was able to process. Beyond this basic reasoning, however, Micah was operating on sheer instinct.

He came to her front door and knocked. When there was no answer, he knocked again, and waited, impatiently, for Adria to answer. She lay in her bed, unable to summon the energy to move.

Micah knocked a third and final time then tried the handle. It was locked. He knew Adria's house, however, with all the long hours they had spent together. He leaned down and retrieved the emergency key from inside the potted plant, lifting the small stone in the middle of the dirt, where the silver key lay wrapped in cellophane, to keep it from rusting.

Micah unlocked the door and entered, locking the door again behind him. He knew where Adria was. He could sense her, his soul feeling for her energy, reaching out for her.

His breathing was labored as he ascended the stairs. In her room, he found the shades drawn. It was so dark, with the stormy sky outside, that despite it being daylight still, her room was almost pitch-black. He dared to turn the small green lamp on her computer desk on, and took in her crumpled form lying in the bed. He felt panicked.

"Adria?" he whispered.

She stirred, feebly, and he rushed to her side. She opened her eyes, taking in his dark, brown orbs, and she did not even have the strength to cry. Her frail hand appeared from under the covers, however, and he grasped it. She immediately seemed to revive, from his touch. Her hand was cold, but Micah would have sworn that he felt electricity and energy flow from within him, out, and into her.

She moved a bit, attempting to sit up in the bed, but could not. He threw the covers back and got into bed with her, taking her up into his arms, holding her tight. He could feel her body shaking now, as she began to cry. Her torso shook with silent sobs. He felt hot wetness on the front of his shirt, and knew this was her tears. His own tears freely flowed.

The magic was working between them, however. Adria was already reviving, regaining her strength. So was Micah, although neither of them would ever regain the emotional control to resist each other.

"Never again without you," Micah said. "No matter what you say, I won't leave you alone."

"No," she said, her voice soft, but with the promise of strength returning.

Micah caressed her arm, her hand. He frowned, feeling cold metal on her finger. He pulled her hand up and looked at it. Adria still wore the ring he'd given her on the 11th. Micah brought her hand up to his lips and kissed her finger, and the ring. Adria sighed.

"This still remains," Micah said. "We'll go, tomorrow."

"Yes."

"We'll live with whatever time we have," Micah said, the tears flowing once more. "And we won't regret anything."

"No."

"Because, Adria," Micah said. "We don't have any choice. I feel it. I know it, now. Without you, I die. And with you, I can't not love you. So, I'm dead anyway."

"So am I."

The heat began to build between them. Once their souls were together, once their strength and vitality were returning, the longing was greater than ever, for both of them. There would be no intervention of fate this time around. They both knew it. They both knew the consequences of their actions, as well, but being without each other had almost led to death.

Finally, they both gave in.

****

Micah ran his hand down Adria's arm and she shuddered. Her breathing came in quick bursts. They both felt the urgency awakening inside the other. Adria pulled at Micah with her hands, and he followed her lead, rolling on top of her, rising above her. He raked his shirt off in one, quick movement, and closed his eyes at the touch of Adria's hands, now warmed by her own physical arousal, on his chest.

Her heart beat far too quickly, as did his. He pulled her up to sit in front of him, and removed her shirt. She was not wearing a bra. He touched her, and she sighed. He pushed her back down and fell on top of her, once more, pressing his body against hers. She was in heaven. She felt his weight, and ran her hands up his back, pulling on him, attempting to get even closer. There was only one way to get closer, she knew.

Micah ran his hands over her breasts, down her sides, along her thighs. He reached down and pulled her sweatpants down, along with her underwear. Adria desperately fumbled with the button and zipper on Micah's jeans, and then pulled at his pants. Within moments, they were both naked, and Micah was caressing Adria, between her legs, gently, with his fingers. She sighed and gasped, moaning in pleasure, lifting her hips with his movements, leading him.

Adria caressed Micah, feeling his stiffness. He breathed in heavy, labored breaths, his head spinning. She was on the brink of ecstasy. She cried out in a burst of pleasure, at the touch of his hand. They had not even kissed yet.

He pushed his weight onto her, kissing her. Their tongues tangled, and heat and electricity jumped between them. Adria opened her legs and pulled at Micah's buttocks, pleading without words. He was mad with desire. He kissed her neck, her chest, he bit the lobe of her ear. He was driving her crazy.

He pushed with his hips, teasing her. Adria kissed Micah's lips, mad with desire. Finally, Micah could stand it no longer, and he pushed his whole body onto her, forcefully. He pushed himself into her, and she cried out in pleasure and relief.

Adria ran her hands over his back, feeling the ripple of his muscles as he worked his way into her, deeper still. She wrapped her legs around him and pushed against him. It was her body's first time, but there was very little pain. What slight discomfort there was, was overshadowed by intense pleasure at the fulfillment of a longing that had run in her so deep, it had pained her very soul.

They made love for several minutes, their souls dancing and singing. Their bodies worked in unison, the act so overwhelming, they were completely lost in each other. Then, as quickly as it had begun, it was over, and Micah lay on top of Adria, his breathing near hyperventilating, his head still spinning.

Adria's breathing was so labored, she made small sobbing noises that could not be helped. She gasped, trying to wind down from the incredible high of their act of love. She laughed and Micah soon joined her. She continued to gasp and laugh, simultaneously.

"I'm not sure," she managed, "but I think that just may have been worth dying for."

Micah looked at Adria then, pulling his body up to see her face. His smile faded and his eyes were pained. Her own smile began to fade, as she realized the implications of her own words. For all she knew, Micah now only had hours to live. Perhaps only minutes. Her eyes welled up with tears. Micah stopped her sadness with a kiss.

She kissed him back. Then he rolled off of her and lay at her side, gazing at her, smiling. She looked at him, feeling awful.

"I've just killed you."

"No," Micah said. "It was my choice."

"Was it?"

Micah continued gazing at her, feeling happy.

"But, you're going to die now, because of being with me."

"I was dying without you," Micah said. "Weren't you?"

She nodded. He was right.

"But, it's not fair," she cried. "So, we're damned if we do, damned if we don't? Where's the justice in that?"

"There is none," Micah said. "Perhaps that's all we ever needed to come to terms with. I came here for you, Adria. Whether I knew it at the time or not. From the moment I heard the words Cannon Beach, our fate was sealed. The moment I saw you, Adria. We were always going to end up this way. There never was any controlling it."

"But, I can't watch you die, Micah," Adria hugged him tightly. "I can't bear it. I'll go mad."

"Perhaps," Micah said, sounding sad. "Perhaps not."

"Yes, I will," she said. "And I'm going with you when it happens. So please don't try and tell me not to."

"Adria, I have no further illusions of any control, on either of our parts. I doubt you have the ability not to follow me," he said. "I don't think that was ever a choice, either, whether I made you promise in the past, or not. Whether I asked you to follow me or not. You will anyhow, won't you?"

"I'm sorry," she whispered.

"Hey," Micah said, pulling her face up in his hand, forcing her to look at him. "Don't be sorry for what you can't help, Adria. I won't ask you to go, but you know how I feel, don't you?"

She nodded.

"I don't want to go anywhere where you won't be," he said.

"Neither do I."

"Then there's nothing more to talk about, is there," he said. "All we can do is just love each other, as much as we can, for as much time as we have. It's the best we can do. Okay?"

"Okay."

"And we'll go ahead with our plans, try not to worry, or think about when, or how, it's going to happen. Tomorrow, we'll go into Portland and apply for our marriage license. We'll wait the three business days. Provided we're both still alive on December twenty-three, we'll get married. Okay?"

"Yes," Adria said, hugging Micah's body.

"And from this moment on, we won't leave each other's side," Micah said. "Because if I'm gonna die, I want every last moment with you that I can get. Deal?"

"Deal."

He kissed her. They made love a second time then fell asleep in each other's arms.

****

Neither of them heard Adria's father come home. Neither of them knew he was there, until he came into Adria's room to check up on his ill daughter.

14. December 16, 2009

"Jayzus H. Key-rist," Richard Allan exclaimed.

The sound of her father's voice woke Adria and Micah. Micah lay frozen in the bed, not moving, feeling as if he was having a bad dream.

Adria sat up in bed, hiding herself with her coverlet. Her heart was doing double time, but this time, there was no pleasure to be had.

"Dad!" She could think of nothing else to say.

"What am I looking at?" Richard said. "No, never mind. I know what I'm looking at. I just don't believe it."

"Dad, it's not what it looks like," Adria said, and then winced.

"Oh, yes it is." He shook his head. "Key-rist."

Mr. Allan turned to leave the room, disappearing behind the door, then pulled it open and stepped back in.

"Hell, I can't," he said, shaking his head.

He turned to leave again, sighing, disappeared, and then came back, once more. He looked at the crumpled form of Micah and squinted.

"Micah, is that you under there?"

"Yes, sir."

"Huh, well at least it's a boy I've met," Richard said. "Huh," he repeated, shaking his head again, looking to be in complete and utter shock.

Richard turned to leave again, and then came back, looking at Adria, then Micah, then shaking his head, yet again.

"Huh." Then he looked at Adria with angry eyes.

"Get dressed, young lady. You too, Micah. Both of you come down stairs. And don't make me wait."

Richard left the room then, closing the door. Adria stood and began dressing. Micah watched her, smiling. She smiled back at him, her heart still thudding in her chest.

"This isn't funny."

"Yes, it is," Micah said. "In my mind, we've been to college. I've graduated high school almost a half dozen times. I've crossed the border, rented in New York, lived in the adult world. We've both reached the age of twenty-something several times already, mentally. There's something kind of funny about remembering our past lives, only to be children again, living under our parent's rules."

"I *am* seventeen, Micah. So are you. My dad doesn't know about our past lives. I just broke his heart."

"We didn't do anything wrong."

Micah stood now and also got dressed. It was Adria's turn to watch him. She flushed, feeling a wave of desire wash over her. She sighed.

Micah walked around to her side of the bed, where she stood, and kissed her. She melted. They kissed for several moments, lost in love.

"Adria!" Richard's voice drifted to them from the living room downstairs.

"Come on," Micah said, taking Adria's hand. "We'll just have to explain to him that we're in love."

"Wait," Adria said, pulling back. "I can't. I can't go down there and look at him."

"Why? Don't be ashamed, Adria. I love you." Micah caressed her cheek.

"I'm not ashamed. I'm afraid to see my dad's face. You're going to die, Micah. And I'm going to follow you. This could be the last time I ever see my dad, and he has no clue."

Adria began to cry. Micah hugged her tight.

"What have we done?" Adria sobbed.

"What we had to do," Micah said. "Come on. Let's get this over with."

They walked downstairs and found Mr. Allan sitting in his recliner. He motioned for the two of them to sit on the couch. Then he stared at them for several, long moments. Adria looked at Micah and he smiled at her, attempting to comfort her. She blushed and smiled back. Mr. Allan saw this and rolled his eyes.

"Key-rist almighty," he said under his breath. "Was this your first time?"

Adria wasn't sure if her father was asking her, or Micah. Either way, the question was laced with underlying meaning, that Mr. Allan could have no clue of. His question sounded much different to both Micah and Adria, than it did to himself.

"Okay, I'll ask you again. Was this the first time you two have done this?"

Micah looked at Adria and shrugged, unsure of what to say. Adria shrugged back, also unsure.

"Let me rephrase the question," Richard said. "How long has this been going on for?"

Micah couldn't take it any longer. The stress was simply too great, as well as the heavy irony of Mr. Allan's questions. He smirked and snorted, unable to help himself. Adria also attempted to hide a smile. Mr. Allan grew visibly frustrated.

"You think this is funny? It isn't funny, you two. Having sex is a very serious matter. A life and death matter, as a matter-of-fact."

"Oh, we know that, believe me," Micah said, almost under his breath.

Adria laughed nervously. This was simply too much for her to take.

"What is so gall darned funny?" Richard yelled. "Do you have any idea how serious this is? Please tell me you used protection?"

Micah looked at Adria in surprise, for neither of them had ever thought of this. Micah raised his eyebrows, thinking hard. He frowned at Adria.

"You know, I don't think we've ever used protection," he said, surprised by this realization.

"Huh uh," Adria shook her head. "You're right, we haven't. Ever."

"Well, it's not like it matters," Micah said.

"Jayzus!" Mr. Allan yelled. "How many times have you guys done it?"

Micah only shook his head. Adria smiled.

"Well, it's too late, then," Richard said, shaking his head. "You two are clearly hell bent on fucking up your lives. Adria, I am endlessly disappointed in you. I trusted you."

"I know, I'm sorry."

"No, you're not," Micah stepped in. "Adria, we had no choice. We couldn't have stopped this."

"Oh, now, I know it may feel that way," Richard said. "I was a teenage boy, once. I know all about out-of-control hormones, believe me. At times, it feels as if you might *die* if you don't do it, am I right?"

"You have no idea," Micah said.

"I have to tell him," Adria said.

"Adria, no."

"Ah, Christ. Tell me what?" Richard looked at his daughter with trepidation. "You're pregnant, aren't you?"

"No," Adria said. "Dad, look."

Her voice shook. She was extremely emotional.

"Don't," Micah warned.

"Micah's going to die," Adria said, the tears now falling.

"Oh, honey, is that what he said? To get you to sleep with him?" Richard glared at Micah, standing up.

"Dad, sit down!" Adria screamed. "Just listen to me, okay? Micah and I are cursed. The curse only sets in after we make love, but once we do, it starts. I don't know how, and I don't know when, but Micah is going to die. And then I have to die to follow him, if we ever want to be together again. I have to follow him into the next life, or we'll be separated forever."

Mr. Allan stood, staring at his daughter for several moments with his mouth hanging agape. He looked at Micah, then back at his daughter, in shock.

"What in the Sam Hill?" he said. "What drugs are you two on?"

But her father's statement had given Adria an idea. She stood and went to the phone. Meanwhile, in the corner of her eye, she saw her father disappear from the room, and heard the garage door opening. Micah remained on the couch.

Adria called up Sam. While the phone rang, her father came back, and Adria's eyes widened as she watched him sit back down in the recliner, staring down Micah, holding something in his right hand. Micah sat frozen.

Sam answered the phone, and Adria sighed her relief. Sam didn't sound very happy, however.

"Sam, I need you to come over to my house, right away."

"Why, what's wrong?" Sam sounded hollowly suspicious.

"Um, my father is sitting in the living room with Micah right now, holding a shotgun on him," Adria said. She looked over at Micah and tried giving him a comforting smile. Micah continued to watch Mr. Allan with caution.

"Why does your father have a gun on Micah?" Sam asked, but she thought she already knew the answer to her question. When Adria told her, Sam closed her eyes, her stomach sinking. She'd expected this, after what she'd read.

"Micah and I made love," Adria said. "And my dad found us in bed, after. I tried to explain, but. I need you to tell my dad everything. Can you bring your notebook and all your research?"

"Sure," Sam said. "I'll be over in five minutes. Okay?"

"Yeah." Adria hung up the phone.

She sat back down next to Micah. Her father continued staring at Micah, glaring.

"Sam's coming over. She'll explain everything," Adria said.

****

No one moved 'til the knock came on the door. Richard got up and answered it, still holding the shotgun. Sam eyed the gun and gulped. She held her notebook in her arms, along with the Tillamook Myth Age, and Adria's dream journal. She walked in and took in the sight of Micah and Adria on the couch together, and she cried. She set her things down on the coffee table and rushed to hug her best friend.

"I'm sorry," Adria said, crying. "We just couldn't help it."

"I know," Sam said, rubbing Adria's back. "I know."

Sam pulled away and looked at Adria in sadness. Then she looked at Micah, choking through her tears.

"Damn you," Sam said.

Micah looked down at his hands, his chin trembling. Richard stood watching the entire scene in utter confusion.

"Is someone going to tell me what the dagnab is going on around here?"

Sam sighed and sat down on the couch, between Micah and Adria. She opened her notebook and simultaneously handed Mr. Allan Adria's dream journal.

"That's a journal I asked Adria to keep, detailing all her nightmares," Sam said.

"I know about her nightmares," Richard said, only giving the journal a cursory glance.

Next, Sam handed Mr. Allan the newspaper printings on William Fenmore and Elizabeth Harris, in 1929, and Devon Rogers and Sophie Prescott, from 1976. She told him to turn to the journal pages marked with blue tabs. Mr. Allan did, and read them. Then he read the news articles and looked at Adria, frowning in shock.

"You dreamed about the past?"

Adria nodded. Sam went on. She explained how Adria and Micah seemed to fall in love instantly, that their attraction to one another was immensely strong, and then she told Mr. Allan about the accident at sea that took the lives of Justin Tremaine and Charlotte Williams, back in 1879. She told him all about the other lives that both Adria and Micah dreamed about.

Then she told Mr. Allan that Adria had gained full memories of all five lives she had led, previous to this one. Sam explained about the curse. Mr. Allan said nothing. He only stared at Sam. Adria could not read her father's expression. When Sam finally finished, Mr. Allan sat, staring at nothing.

"I told you this was a bad idea," Micah said. "He won't believe us."

"It's not fair not to tell him," Adria said. "He's my father. At least give me the chance to say goodbye. So he knows it's not suicide!"

"Suicide?" Mr. Allan looked at Adria in fear.

"She has to kill herself, to follow Micah," Sam said.

"Sam?" Richard stared at her. "You believe all this horse shit? You're actually sitting here, condoning the notion of my daughter killing herself? What is wrong with you? Get out of my house, right now!"

"Wait, Dad! She's only trying to help. Did you read the Tillamook book? Did you figure something out?" Adria asked.

Sam nodded her head, but she looked infinitely sad. Mr. Allan scoffed.

"What are they giving you kids to take these days," he said.

"Look he ain't never gon' b'lieve us, Celia," Micah said. "Best to jest leave off tryin.'"

"If you haid the chance to say g'bye to yo daddy, wouldn' you wanna take it, John?"

"Celia, he ain't never gon' b'lieve it," Micah said. "No one whill."

Micah's voice had changed. So had Adria's. Mr. Allan stared at them both, his mouth falling open again. The couple continued to fight.

"Si tuvieras la oportunidad, ¿no te gustaría que decir adiós a tu hermano, Rafael?" Adria said. (If you had the chance, wouldn't you want to say goodbye to your brothers, Rafael?)

"¿Qué hermano? El que me apuñaló con un cuchillo? *Ese* hermano?!" Micah looked at Adria in disbelief. (Which brother? The one who stabbed me with a knife? *That* brother?!)

Adria groaned in frustration.

"Me preocupo por mi padre. Y tu no te preocupas por el tuyo," she said. (I worry about my father. So, you don't care about yours).

"Haces daño a mi corazón, Amaya," (You hurt my heart, Amaya) Micah said. "Siento tu dolor. Me encanta lo que amas. Pero tu padre nunca nos va a creer." (I feel your pain. I love what you love. But your father will never believe us).

All the while, Mr. Allan only stared at his daughter and Micah, looking shell-shocked. For, he knew his daughter well enough to know she did not possess the where-with-all to speak Spanish. She'd taken French for her language requirements at school, and had faired poorly in learning it. Mr. Allan knew his daughter very well, in fact. The voice he'd heard her use, while talking as Celia, was not his daughter's. Neither was the voice of Amaya.

Sam looked at Mr. Allan with sympathy. Mr. Allan only stared back and forth between Adria, Sam, and Micah. He sat down in his recliner looking stunned.

"What did you find out about the curse, Sam?" Adria asked.

"You're not going to like it," Sam said. "I know I don't."

Sam looked at Adria with dread and sadness. Adria and Micah merely sat, and waited, to learn of their own fate.

15. The Seven Lives of Tanook the Hunter

In the time just after the great expansion, when the Clanock tribe came to live on the edges of the Nehalem, a great war was raging between the Sea Gods, who lived in the tunnels of the Great Sea Rock, and the peaceful Nehalem. The waters raged with their battles.

A great hunter of the Clanock tribe, Tanook, dared to fish one day, at the Great Sea Rock. The Gods were quieted, and many fish were to be found there. Tanook provided for his clan, for they were in a scarce season, and the fish were greatly needed.

So Tanook dared to enter the waters of the warring Gods, and the Sea Spirits were angered. The Nehalem and the Sea Gods began to fight, while Tanook sat helpless in his boat. The Tunnel Spirits tried to take Tanook, but the Nehalem fought for their people, for they were their true Gods.

The war continued, and Tanook called to both sides, for a truce. A bargain was set, and Tanook agreed to sacrifice his life. The Tunnel Spirits took his life, but the Nehalem gave it back. The Gods began to fight, once more.

The Spirits of life and death made an agreement. They drew a line in the waters, and the wars ended. The storms would die no longer at the mouth of the Nehalem, but at the Great Sea Rock. This would give more food to the Clanock tribe.

But the Clanock tribe would never be allowed to set foot in the sea at the Rock, for this was the territory of the Sea Gods. Tanook accepted his curse, and the waters of the Sea Gods were also cursed, to keep the tribe away.

Tanook walked out of the sea, but the Tunnel Spirits had marked him. The Nehalem had also blessed him. The truce was set for seven lives.

Tanook returned to his tribe, and the waters fought no more. The Sea Spirits took his life, when he reached twenty years of age, for this, the waters had agreed to. When

Tanook died, the Clanock named the next baby after him, and his life was restored by the blessing of the Nehalem. The truce continued, and Tanook was taken by the Sea Spirits six times, for this the Gods had also agreed upon.

The Sea Spirits always took Tanook's life. Always a baby took its first breath, as Tanook, the man, took his last. Tanook lived for one-hundred-and-twenty years. His sixth life, he recalled the others, and went mad.

The Sea Spirits cursed the villagers to take his life, for they feared for the safety of their people, for Tanook was cursed with a great rage. This was the sixth life.

The Nehalem kept their agreement with the Tunnel Spirits, and so, in his seventh life, Tanook's life was restored, and the Tunnel Spirits lifted the curse of death. Tanook led the village as a great hunter, and the curse was no more. Tanook lived to one hundred years, and so, he lived two-hundred-and-twenty years.

The Clanock tribe never fished at the Great Sea Rock again, for those waters were cursed with Tanook's Truce. The Nehalem and the Tunnel Spirits rested, and the waters were drawn with a line. The Clanock tribe paid their debts, with the six lives of Tanook, and so he lived to be a great hunter, once more. This is how the Clanock Tribe came to be named the Tanook Tribe.

****

Sam closed the book and looked at Adria and Micah. Then she looked at Mr. Allan. No one spoke for several moments. Then Mr. Allan shook his head.

"No," he said. "This is just too much. You're asking me to go way out on a limb here, to even believe that my daughter's been reincarnated. And Micah, too. Now you want me to believe some ridiculous legend of some lost Indian tribe? You people are out of your minds."

"So, this explains everything," Adria said. "When Justin and I drowned off of Tillamook Rock, we did so in cursed waters."

"Yes," Sam said. "And the curse of the truce that Tanook struck was placed on both your heads."

"But it said that Tanook always died at age twenty, didn't it?" Adria said, frowning.

"Yes, but Tanook was only one man. Throwing two people into the water at once? I don't know. The story doesn't explain how the curse works with two people."

"Well, we've figured that one out, anyhow," Micah said. "Charlotte and I were in love. We were engaged. She jumped into the water to try and save me. We were already bonded by love. I guess the Tunnel Spirits decided that was the kick-off of the curse? When we consummate our love, I guess."

"Uck," Mr. Allan said. "Please don't ever say that again."

"Look, it's a curse," Sam said. "If the deal is for the two of you to die, the Spirits will find a way. The two of you hooking up is as inevitable as Micah's death. The curse has to be brought about, as part of the deal between the Gods. Therefore, if the curse can only be wrought upon the two of you when you... you know... then it stands to reason that you won't be able to resist doing it. Not for long. If you could, then the curse would never happen, and the six lives would never be paid. Your loving each other is part of the curse."

"It's still all speculation," Micah said. "Since Tanook was only one person, and we're two. We have no idea how the curse is changed, by putting two people into the truce."

"Maybe not," Sam said. "But, I know this – Tanook was cursed to die six times. In the seventh life, he was born free of the curse. The seventh life was his reward for paying with his life six times before. And you guys are on your sixth life right now."

Adria looked at Sam, her eyes growing wide with the realization of her remarks. Sam looked back, her eyes sad and pained. She took in a deep breath.

"There is a way to end the curse, Adria. It will be lifted... Once more," Sam said, her eyes filling with tears. "You and Micah have to die one more time. Then, you'll be reborn, without the curse."

"What if you're wrong," Adria said.

"I don't think so," Sam said. "You think I want to be right? I wish I'd found an answer that would keep you both here. But the legend clearly states you have to die six times. The seventh life will be granted by the Nehalem, and the Tunnel Spirits will lift their curse."

"My daughter is not going to die," Mr. Allan said. "I don't care what that book says. I don't care what the two of you think you remember. Adria, you are not going to die."

"It can't be helped," Adria whispered. Micah took her hand, behind Sam's back.

"Micah will die," Sam said. "The curse will find a way. In the legend with Tanook, the Spirits cursed the villagers to be the ones that killed him. And Micah, you were killed by people, in every life, weren't you?"

"A farmer shot me," Micah said. "A car hit me. My brother stabbed me. A frat guy crushed my skull. A mugger stabbed me."

"But, all these things were caused by the curse," Sam said. "Including the Spirits using other people to hurt you."

Sam looked at Mr. Allan then, eyeing the shotgun sitting next to him. Richard looked at Sam, then at his own gun.

"You think I'm going to shoot Micah?" he said. "Are you out of your mind?"

"It's the first thing I thought, when I saw the gun," Sam shrugged. "I thought, 'is this how it's going to happen?' The truth is, we have no idea how or when. But, it will happen. And I don't think we have very long, either."

"What do you mean?" Adria said. She squeezed Micah's hand tight. He squeezed it back.

"Remember what I told you, about the pattern I suspected in your past lives?"

"What pattern?" Micah asked.

"When you and Charlotte drowned, when the curse first began, you both were immediately born, the same day you died. But the next several lives, after you died, there was a pause. Seven years the first time, two years the next, a year after the third death. Then, the turnaround started coming faster. A few months. The last two lives, you and Adria were turned around again immediately. You were born, the last two times, on the same day you died. Within hours. The curse seems to be speeding up the closer you get to the end of it all. And now I understand why. The curse is winding down, it's playing itself out. The closer you get to your last death, the faster it all goes. That's why, I suspect, you were so compelled to sleep together. To hasten the final curse. The final death."

"Once more," Adria whispered.

Sam looked at her and nodded. "I hate this. I hate knowing this. I wish this was your seventh life. But, it's not. The next one is."

"And after everything we've been through," Micah said, looking at Adria.

"I know you won't give up now," Sam said, looking down at the floor. "And I can't say that I blame you, either. I don't want to lose you, Adria. I love you. You're my best friend. I can't imagine going through the rest of my life without you to talk to. But, I know you can't be without Micah. You can't help it. I don't want to understand, but I do."

"I have to die," Adria said, beginning to cry.

"What?" Mr. Allan said, but his voice was weak.

"Once more," Sam cried, nodding. "Then you and Micah will be free to be together. No more curse. No more death. You have to die, once more."

"There has to be some other way," Adria said, the tears now falling. Micah cried silently on his side of the couch, still holding Adria's hand.

"There has to be a way to break the curse," Adria said.

"No," Sam said. "It has to run its course. There is no breaking it, just letting it run out. This is the last time. I can't see any other solution. You'll be immediately reborn, into your seventh life. The seventh life, you'll find Micah, and the two of you will be free to be together."

"If the curse is lifted, maybe we won't find each other?" Adria said sounding frightened.

"I'll find you, Adria," Micah said. His eyes had a fire in them. "I'll find you, don't worry."

"This is insane," Richard said. "I cannot listen to this anymore."

"Papá, por favor. Te amo. Necesito tu ayuda. Por favor cree," Adria said. (Daddy, please. I love you. I need your help. Please believe). Only two people in the room understood what she'd said; she and Micah.

Mr. Allan turned then and looked at his daughter with tears standing in his eyes. He did not want to let any of what he'd heard in, but he heard his daughter's voice, and he recognized that she was someone else. Or, that she had been. He looked into her eyes, and his own eyes grew wide with the realization that everything he'd been told was true.

Adria stood, the tears streaming down her cheeks, and rushed to her father's waiting arms. Mr. Allan hugged his daughter, tears streaming down his own face. He looked over Adria's shoulder, and his eyes locked on Micah's. Micah was also crying. Mr. Allan sighed and closed his eyes then, holding his daughter more tightly than ever.

16. December 16-17, 2009

On the night of December 16, Mr. Allan agreed to let Adria sleep over at Micah's house. He couldn't believe he was doing so, and he felt half-crazy. But what they had already discussed, as well as their plans for the next day was also plain crazy, he reasoned. The fear was in his heart. It was in Sam's, as well.

Everyone looked to Micah, wondering when and how he would be killed. They also wondered how long they had with Adria. Everyone was in some form of denial, but when it came time to let Micah out of their sights, all three of them felt completely panicked.

"No, we said we wouldn't spend any time apart, from here on out," Adria said.

"Well, Micah has to go home at some point, Adria. Don't you think his Dad is going to wonder where he's at?" Mr. Allan said.

"We have to be together," Adria said. "What if he dies while we're separated?"

"You never have been before," Sam said. "That's not how the curse works. In fact, Micah has a better chance of dying because you're near him, than if he's away from you."

"But," Adria stammered. "I can't just let him walk out of this house and not go with him."

"What time does your Dad go to work, Micah?" Sam asked.

"He goes on at eight," Micah said. "Sometimes he leaves earlier."

"Okay," Sam said, thinking. "I'll walk Micah home."

"No, I'll drive him," Mr. Allan said.

Everyone was worried. Micah sighed.

"Micah, once your Dad leaves, I'll bring Adria over. And," he sighed. "I can't believe I'm gonna say this. Adria will spend the night at your house. She'll leave in the morning, before your Dad gets home. What time does he come home?"

"Eight," Micah said.

"Fine. Adria will come home a little before eight. She'll get ready, and so will you. We'll pick you up at ten. How does that sound?"

"Okay," Micah nodded. He was overwhelmingly grateful for Mr. Allan's cooperation.

****

Their plans went ahead without a hitch and at eight-thirty that night, Adria found herself in Micah's bed, and they loved one another. The curse was already set in motion, and they were no longer afraid of the consequences, for it was far too late for that. They loved each other then fell asleep in each other's arms. In the morning, Adria reluctantly left Micah's house.

"You won't go anywhere, will you?" She stood at Micah's front door and looked at him, pleading.

"Unless I slip in the shower, I don't see how I'm going to die in the next few hours," Micah smiled, trying to reassure her.

"It's not funny."

"I'm in the house alone, Adria. This isn't Final Destination," Micah said. "You have to be with me, remember? I'm in more danger with you here, than when you leave."

"Should I stay away, then? I should stay away," Adria turned to leave. He pulled her back and kissed her. Then he pulled away and gazed at her.

"No," he said. "I'm going to die, no matter what we do or don't do, from this point on. Remember? It won't be your fault, Adria. This is the last time, remember? Once more. We can do this. We can get through this."

"But, my Dad," Adria began to cry. "And my Mom. And Sam."

"I know," Micah hugged Adria tight. "It sucks. Everything sucks. But, it's all almost over, Adria. I can feel it, can't you? I know Sam is right. It sucks, but we have to get through this. Just one more time. Otherwise, it was all for nothing."

"I love you."

"I love you, too," Micah said. "Now go. Get ready. Get ready for me to marry you."

****

December 17, 2009. 10:30 a.m.

"I sure wish I could explain this to your mother, but," Mr. Allan trailed off.

He drove his old Jeep Cherokee through the rain. In the passenger seat, Sam sat, intermittently looking back at Adria and Micah. She smiled. She simply couldn't help herself.

In the backseat, Micah and Adria sat holding hands, gazing at one another lovingly. They were going ahead with their plans, and things were going faster than previously expected. Adria pointed out to Micah that all of this could only have been possible by telling her father the truth. Micah had relented, nodding.

They were on their way to Portland. Mr. Allan had miraculously agreed to sign his consent for the two of them to get married. They only needed the consent of one parent. Micah was not about to ask his own father. Mr. Allan and Sam would be their two witnesses.

"Well, let's just see how busy the clerk is today," Mr. Allan said. "It is a Friday, and it's just before the Holidays. They may not be able to do it today, five minutes or not."

"It has to happen," Adria said, still gazing at Micah. "As long as we don't die during the drive, this will be the first time Micah and I will have pulled off getting married."

Mr. Allan took in a deep breath and sighed. His only reason for consenting to allowing his daughter to marry

Micah was because he held onto the slim hope that marriage might break the curse. If they had never made it that far before, perhaps it would have an effect?

Sam was not holding her breath on this one, however. She did not want to believe her best friend needed to die one more time, but to her, it was spelled out plain and clear. The legend left little margin for hoping otherwise.

In Portland, they waited in the county clerk's office, in a semi-long line. When they reached the window, the clerk seemed fairly unsurprised that a father was consenting to allow his seventeen-year-old daughter to get married. Mr. Allan babbled nervously.

"You know what they say," he laughed. "You have to let 'em learn from their own mistakes. Hell, if I don't go along, they'll find their own way, right?"

The clerk looked down, filling out the forms, and typed on her computer. She sighed.

"Please, I've seen it all. Besides, I'm sure you'll be back in a few months, for the annulment," she looked up at Mr. Allan from under her glasses and smiled ruefully.

"Uh, yeah," Mr. Allan laughed.

The entire process took only ten minutes. Mr. Allan paid an extra fee to waive the three-day waiting period, and the ceremony was scheduled for two hours later.

"All the marriages are performed between three and five," the clerk sighed. "Have some lunch."

It was impossible for Sam or Mr. Allan to convince Adria to leave the Clerk's Office. She was deathly afraid the Cherokee would be hit by a semi, or that a car would careen onto the sidewalk. She was endlessly fearful that something would happen to Micah in the next two hours that would prevent them from getting married.

In the end, Mr. Allan brought sandwiches back to Micah and Adria. He took Sam with him on the walk, and they went around the corner, to a deli. While waiting in line, Mr. Allan mumbled, half to Sam, half to himself. She only nodded, feeling sorry for him.

"You know we've all lost our minds, don't you? Flipped our lids. Gone off the deep end. Hell, I'm the craziest one of you all. Nutso."

Back at the court building, Micah and Adria sat together, holding hands. Adria looked around fearfully at the people waiting in line, wondering if one of them might go postal and pull out a gun. Micah felt Adria's tension and sighed.

"Worrying won't help," he said, watching her eyes. "We're supposed to be enjoying the time we have."

"Micah, you could die in the next five minutes, for all I know."

"Then let's make those five minutes count," he said, gazing at her.

Adria was immediately lost inside his eyes. She sighed and kissed him. When the food arrived, neither Micah nor Adria ate. They only stared at each other. Mr. Allan watched this, awe struck and baffled all at once.

"Souls connected?" He frowned at Sam.

Sam only nodded, eating her sandwich. She spoke with her mouth full.

"You can't doubt that, can you? I mean, look at them. No wonder they had sex."

Mr. Allan closed his eyes, wincing. Then he shook his head and watched his daughter's face. Despite himself, he smiled. He'd never seen Adria so happy in her entire life.

****

At three in the afternoon, all the waiting couples were called into a line. There were five of them. Micah and Adria were first to jump in. Adria looked at Micah in complete awe and surprise.

"This is really going to happen, isn't it?"

"Unless the roof falls on our heads," Micah shrugged, smiling at her.

"Don't say that."

They were ushered into a small office and the county clerk made both Adria and Micah swear on a Bible. Sam and Mr. Allan stood to either side of the couple and looked on. Mr. Allan felt like he was dreaming. He was crazy for doing this, he thought. Then he stood and watched his daughter get married, and his eyes filled with tears.

The clerk simply asked Micah if he would take Adria as his lawfully wedded wife. Micah said yes, his eyes never leaving Adria's face.

The clerk asked Adria if she would take Micah as her lawfully wedded husband. Adria said yes, gazing at Micah. They had purchased cheap rings from the clerk's store. Mr. Allan couldn't believe there was such a thing. The rings, they now placed on each other's fingers.

The clerk then announced that by the power invested in her, Micah and Adria were married. She gave Micah permission to kiss Adria, and he did. When they stopped kissing and pulled away, Adria looked at Micah in complete disbelief.

"I can't believe it," she said. "I was certain something would go wrong. An earthquake, food poisoning, something."

"Why do you think I didn't eat," Micah smiled, winking at her.

How could he have such a sense of humor about this? Adria wondered. Perhaps it was his defense mechanism? After all, Adria realized, it must be frightening for Micah, wondering how and when he was going to die. He was going to go first.

Micah gazed at Adria and caressed her face. Then he looked at Mr. Allan and nodded his head.

"Thank you," he said.

Mr. Allan came over and surprised everyone by hugging Micah tightly, and clapping him on the back.

"Micah," he said, "You better treat my girl right."

"I will, sir."

"I want to talk to you, when we get back home," Richard said.

Micah nodded.

****

On the drive back to Cannon Beach, Micah and Adria kissed in the backseat, and Mr. Allan and Sam did their best to ignore them.

"Sam?" Richard said, almost under his breath. "Do you think this undid things?"

Sam immediately knew what he meant. She looked at him and shook her head, not wanting to lie. He nodded. Micah and Adria were too caught up in each other to notice.

"But, you could be wrong, right?"

"Sure," Sam said, but her voice was hollow. "I could be wrong."

"But?" Richard said.

"But, it's a curse," Sam whispered. "I don't think it will allow anything to happen that would undermine it. The fact that they got married, and nothing stopped them, tells me that marriage was never an obstacle for the curse. They just never made it that far before now. They also never knew in any of their past lives that they were running out of time. They thought they had their whole lives. They never rushed to get married, two months after meeting."

Richard nodded, following Sam's reasoning. He sighed.

"I can't lose my daughter," he said.

"We may not have any choice."

In the backseat, Micah and Adria were lost in each other.

Once back at Adria's house, however, Richard pulled Micah aside and sent Adria upstairs. She looked at her dad fearfully.

"I'm not gonna hurt Micah," Richard said. "And I won't let him out of my sight, okay? I'll send him up when I'm done."

Adria nodded and went upstairs, reluctantly. Micah sat down at the kitchen table, across from Mr. Allan. Mr. Allan launched straight into what he had to say without any hesitation.

"She's not going with you, Micah," Richard said. "She has too much to live for."

Micah surprised Richard by nodding. He scoffed.

"I don't want Adria to die," Micah said. Sam stood in the corner, listening.

"I can't help dying, that I have no control over," Micah said.

"If you're dead, you can't stop Adria," Richard said. He turned to look at Sam.

"Oh, no," Sam said. "You can't expect me to stop it."

"I want you to stick to these two like glue," Richard said. "When the time comes, Sam. I want you to stop her."

"I can't do that," Sam said. "I can't take that choice away from her."

"Sam?" Richard frowned at her in shock. "You'd let Adria kill herself? You'd stand by and let it happen?"

"No," Sam said. "I don't know. I don't know what I would do. I can't imagine how any of this is going to take place. I may not even be there. I can't be there every moment, Mr. Allan."

"I want you to try. Obviously, I can't. I have to go back to work tomorrow. I don't want to leave Adria alone, though. Thank God it's Winter Break. The next few weeks, you can be with Adria, can't you? You can walk with them back and forth, each night. You can tell Emily that Adria's sleeping at your house. Micah, you and Adria won't be able to be together every night."

Micah nodded. He knew.

"I mean, your Dad has to have nights he's home," Richard said. "And I can't do anything on the nights that Adria's with her mother. That's starting next Monday. Next week, you'll have to be away from each other, on the night's your Dad's home, and she's at Emily's. And for God's sake, do not tell anyone that you two are married, you got me? If Emily catches wind of what I did, she'll string me up."

Micah nodded again. Mr. Allan looked at him, concerned.

"Are you scared?"

Micah nodded. "But, not to die. I'm scared to leave Adria all alone. I know how much pain she'll be in. I don't want to hurt her."

Mr. Allan gazed at Micah with sudden adoration and love. He smiled.

"You're not afraid to die? You're afraid to break Adria's heart?"

Micah nodded, looking down at the table.

"Jayzus H. Key-rist," Richard whispered. He looked at Sam, slapping his hands on the table.

"There's gotta be a way to stop this," he said. Sam shrugged.

"Micah," Richard said. "No knives. Is there a gun in your house?"

"No, sir," Micah said.

"Good. No driving. No hiking. From now on, you and Adria will only remain indoors. And sleep on your back, don't sleep face down."

"He's not a baby, that's SIDS," Sam said. "No fights, Micah," she added.

Micah nodded. "But, if it's going to happen, it will."

"Well, I'll tell you what's not going to happen," Richard said. "My daughter is not going to commit suicide."

"Mr. Allan?" Sam said.

"What?"

"Um, the last time Micah and Adria were apart, they both nearly died," Sam said.

"So?"

"So," Sam took a deep breath. "If Micah dies and Adria doesn't follow him, they'll be separated. I don't know, if that happened, what it would do to Adria."

"What are you trying to say?" Richard stared at Sam.

"That she might die even if she doesn't kill herself. She might die anyway, from sadness, or, whatever. Whatever happens to her when she's away from Micah."

"I don't believe this," Richard said.

"I don't know if she can choose to stay behind," Micah said. "She's always followed me. I think it's part of the curse. I don't think she has any more choice in the matter of dying than I do."

"Bullshit," Mr. Allan yelled. "Suicide is a choice."

"Like having sex was?" Micah said. "I'm sorry, Mr. Allan, but you just don't understand. We never had any choice. We never had any control. And I don't think Adria can stop herself."

"Then Sam will!"

"Not if it means I'm the one who kills her!" Sam said. "And if I stop her and she gets sick and dies, it will be too late, Richard. She'll die anyway, and she and Micah will be separated. A few hours difference in their deaths, even, could spell a difference of years in their rebirths. I don't know how it works. All I know is, they have to die at the same time. Within minutes of each other."

Micah nodded. "She's right. I know it. I feel it, in my memories. I can only wait for her for so long. I get pulled away, and if she's not with me, we're separated by time. It's different in death. Hours could mean I'm born right away, and Adria isn't born for decades."

"This is nuts," Richard said. "I took you, Micah. I drove you myself. I signed the papers. I allowed you to marry my daughter, in the hopes it would put an end to this whole crazy thing."

"Is that why you did it?" Sam said. "Because you'd hoped?"

Mr. Allan looked down at the table. He nodded.

"And I know it's what Adria wants. Micah makes her happy. You think I don't remember what it was like before? With the nightmares? With how thin Adria got, how pale, how sick? And I knew," Richard pointed at Micah, "I knew when she got better, it was when she was with you. I thought she was just happy and in love; her first real boyfriend, la-tee-dah. But her hair," he trailed off. "Her eyes."

"That's what will happen to her again, if we're separated," Micah said. "I don't want Adria to die. But I need her. And she needs me."

"*I* need her," Richard said. "I can't lose my child. How will I explain all this to Emily, huh? She won't even know. She won't understand."

"Look at it this way," Sam said, wiping her tears away, for she'd begun to cry. "Adria won't really be dead. Adria will, yes. But her soul will still live. And she'll be reborn, along with Micah. And next time, this won't happen. All this pain, all this ugliness, it will all be over with. And she'll be out there. With Micah. Somewhere in the world. She'll exist. She won't really be dead. She'll just be somewhere that we can't see her anymore."

Sam wiped furiously at her own face now, fighting off the tears that were spilling down her cheeks. These revelations were what she'd come to deal with the last several days. It was why she'd stayed away from Adria. She'd needed time to process the truth of it all. She'd needed time to grieve. She looked at Micah and smiled through her tears.

"I can't hold Adria back," she said. "No matter how much I love her. Please understand, Micah. I'm not killing her. I'm just letting her go."

Micah stood. He walked around the table and embraced Sam tightly, crying.

"Thank you, Sam."

"For what?" she asked.

"Understanding."

"No," Richard shook his head, still in full denial. "There has to be some way around all of this. Maybe Micah simply won't die? I'm still not sure I even believe any of this."

"Then, we'll all just have to wait and see," Adria said from behind them all.

She stood in the kitchen entryway, looking sad. No one was certain how long she'd been listening. Adria looked at Micah and Sam and smiled.

"Should I be jealous?"

Micah let go of Sam and walked over to embrace Adria, kissing her. He smiled.

"No," he said.

"Dad?" Adria said. "Are you done?"

Richard looked at Adria and nodded. Adria looked at everyone.

"All we can do is wait," she said. "If you don't mind, I'd like to be alone with my husband."

Micah gazed at Adria, his eyes only for her. Richard nodded again. Then he exclaimed out.

"Shoot, I almost forgot."

Richard reached inside his pocket and pulled out a box. He handed it to Micah, who blushed and stuffed it into his own jeans pocket.

"Indulge me," Richard said. "Be good."

"Goodnight, Dad," Adria said. "Goodnight, Sam."

"See you soon," Sam said.

****

In Adria's room, Micah pulled the box of condoms out of his pocket and looked at Adria, his crooked grin making her feel lost and happy. She rolled her eyes, laughing.

"What do you think?" he said. "Should we try and act like we might live long enough?"

"What would be the point?" Adria said. "I think a baby is the least of our problems. It would have happened by now, if it were even possible. And by that, I mean, in any of our lives."

"Yeah, I know what you meant," Micah sighed.

He walked up to her and kissed her. She melted in his arms.

"How do you feel about being Mrs. Adria Foster?"

"Wow," she said. "I really am, aren't I?"

"You really are," Micah said. "What if the curse can be undone?"

"Micah," Adria said. "Please, don't. Why even bother?"

"No, think about it. We never even knew before. We do this time. The curse is for our lives. But what if there was another life involved? It may be rushed, but... what if you were going to have a baby? That's a new life, Adria. One that was never involved the day we fell into the water off Tillamook Rock. Do you really think the Tunnel Spirits would take a life away, that wasn't even involved in the original bargain?"

"Micah, you're reaching," Adria said. "There is no stopping the curse. You heard what Sam said. Nothing that might stop it could ever be allowed to happen. Our being married was never going to stop it."

"So, what are you saying?"

"I'm saying that if me getting pregnant could stop the curse, I simply won't become pregnant," Adria said. "We could do it a dozen times a day, and a baby won't ever happen."

"But, what if you're wrong?" Micah said. His eyes were twinkling.

Adria frowned at him. She didn't want to hope. Micah looked at the box of condoms and then smiled at Adria. He threw them over his shoulder and embraced her. She sighed.

"Mrs. Foster, would you do me the honor of allowing me to make love to my wife for the very first time?"

"You think you need to ask?"

They made love, again, only this time as husband and wife, and it was wonderful. Micah and Adria were happy.

17. December 18, 2009 - January 21, 2010

They made love several times on their wedding night. Several more times the following week. It was wonderful. After the first few days together this way, Adria began to worry less and less about Micah's impending death. She simply became swept up in her love for him.

There were times when they were separated. Then, Adria grew anxious and gloomy. She worried during the long stretches that she was alone, away from him. During these times, she called Micah, or texted his phone, or chatted with him online. When she was unable to have contact with him, overnight, she did not sleep. She wrote songs. It was the only thing that helped.

Sam stayed with her on the nights she could not be with Micah. They spent long hours talking about everything. Sam and Adria became closer friends than ever. They talked about the impending doom that lay in wait.

"How do you think it will happen?" Adria asked, one night. They were at her mother's house.

"I don't know," Sam said. "You never see it coming, right?"

"No. It's always been sudden and unexpected. Completely jarring."

"And you've always been alone?"

"No," Adria frowned. "Never. It's always been with other people around. Except in the field, with the farmer. In 1929 there were people everywhere. William just... was in the street, not paying attention, and the car... they weren't looking, either."

"So, John was shot because he crossed the fence?" Sam asked.

"The fence was down," Adria said. "He didn't know no betta'. Couldn' tell he was off prop'ty." Adria became Celia.

"You've never been anyone else, without Micah around," Sam said.

"Sorry," Adria said. "You're making me think about it."

"For a reason," Sam said. "John died because he crossed a line. William died because he stepped out into the street and didn't pay attention, right?"

"Yes?"

"Then, Rafael engaged in a fight with his brother," Sam said.

"It wasn't his fault," Adria defended.

"Anyway," Sam said, "Devon got into a fight as well, right?"

"Again, not his fault."

"And then Eduardo got mugged?"

Adria nodded.

"At three in the morning? What were you guys doing out at three in the morning, in a bad neighborhood?"

"Look, it's not our fault," Adria said. "When you come from the worst cities in Mexico, Hermosa Beach doesn't seem so dangerous. We didn't know. Dale un descanso." (Give it a rest).

"Huh?"

"Nothing," Adria mumbled. "You're saying it's all Micah's fault?"

"No, I'm saying that Micah's actions are just as out of control as everything else. At some point, he'll do something stupid. He won't look while crossing the street. Or he'll pick a fight, like with Kane, maybe, and he'll get kicked in the head. Or he'll be clumsy and trip down some stairs. I'm saying, the curse will find a way to make it happen, even if it's through influencing Micah's actions, somehow."

"That's murder."

"That's the curse," Sam said. "But, it seems to actually happen with other people around. Many times, a third person, who kills Micah. Like the farmer, Ricardo, that frat guy, the mugger. The car hitting him was less intentful, but that's the only instance of it."

"So, what are you saying? You think Micah will be murdered?"

"Maybe," Sam said.

"Who...?" she started to ask, but then stopped.

Adria saw the dark, glowering face of Westley Kane, and she felt a sinking dread in the pit of her stomach.

"Kane?" she looked at Sam.

"It is pretty weird that Micah chose him to pick a fight with, isn't it? On his very first day at school? The day he met you, Adria. And when I asked him why he chose Kane, Micah couldn't give a decent answer. Because it wasn't his choice, maybe? Maybe the curse led him to fight with Kane?"

"You think they'll get into another fight?"

"It's a pretty good bet," Sam said.

"But, there's no way to know that's how it will happen."

"But, it's a pretty good guess. Remember the way Kane kept looking at Micah? Watching him?"

"Then, what should we do?"

"I don't know," Sam said. "Just, be on the lookout for Kane. And if Kane tries to start something, then Micah just needs to back off, no matter how much he might feel driven to fight. He needs to resist the urge to start anything."

"He won't start anything, not now," Adria said.

"He can't finish anything, either," Sam warned. "If Kane approaches him, Micah needs to walk away."

Adria sighed and got up, pacing. She sat down at her keyboard and turned it on. Sam sat up, looking excited.

"Finally," she said. "What have you got for me tonight?"

"Something I started writing when Micah and I were apart. You know, before?" Adria led.

"Yeah, I know."

"I wrote the rest of the lyrics a few nights ago. When Micah was home with his dad."

She began to play the piano. It was slow and sad, but at times, almost angry. The intro was fairly short, just a few, simple chords, then Adria launched into the words with energy and purpose.

It seems like ages now,
Since you tore your story out...of my life.
The pages burning, ashes flying,
With anecdotes of you.

When you took away my joy,
I felt the pain that burdened you.
And when you reeled, and span away,
You brought your monsters to my point of view.

But if you ever do need me,
I hope you find out where I'm going to, Oh you lost boy.
And if you fall down on your knees,
You know I will be praying for you...

I wonder if you're still,
A part of someone's world?
I wonder if ten years from now,
I'll still feel your hurt?

When you took away my joy,
I felt the pain it burdened you.
And when you reeled, and span away,
You brought your monsters to my point of view.

'Cause if you wanted to be free,
You would have chosen to come with me, Oh you lost boy.
And if you needed to be loved,
Why did you choose to walk away from me? Oh....

Oh you lost boy. No...

You lost boy...

It seems like ages now,
Since you tore your story out...of my life.
The pages burning, and ashes flying,
With anecdotes of you.

When you took away my joy,
I felt the pain, how it burdened you.
And when you reeled, and span away.
You brought your monsters to my point of view.

But if you ever do need me,
I hope you find out where I'm going to. Oh...
And if you fall down on your knees,
You know I will be praying for you...

...If you ever do need me,
I hope you find out where I'm going to, Oh you lost boy.
And if you fall down on your knees,
You know I will be praying for you...

You lost boy...

"Jesus, Adria," Sam said. "You fucking rock."

****

On January 2, 2010, school resumed. Adria was nervous. This was the first time Micah would be around so many people, since the curse had set in. She was a total wreck that first morning in the hallway. She rushed up to Micah at his locker and looked at him with relief.

"Everything's okay?"

"Of course," Micah smiled his crooked grin at her. "Nothing out of the ordinary."

"I can't stand this," Adria said. "It was better not knowing."

"Then we wouldn't have gotten married," Micah said. He leaned over and kissed Adria once, and she lingered, her eyes remaining closed. Micah smiled, sighing in frustration. He twisted his wedding ring around on his finger.

"If anyone asks, it's just a promise ring, right?"

"Yeah," Adria said, opening her eyes. "Promise me you'll be careful? About Kane?"

Adria had talked to Micah about what she and Sam had discussed. He'd listened, intently. He wanted to support Adria, but Micah held little hope in staving off his impending death. He only kept up appearances to comfort his wife. He smiled at this thought.

"What?"

"You're my wife," Micah whispered.

"I know," Adria laughed. "*Tonto*."

"I know you are, but what am I," Micah said.

"I'll see you in history?" Adria said, looking anxious again.

"You know, if you keep up all this worrying, you're never going to even make it to the end of this week, Adria."

"I'm sorry. This is driving me crazy. I'm waiting for the worst thing in my life to take place. I'm waiting for my worst nightmare to come true. Plus, every day, I wonder if I've just said goodbye to my mom for the last time. Or my dad. Or Sam. Every time you walk away from me, Micah, I wonder if the next time I see you, I'll be holding your lifeless body in my arms."

Micah leaned forward and put his forehead against hers. His eyes were closed, and so were Adria's.

"I'm so sorry, Adria," he said. "I feel like I let you down. So badly."

"I let us down, too," she said. "It's both our faults."

"It's neither of our faults," Micah said. "This shouldn't have ever happened. I mean, what for? For drowning in the wrong spot of water? It's ridiculous. We're not even Tillamook. Foster is an Irish name."

"It doesn't matter where we came from, it only matters where we died," Adria said. "We died in a cursed spot."

"This sucks," Micah said.

Adria nodded. The rest of that first day went by extremely slow for both of them.

****

The next day passed, and the next, and the next. The first week of school in the New Year went by, and nothing happened to Micah.

The second week passed by, and Adria began to relax a little. Micah seemed to relax as well, but inside, he was an anxious knot of raw nerves. He hid it well from Adria, however, as he did not want his own anxiety to rub off on her in any way.

If he could make whatever time remaining between them as comfortable for Adria as possible, Micah was intent on doing so. His worst fear, in his mind, was not his own death, or even any physical pain that might accompany his injuries, but of having Adria by his side, and seeing the pain in her eyes; the heartbreak written all over her face.

Micah played the images of Adria crying over his body in his head again and again, and it drove him mad. He would do anything not to hurt her that way. It was all he cared about. He loved her so much.

As the weeks passed, they fell into a pattern. On the weeks Adria was with her dad, Micah stayed at her house, once his own father had left for work. Micah's father had Tuesday's and Wednesday's off from work. Those days were his weekend. So, every Tuesday and Wednesday, when Micah's dad was home, he and Adria were separated. But always, Micah never left the house in the evenings. He never had any reason to.

The weeks that Adria was with her mother, the couple was also separated. Adria began spending the night at Sam's house every weekend she was at her mother's. Then, she would simply go to Micah's house, instead. Otherwise, she and Micah would spend hours on the phone, many times, just listening to each other breathe, while lying in bed at night.

Adria's mother came into her daughter's room on several occasions to find her daughter fast asleep, with the phone lying next to her head, on her pillow. She would pick up the phone and listen, only to hear Micah's soft breathing as he slept. Then, Emily would hang up the phone and smile down at her daughter. It had not been lost on her that Adria was well, once more, no longer suffering from horrible nightmares and not eating.

Adria was happy, and Emily was well aware that her daughter had a boyfriend. She'd met Micah a couple of times. She had no idea, however, of how serious things were. She had none of the knowledge of her ex-husband.

****

Richard Allan spent his time researching curses. He tried to find an answer, a way to break the hex on his daughter's head. But, he could find nothing. There seemed to be no answer.

As the weeks passed by, everyone began to relax, for they all simply could not walk around in a constant state of anxiety. None of them had the energy to keep up with that pace.

Richard Allan started wondering, as spring came around, if the curse might not, indeed, have been broken by Micah and Adria's wedding.

18. March 23, 2010

On Tuesday, March 23, it happened. Adria and Micah were walking down the hallway, holding hands, when Micah was violently shoved up against a locker. Kane seemed to come from out of nowhere, and suddenly he was in front of Micah. Micah's hand was ripped from Adria's with the force of Kane's push.

His body hit the lockers, and the hallway instantly went quiet. The entire student body was well aware of the on-going feud between Micah Foster and Westley Kane. There had been two altercations between the boys, both on campus. Both times, Micah had drawn blood, and the pulverizing that had been heaped upon Kane in the second altercation had already reached mythical status in the hallways of Seaside High.

What no one realized after the second altercation, however, was that Kane was simply biding his time. He'd been publicly humiliated by Micah, twice. He intended to redeem himself, and make Micah pay. He would not be caught off-guard by Micah ever again, he'd vowed to himself.

Kane had taken the time to heal. Then, he had waited, and watched. He'd been calculating his attack on Micah, planning it for months. It was Kane's intention to make certain that this time, Micah would be expelled. He would also make certain that this time, Micah's blood would be spilled, and not his own.

The hallway sat in dead silence. Adria's heart pounded in her chest, so loud, she could hear it in her own ears. Her head was spinning. Was this it? She couldn't breathe.

Micah stood, stunned, his back up against the locker, and stared at Kane, his eyes wide and surprised. The fire and rage that had once burned deep within him, had long ago died down, the moment he was with Adria again.

From the moment they'd made love, the darkness inside him, and the raging inferno, had been expelled. He had no desire to fight Kane. He also knew what it could mean for him, if he did. He had no intentions of engaging Westley Kane in any kind of physical altercation.

Micah looked past Kane, to Adria, and her eyes met his. They locked on each other. Adria's eyes pleaded with him, and he knew what he must do. He'd promised her, if this ever happened, that he would do nothing.

"Come on, you fuck! Let's see you throw a punch today, huh?" Kane screamed at Micah. "Now that I'm not sitting down, at a table, unprepared. Huh?"

Micah moved to walk away, and Kane shoved him up against the locker again. Again, there was a loud banging noise, and several people in the watching crowd gasped. Adria winced, shutting her eyes in pain.

Micah bit his lip as the handle of the locker behind him dug into his skin. Already, a bruise was forming there. He felt fire begin to rise inside him, and he tamped it back down, quickly, extinguishing it. He looked at Adria again, and saw the pain in her eyes, the fear. It was all he needed to see, to keep his hands limp at his sides.

Kane was furious at Micah's resistance. He felt like a fool. He felt as if he was standing in the hallway, and suddenly realized he was naked. Everyone was looking at him, he knew. This was not the way things were supposed to go. This was not what Kane had planned. He'd wanted to redeem himself.

Kane threw a punch at Micah, and it landed on his cheek with a sickening thud. The crowd gasped again. Micah went down on the ground, his cheek already swelling and bruising.

"Micah!" Adria screamed.

"Get up, you fucking coward! You're not so tough now, are you?!" Kane screamed, slowly backing away several feet.

Kane ran at Micah and kicked his leg, hard. The crowd winced and gasped, once more. In the back of the crowd, a freshman girl went running off, to fetch adult help.

No one wanted to see Micah get hurt. Although he'd been the new kid, and kept to himself, his fights with Kane had made him a living legend among the students.

Kane was a jock, known for his temperament. His popularity was laced with equal hatred and contempt, among the students he'd bullied over the years. Many of the teens attending Seaside High were more than happy to see Kane take a beating on the day Micah first arrived.

The second fight, in the cafeteria, some weeks later, had been gruesome, but many believed it had put Kane firmly in his place. Micah was popular among the students, even if he had no clue.

Micah took the kick, wincing, but he did not move, nor did he stand to defend himself. Kane was beside himself, not knowing what to do. Adria suddenly became very afraid. Visions ran through her head, of Kane beating Micah to death. Something Sam had said to Adria weeks ago, now ran through her mind, giving her the chills.

"...Or he'll pick a fight, like with Kane, maybe, and he'll get kicked in the head."

Adria was suddenly certain that this was exactly what was about to take place. She could not watch Micah die again. She knew it. She reacted instinctively. She stepped in front of Kane and screamed at him.

"Leave him alone!" she said. "Hasn't there been enough fighting already?"

Kane stared at Adria in rage and disbelief. A *girl* was fighting Micah's battle for him, now? People were laughing at him, he knew. In his mind, Kane was humiliated all over again. He ignored Adria, craning around her, at Micah's crumpled body, where he still lay on the floor.

"Get up you chicken-shit-fuck!"

Kane grabbed Adria by the shoulders and shoved her forefully up against the same locker he'd shoved Micah just minutes earlier. Her head hit the locker and she felt dizzy. Kane had shoved her with great force. He had also done so just as Mr. Prince came running up with the freshman girl leading the way.

"What's going on here?" Prince said. "Adria, are you all right?"

Adria shook her head, not to say no, but to try and clear it. She reached behind her and touched the spot that ached. It felt warm. She pulled her hand away and her fingers were covered with blood. Her head was bleeding.

"Oh, dear God," Mr. Prince said. He turned and looked at Kane, glaring. "Kane, you're out of here."

"What?!" Kane stared at Prince, disbelieving.

"You heard me," Prince said. "You picked a fight with Micah. We had an agreement, that the two of you would leave each other alone. Both of you. Did Micah fight?"

Prince looked around at the crowd. No one spoke.

"Well, everyone's been watching. Did Micah fight with Kane?"

"He didn't do anything, sir," the freshman girl said. "He was just walking, and Kane pushed him. He punched him, and Micah didn't do anything. He just took it."

Prince nodded. He looked down at Micah, who stood now, to see if Adria was okay. His left cheek was badly swollen and bruised. All he cared about, however, was Adria. He took her face in his hands and cradled it. She began to cry.

"I thought you were dead," Adria cried.

To Prince and everyone else watching, Adria's statement seemed to be the product of her head injury, making her overly dramatic. Kane, however, glared. Prince turned back to Kane, looking furious.

"Kane, you pushed a female? You picked a fight with Adria?"

"She got in my face!" Kane defended.

"You hit her boyfriend, you jerk," a boy said from the crowd. "Then you kicked him while he was down. You're a fucking coward, Kane."

"Yeah," several students chimed in.

"Westley, I'm sorry, but I have no choice. It's one thing to fight with Micah again. That, alone, would have done it. We had an agreement. You tripped him last time. You caused that fight. But, you can't go hitting girls. Period. Zero tolerance. I'm sorry."

"But," Kane said.

"Come to the office. We need to call your parents," Prince said.

"This is bullshit!" Kane said. "He picked a fight with me, his first day of school, and all he got was detention?! It's not fair! I go to the hospital, and he only gets suspended for two weeks? But I'm out?! It's not fair!"

"I decide what's fair," Prince yelled. "If you had to pick a fight with Micah, Kane, you shouldn't have done it on school property. We had a deal. You broke it. Micah didn't. End of story. You're gone. I'm sorry. Now go to the office. Now!"

Kane turned and walked down the hallway, defeated, the crowd of students parting for him. Adria and Micah watched him go, feeling nothing but dread. Kane spun around then, quickly, and fixed an icy stare on Micah.

"I'll be seeing you," Kane pointed and glared death at Micah.

A chill ran up Adria's back. She knew. She knew right then, at that very moment, that Kane would kill Micah.

****

"We have to leave," Adria said.

She paced the floor of her Dad's living room. It was her week with him, again. Micah sat on the couch, his face in his hands. He said nothing.

"We have to get as far from Cannon Beach as we can," she said.

Sam sat in the recliner, listening. She'd missed the fight. When she heard about it, she came running to Adria's locker. Adria had gone to the nurse's station, but her head injury hadn't required any bandaging. The nurse couldn't bandage through her hair. She'd simply held a cloth on her head until the bleeding stopped. The injury wasn't so bad, after all.

"Head injuries always bleed a lot," the nurse sighed.

She looked at Micah's cheek and gave him an ice pack. By the time they returned to the hallways and headed to Adria's locker, Sam had heard the news and was waiting for them. Now, she sat in Adria's living room and only took everything in, thinking.

"Is anyone listening to me?" Adria screamed. "We have to leave, before Kane kills Micah!"

"Adria, we can't run from the curse," Micah said. "If we leave, I'll only die some other way."

"No!" Adria wailed. "I won't accept that. It's suicide to stay here. Kane is going to come after you, Micah. I just know it."

"Where would you go?" Sam said. "If you leave, I can't go with you, and I promised your dad I'd stick to you like glue."

"Yeah? Well where were you today?!" Adria screamed.

"In class!" Sam yelled back. "This isn't my fault! I can't be with you every moment, Adria."

Adria looked at Sam, blinking. She realized how out of line she was.

"I'm sorry," Adria said. "I'm sorry, Sam."

"So am I," Sam said.

"I'm staying here," Micah said. "If we leave, Adria, you won't see your dad. Or your mom. And if I die anyway, and we're far from home, you'll have wasted what little time you have left with your family."

"You're my family, Micah," Adria said. "Why would we stay here, when it's so dangerous?"

"Because," he said, "we can't run from this, Adria."

"Micah's right," Sam said. "Besides, I don't want you to go."

Adria began to cry and hugged Sam tight. When she pulled away, Sam looked at her, her face loving, like a mother.

"You can't run from it, Adria. Because, look what happened today? Micah didn't do anything. He did exactly what we told him to, which was nothing. He never laid a hand on Kane. Kane did this to himself. Things will happen, Adria. Things beyond our control."

"It's my fault," Adria said. "Westley got expelled because of me. I got in the way, and he pushed me. That's why Prince kicked him out."

"Right, but he pushed you, Adria," Sam said.

"Because I got in his face," Adria said. "Oh, God! I caused this!"

"No, you didn't," Micah said. "Kane would have never even picked on me today, if I hadn't fought with him first, Adria. You had nothing to do with that. I picked him, remember? The first day of school."

"It's the curse," Sam said. "There is no fault, here. For anyone."

"Kane tripped Micah, that day in the cafeteria. You're telling me the curse made him do it?" Adria said. "That's stupid."

"Well, for all we know, Kane will have nothing to do with Micah's death!" Sam yelled. "We're grasping at straws, here. We can't know. There is no stopping it. It's going to happen, one way or another."

Adria turned and left the room then. She ran up the stairs and into her room, slamming her door. Micah could hear her pacing in her room, her footfalls moving across the ceiling. He looked up, sighing in frustration.

"I don't know what to do," he said. "I just wanted to enjoy our time together, what little of it we might have. I didn't want it to be like this. She's always on edge. From the moment we leave the house, 'til we return indoors. Even then, if I leave to go to the bathroom, she paces outside in the hallway. She thinks I'll slip and hit my head on the sink. Or a stray bullet from some kid's target practice will fly through the wall. Her head is spinning around, Sam. She's going crazy."

"I know. So am I. You can't blame her, can you? Did you guys really have to do it?"

"It's a little late for that now, Sam."

"So? Did you really have to sleep together? You couldn't resist?"

Micah closed his eyes and thought back to where he'd been, mentally, physically, emotionally, the day he'd come to see Adria in her room. He felt the emptiness inside of him, and he shuddered. He opened his eyes and looked at Sam. His face was filled with hurt and pain.

"Fine," Sam said. "I just hate this. This sucks, you know? For everyone."

"I know," Micah said. "But, I wish we could just be normal. Just be happy together."

"You're not happy?" Sam asked.

"I am," Micah said. "Of course I am. I just wish...I'm not even sure what I wish."

"I know what you're trying to say, Micah."

She sighed. Then she looked at him, her eyes twinkling.

"I have an idea, but I think it might be an awful one. I'm sure Adria will never say yes, but... it's worth a try."

****

Upstairs, Adria sat down at her keyboard and turned it on. She began to play. She'd been working on a song the last several weeks, when she was alone at night and could not sleep. She put all her feelings of fear and hope into it. She began to play it now.

Downstairs, Micah and Sam had finished talking. They heard the piano chords as they first began to sound. Sam smiled. She nodded to Micah and they both went to listen. Micah loved it when Adria sang. She hadn't done so for him in a while.

The two of them entered her room and sat on the bed. Adria didn't even notice them. She was still playing her chords, her back to them. The music was sad and soft, the piano echoing off the walls. It drifted between major and minor, lifting their spirits, then dropping them down again. When Adria began to sing, Micah's heart broke. So did Sam's.

****

If you saw me at this moment, would you run away?
Would I even have the courage, to know what to say?
'Cause when I see your eyes I lose my strength,
To do what's right.
I'd give up all life's moments now,
For just one night...
It may be wrong...
It may be wrong...

But if you ever thought I'd love you less,
Without you here...
Or that I might just prefer my life,
Without you near...

For once more,
Take my hand and lead me to the place we knew before.
For once more,
Take me to the furthest place from where I was before.
For once more... I'd give up all life's moments.

You know that I would do it all again, without a thought.
Even knowing how it always ends, it's no one's fault.
'Cause when I see your eyes I lose my strength, to walk away,
And suddenly I lose my voice, I lose my rage...
This can't be wrong...
It can't be wrong...

So if you ever thought I'd love you less,
Without you here...
Or that I might just prefer my life,
Without you near...

For once more,
Take my hand, try not to think, or worry for no one's,
Keeping score,
The only thing that matters here,
Is you and I were born.
For once more... I'd give up all life's moments.

If you thought that I'd forgotten how it feels to love,
Or that I couldn't remember how it felt to touch.
I remember every moment now, of every day,
I remember every lifetime we had ripped away.
Oh, I remember...
I remember...

If you ever thought I'd love you less,
Without you here...
Or that I would just prefer my life,
Without you near...

For once more,
Take my hand, try not to think of what we shouldn't do.
For once more,
Take my hand, there's nothing left, that I wouldn't do.

For once more,
Take my hand and we'll go there. Don't worry for no
one's,
Keeping score,
The only thing that matters now,
Is you and I were born.

For once more,
I'd give up all life's moments...

****

Adria sat at the keyboard for several moments, not moving. Micah stared at her. Sam was crying. She shook her head. Then she stood and left the room. As she walked away, she mumbled under her breath.

"What a fucking waste."

The door slammed behind Sam as she left, running down the stairs. The front door could be heard slamming downstairs. Adria's body gave the minutest hint of a jump at both slams. Micah closed his eyes. *Everything is turning into shit.*

Adria was right, it was better not to have any clue what was coming. He opened his eyes again, as he felt the bed depress next to him, under Adria's weight. She sat next to him, but did not look at him. When she spoke, Micah knew the darkness of it all was taking her mind apart.

"Maybe we should do it ourselves," she said. "Just, take a big bottle of pills, each, and lay in the bed, in each other's arms."

"Adria," Micah whispered.

"I can't do this," she said. "I can't live like this. Waiting. Waiting for you to die, Micah. I love you so much. I don't want to find you in the next life. I want you in this one. I want this life. With you, my dad, Sam. I'm happy here. I don't want to have to start all over again. And I can't watch you die, Micah. The pain. It'll hurt so much," Adria broke down into sobs, and Micah held her, crying himself.

"This is madness," he said. "This is sheer madness."

Adria clung to him. She pulled on him. She was still sobbing when she began kissing his right cheek, the one that wasn't bruised and swollen. She was desperate. So was he.

In an instant they were making love, and Adria cried the entire time, so overwhelmed by her sadness and joy, both, at once. Micah felt her body underneath him, and he couldn't imagine how they ever managed to resist being together.

He fell onto, into her, was enveloped by her softness, her warmth. He loved her so much. He only wanted to make her pain go away. He only wanted to be with her. He reveled in her body, in his desire for her. He brought her to the brink of ecstasy, and over. She clung to him, hugging him tight. He could feel her panic, her desire to be as close to him as possible. He buried his face in her shoulder, and loved her even harder. She cried out, her pleasure overflowing, climaxing for a second time.

When the act was complete, they lay together, not sleeping, but spent, nevertheless. Micah stroked her arm, and Adria stared at his skin, her eyes falling out of focus.

"Who do you think we'll be, next time?" she asked.

"I don't know," Micah said.

"I hope we're American," she said.

"We always have been," Micah said. "Except for the last time. And we both ended up in Hermosa Beach."

"But, our lives, growing up," she said. "That was awful. For both of us. And look at what you've been through in your life, now? With your mom."

"It's not so bad," Micah said. "It could have been a lot worse."

"I hope we have wonderful lives next time," Adria said. "I hope I have wonderful parents, like this time. And I hope we live on the same block, and play together as children."

"Adria, we've never met as children. Even when we lived blocks from each other."

"I didn't say I wanted to live only blocks away from you," she said. "I said I want to live on the same block. Nextdoor neighbors would be perfect. Do you think that's even possible?"

"I don't know, Adria. But, whoever we end up being, wherever we're each born, I know I'll find you."

"How can you be so sure?" she said. "If the curse is the only thing that's drawn us together every time, then once it's lifted, there won't be anything to bring us together."

"Yes, there will," Micah said. "My love for you."

"You won't even remember me."

"Maybe I will," he said. "We both remembered this time. We remember every person we ever were. I even have vague memories as Justin Tremaine."

"You do?" Adria peered up at Micah's face. "I don't remember anything from that life."

"It's not much," Micah said. "I just remember your face. I remember us, in the boat. And you, smiling at me. I remember that we'd just gotten engaged, and you wanted to have the wedding near Cannon Beach. When we got here, to look around, and you saw the town, you thought it was beautiful. You said it was where you wanted to get married."

"You remember that?" Adria asked. "Why don't I remember that?"

"I don't know," Micah frowned. "But, I know that even in that life, we were just as in love as we are now, without any curse compelling us to be together."

"So?"

"So," Micah said, sighing and rubbing her arm. "I don't think the way we love each other is because of the curse. I think that's just because we're us. Let's say, two guys had been in that boat. Do you really think if two random surveyors had drowned in those waters, they would have been born and found each other? Or that the curse would need to take effect with them seeing each other?"

"Um, you're kind of grossing me out with this scenario," Adria said.

"Sorry," Micah laughed. "I just meant, I think we find each other, because we're us, is all. It has nothing to do with the curse."

"Then, why does the curse only take effect once we sleep together? What does that have to do with anything?"

"You really don't remember that life, at all?" Micah said.

"No, why?"

"The day we drowned," Micah said. "Was the day we first slept together."

"What?" Adria looked at Micah in shock. "And you're just now telling me this?"

"I only remembered a few nights ago," Micah said. "When we'd been apart for several nights. It still hurts, even though we're together."

"I know," she said. "So, we slept together, when?"

"That morning. We got engaged the night before. We were so happy, I guess, it just happened. Then we drowned. In cursed waters."

Adria laughed. Micah was relieved.

"So, when we died and were cursed, the events of the day decided how the curse would take effect, because we were tied together?"

"That's what I think," Micah said.

"So, death only comes once we repeat the actions of our last day of life," Adria said. "Except, this time, we actually got married. This time's different."

She looked at Micah with hope. He was not smiling, however. Adria knew something was wrong.

"Micah?" her voice was low. He took a deep breath.

"It's going to happen soon," he said.

She stared at him for a prolonged moment, digesting his words; letting them in. She saw the truth of Micah's statement in his eyes, and her eyes welled with tears.

"No." Adria clung to him and began to cry.

"Adria," Micah said. "Shh. Please don't cry."

"How do you know?"

"I can feel it," he said. "Lately. The closer it gets. And today, when Kane hit me? I felt it. I knew I wasn't going to die today, but… soon."

"How long?" her voice trembled.

"I don't know," Micah said. "Just… soon."

"I can't, I can't," she said.

"We don't have any choice."

"We can run," Adria said. "We can go far away."

"It will follow us," Micah said. "I feel that, too."

"Is it going to be Kane?"

"I don't know," Micah said. "Maybe. Probably."

"You know?"

Adria looked at Micah. She felt shocked, in disbelief. Micah sounded so calm. He paused for a moment, thinking. Then he nodded.

"But, if it wasn't him, it would be someone else. Or something. I have a feeling if we tried to run, or escape it, we'd only speed things up. And I want the next few weeks with you, Amaya."

"You know you have weeks?" She didn't acknowledge that he'd called her by her name in the previous life.

Micah nodded. "Barely. But it's just enough time."

"For what?"

"The Prom," Micah said.

"The Prom?" Adria looked at Micah, again in disbelief. "You're going to die, and you want to take me to the Prom?"

"Maybe another rave first, too. That would be nice."

"Micah, you've got to be joking me."

"Adria, listen to me. I'm going to die. I'm going to be killed. And all I want, my last few weeks, is to be with you. And I want to take you to a couple of stupid dances, okay? Just think of these things as my last wishes."

"If you only have a few weeks left, then so do I," Adria said.

"Yes. Unless you stay, when I go."

"No."

"I'll understand if you do," he said.

"I would never do that, Micah. Not when our next life is free for us to live. Sam's right, isn't she?"

Micah nodded. He felt that, too.

"Everything's coming to an end," Micah said. "And we know everything. We remember everything. You'll probably remember being Charlotte, soon. Then, you'll feel what I feel. And you'll feel it closing in."

"Are you scared?"

"Of course," Micah said. "But not to die. I know I'll be born again. I'm scared of hurting you, Adria. It pains me to see you sad, even now. I shouldn't have told you."

"No," Adria said. "Now I know. I can say goodbye. To everyone. To everything. There are some things I need to do. Something for Sam. And I need to spend some time with my dad. And my mom," Adria began to cry again. "I'm their only child."

"My dad will be sad, too," Micah said. "But, I can't do anything about that."

"Won't you even try to get closer to him?"

"I don't know," Micah said. "Maybe."

"Prom is in less than two weeks, Micah. Do we have that long?"

"I think so. But, it'll be close."

"How do you know this?"

"I can't explain it. You'll feel it, too, I think. Soon."

"I can't believe this is really going to happen," she said.

"You'll be okay," Micah said. "Everything's going to be okay, Adria."

"I wish I could save you," she said. "We just won't leave the house. We'll stay inside."

"Then, we'll only have spent our last days together, hiding," Micah said. "Let's go out with a bang, Adria. Let's just live. Let's just be together, and be happy."

"How can you say all this?!"

"I only want to be with you, Adria, that's all. Will you grant me that? Before I die?"

"I'm going to die, too," she said. "Right after you. Maybe even with you."

"No, after," Micah said. "You shouldn't go unless you're certain I already have. You'll feel me, Adria. When I go. You'll feel me, remember?"

"I 'member," Adria said, becoming Celia, if only for a moment.

She closed her eyes and remembered being Camila on New Year's Eve, 1954. She remembered feeling Rafael's soul, waiting for her. She even remembered the feeling of her own soul flying to meet him. It was all darkness, and yet, she could feel him surrounding her. It was pure joy.

"I remember," she said again, this time as herself.

"You'll feel me when I'm gone, all around you, Adria," Micah said. He nodded. "Then, you'll know it's time. If you choose to go with me."

"I will," Adria said. "I promise."

Micah held Adria in his arms and squeezed her. All he wanted was to be with her.

"Song?"

"Starting to Turn. Andrew Paul Woodworth," Adria said. "It fits. You pushed it in there, this time."

"I'm sorry."

"In my next life, I hope I still hear music," Adria said.

"And I hope you still sing," Micah said, smiling. His heart was in a constant state of pain – and joy.

"And I even hope you still like raves," she laughed.

Micah laughed with her. Adria smiled at him.

"Everything's going to be okay, Adria."

She clung to him. She held onto him, tight.

He held her tight as well, and tried to memorize the feel of her body. He etched the sound of her breaths into his sub consciousness. He committed to memory her laugh, her smell, her way of thinking. Micah breathed Adria in. He learned her. He felt her soul, and he knew it. He knew he would be able to find her in the next life. It was almost already upon them.

19. March 24-27, 2010

"Dad?" Adria said.

Her father was sitting in the kitchen, at the table, drinking a cup of coffee. He looked tired. He had dark circles underneath his eyes. It pained Adria to see her father this way. She knew his pain was because of her. She sat down in the chair adjacent to him at the table.

"Yeah, sweetie?"

"I need you to buy some stuff for me," she said.

"What stuff?" Richard asked.

"Recording equipment, for my studio," Adria said. "I know we had a deal, for me to earn the money, save up my allowance, but," she trailed off.

She did not want to tell her father about what Micah knew. She didn't have the heart. Her father looked at her now, and he read it in her eyes, anyhow. He knew from what she was asking for, as well. She took a deep breath and continued.

"I want to record my songs. For Sam," she said. "So she can have them."

"Baby," Richard said. His voice shook.

"Please?" Adria said. "I need to do this."

Richard stared at his daughter for several, long moments, thinking. Then, he nodded, but said nothing else, save for asking her when she wanted to go.

"Today."

Richard looked at her again, his face pulling taught with concern and panic. She returned his gaze, unblinking.

"Also, I need to buy a dress. For Prom."

"When is Prom?" There was hope in her father's voice.

"In nine days," Adria said. "On the third."

"It's a right of passage, you know?" Richard said. "Everyone should go to their Prom."

"And I will," she said.

She smiled at her father. He smiled back, but there were tears in his eyes.

"The third? That's next weekend. You'll be with your mother that week."

Adria nodded.

"Think she'll let me stay out all night?"

"Your mother?" Richard said. "I don't know."

"Can you ask her, for me?"

"Honey, I don't know."

"Please, Dad?" Adria asked. "Please? So I can be with Micah."

"Do you understand what you're asking me, Adria?"

"Yes," she said. "Please?"

Richard thought about it, hard. Then, he sighed and nodded his head. She smiled at him.

"Daddy?" Adria began to cry.

"Baby?" Richard responded with tears of his own.

"I love you," she said, dissolving.

Adria scraped out of her chair, and rushed at her father, hugging him fiercely.

"I love you, Daddy. And I couldn't have asked for a better father. Not ever."

"Adria," her father sobbed. "Oh, baby. Please."

"I'm so sorry," she hitched. "I'm so sorry."

****

But there were forces at work all around them, and even Richard was beginning to feel it. A storm was growing, building, and there was no one who could stop it. They all sensed this.

****

That afternoon, Richard took his daughter shopping. They laughed, and they ate lunch together in the shopping center at Seaside. Adria got the equipment she needed, and a

Prom dress. On the drive home, she sat in the passenger seat of her Dad's Cherokee and smiled. Richard was happy to see Adria smile. She hummed quietly to herself.

That evening, she locked herself in her room, and while her father was gone at work, she played, sang, recorded, and mixed. She laid down all her songs, including her covers, and her originals. It took all night, and Adria did not sleep. It was a Wednesday, so Micah's Dad was home. They couldn't be together, anyhow. Micah texted her every twenty minutes or so, with a simple message.

Still here. Still breathing.

He knew she was taking the time to do what she needed to do, to prepare. They'd never had the chance for preparation before. They'd never gotten to say goodbye. But this was the last time, and they both knew it now, regardless of what Sam had learned in Tillamook legend, or not. The tide was turning. Everything was coming to an end.

****

March 25, 2010

Adria and Sam drove into Seaside together for school. They barely conversed on the walkies the entire way. Sam sensed something was up, however. The last five minutes, she couldn't help herself, and she walkied Adria.

"Did Micah ask you to go to the Prom?"

"Yes," Adria said.

"Did you say yes?"

"Yes."

"You did?!"

Sam was surprised. She'd figured, what with Adria's paranoia about being out in public with Micah, and her shunning of crowds, that Adria would refuse to go.

The whole thing had been Sam's idea, however. She thought a normal teenage activity, like a school dance, might give Micah the opportunity he was looking for with

Adria. It's what she'd talked to Micah about, the day he'd been beaten by Kane. The day Adria wanted to slink out of town, to hide. Micah simply wanted the opportunity to forget he and Adria's worries and enjoy being together.

"Yes," Adria said. "It's what Micah wants. A dying man's last wish."

Sam sighed. "You know I'm going, right?"

"You are?"

"Yep. I have a date."

"Who?"

"This guy in Math asked me," Sam said.

They reached Seaside High and pulled into the parking lot. For a brief moment, Sam felt as if everything between she and Adria was as it always was, as it should be – as it had been, before everything turned to darkness. For a few, brief moments, she had her best friend back and everything was normal. It was an illusion, but one that Sam was more than happy to indulge in. She got out of her car and laughed at the look on Adria's face.

"When did you get asked?"

"The same day, after Kane got kicked out of school," Sam said. "I think I'm popular by association, now."

"Huh?"

"Um, Micah's this living legend at Seaside now," Sam said. "And everyone knows you two are together. You guys are like, this star-couple."

"What?" Adria laughed.

"Yeah, you're the duo that toppled Westley Kane," Sam said. "Everyone loves Micah. Can you believe that? The new kid; here less than a whole school year, and he's more popular than anyone."

"But, no one ever talks to him, or me," Adria mused.

"They sit and watch, in awe," Sam said. "Almost as if everyone can sense there's something special going on." The illusion was broken.

"The villagers, in on the curse," Adria nodded. Her eyes looked far off.

"So, we'll go? Together?" Sam asked.

"Sure," Adria said. "We can caravan. And after, Micah wants to go to this party thing. He got invited."

"Where?" Sam looked worried.

"Phillip Moore's throwing a party at his house, here in Seaside. Everyone's invited."

"That's a bad idea," Sam said. "Phillip Moore? And you still don't think you and Micah are popular, now? You shouldn't go. What if something bad happens?"

"Then, it will happen, anyway. Besides, it's what Micah wants, Sam," Adria said. "He wants to give us as normal a life as he can, while we're still here. Maybe he's right, maybe we should just relax and enjoy it. If it's all going to end anyway, why stay locked up in our rooms?"

"But, you shouldn't tempt fate," Sam countered.

"You're the one who said the curse will happen, no matter what we do," Adria defended.

"I know," Sam said. Her voice was apologetic. This curse was going to drive them all insane before it was through, she thought, in the back of her mind. "But, I guess I'm still in denial."

"I know," Adria said.

The world was toppled and upside down, yet everyone involved, whether they were aware of the involvement or not, attempted to operate under normal conditions, anyhow.

****

At Adria's locker, Sam stared at her. She was worried. A shadow was on her friend's face. In a moment, she learned why. Adria produced a CD from her bag and handed it to Sam. On the front of the silver disc, in black permanent marker, the words "Adria's Songs," was written. Sam held the CD in her shaking hands. Her eyes welled up with tears. She looked at Adria's face – and knew.

"No," she whispered.

"So it won't seem like a complete fucking waste," Adria said. "So you'll always be able to hear me singing."

"No!" Sam yelled.

She pulled Adria into her arms and sobbed. Micah was heading down the hallway, but when he saw Adria and Sam this way, he held back, waiting. Oddly, the students in the hallway that passed seemed to ignore the scene as if they saw nothing.

"When?" Sam asked.

"Soon, that's all we know," Adria said.

"After Prom?"

"Maybe," Adria said. "Maybe before. But, we're just going to go ahead, as if it will still happen. Prom, I mean."

"This is crazy."

"I know," Adria said. "Sam?"

"Yes?"

"I don't want you to be sad."

"You know I will."

"I know," Adria frowned through her tears. "But, everything will be okay. I won't be dead, okay?"

"Adria, please," Sam cried. "Please."

"I have to, you know that," Adria said. "I can't leave Micah alone. Not when we're this close."

"I hate this. I hate him."

"No, you don't," Adria said. "You don't, Sam."

"I do," she cried.

"But, I love him, Sam. So much. I don't have any choice."

"I hate knowing all this," Sam said. "How can any of us stay sane?"

"I want you to help my Mom and my Dad get through it," Adria continued. "I know I'm asking a lot."

"Yeah, you are," Sam said.

Micah finally approached the two girls, looking worried. Sam sighed.

"I'm trying really hard not to hate you, Micah," she said.

He nodded, looking down at the floor. He put his arm around Adria and she sighed, feeling instantly comforted by the effect of his touch. Sam saw this and closed her own eyes, sighing.

"Fuck," she said, and walked away.

****

March 27, 2010

Adria didn't bother lying to her father. She told him she was going with Micah, into Portland, to a rave. He nodded and let her go, but only after she reassured him.

"I'm coming home in the morning, Dad," she told him.

"For certain?"

She nodded. Micah was right, she was beginning to feel what he'd already been sensing. She felt the curse approaching, but somehow, she sensed it was not quite upon them, just yet. In a way, it lent a small modicum of comfort to her and Micah, for they felt they could relax tonight, and simply enjoy each other's company. It was all Micah wanted. In the end, it was really all Adria wanted, as well. For tonight, she felt she and Micah were safe from harm. She told her father this.

"And Prom is in one week," Richard said.

Adria nodded. Richard nodded back. He gave his consent for her to go. He felt crazy doing so, but after all, Micah was her husband, now. And still, no one knew, except for him and Sam. Richard shook his head, feeling loopy.

Micah came to the door to pick Adria up. Mr. Allan pulled him inside and asked him the same thing he'd asked Adria, about whether they'd be returning home in the morning. When Micah nodded, Richard saw the look on his face, and he was finally, fully comforted.

"Not yet," Micah said, and Richard nodded again.

He perfectly understood the language being spoken between them. It was crazy, but still, it was so. He hugged his daughter and told Micah to be careful. He told Micah to care for Adria, and he nodded. After the door was closed, Mr. Allan stood in the living room, taking in the silence, feeling deathly alone.

"We've all lost our minds," he whispered.

****

On the drive into Portland, Adria felt relaxed. She smiled. Micah smiled at her joy. He could feel it radiating off of her in waves. She looked at him, her eyes slowly traveling over his entire body as he drove. He was gorgeous.

The weather was turning and Micah only wore a white undershirt tonight, no black sweatshirt. Adria wore a spaghetti strapped, white tank shirt and shorts. Micah also wore black dress pants. He looked good. Adria sighed. Micah smiled. He could feel her thoughts, sense her feelings. The closer the time came, the more connected they were.

"Song?"

"Don't Walk Away, by Ryan Levine," she said.

"That doesn't fit," he frowned. "I'm here."

"It doesn't always fit," Adria said. "It's just what I hear. I know you're with me, Micah."

"Always," he said.

He reached over and took her hand, pulling it to his lips, kissing it. Then, he laughed, smiling a wicked grin.

"What?" she asked.

"Nothing, just, in a little while, I'm gonna wipe that Ryan Levine right outta your head," he smiled. "And put a little Underworld in there."

And he was right. Once inside the venue, it wasn't long before Cowgirl was playing, and the masses writhed with pleasure and energy. Adria was immediately lost in the sweeping motions of the crowd, as a communal sense of connectivity rippled through everyone.

Micah didn't need to coax Adria into dancing this time. Nor did they have to hold back on their own public displays of affection. In the line, they stood in each other's arms, kissing wildly, blending in with all the other couples. As soon as they got inside, they jumped in with the dancing masses, and for the next four hours, they shook, caressed, writhed, grinded, touched, swayed and sweated. They were free. Released. For those few hours, the world fell away, and, once more, Micah revealed part of his soul to Adria in the only way he knew how – by pulling her along with him. In many ways, their dancing this way, together, made Adria feel closer to Micah than even when they slept together. She actually felt as if dancing with Micah this way was a strange form of making love with him. He felt the same way.

At 4:15 in the morning, they spilled out of the warehouse, in each other's arms, laughing and reveling in their joy, along with the last of the crowds that remained. Back inside the van, Micah looked at Adria with intense longing. She could feel his desire burning. The air was heavy. She felt short of breath.

"I've begun to wonder, the last few times, if this is the last time we'll ever make love," Adria said.

"It won't be," Micah said. "Because we'll be together again, Adria. In the next life."

She looked at Micah on his side of the van, behind the wheel. He absently shook his thick bangs out of his eyes, and she laughed. He looked at her, his eyes shining.

"You want me to cut it?" he asked.

"No," she said. "I want to remember you exactly the way you are right now."

Micah smiled his crooked grin at her, and she sighed, her heart melting. God, he was beautiful. He looked over his shoulder, into the back of his van, a devious grin breaking out on his face. He looked back at Adria and she sighed again, climbing over her seat, into the back.

"Huh," she said, as she felt the soft blankets under her knees. There were soft pillows as well. She smelled a pleasant scent. Strawberries? Something sweet.

Micah climbed in behind her and exhaled. She reached for him. It was dark.

"Wait," he said.

The cab filled with a soft light then, as Micah turned the knob on an electric camping lantern. Adria laughed.

"You planned this all out, didn't you?"

Micah shrugged. He looked at Adria, worried.

"Is it too… campy? Trashy? In the back of a van?"

"Shut up," she sighed. "Husband."

She grabbed him then, overcome with lust. She loved him so much. She wanted him so badly. Something inside her felt urgent, as if her body somehow recognized that the time for physical love was running out. There wasn't much time left at all. She pulled his shirt off, undressing him. He let her. She quickly undressed herself then pushed on Micah's chest, asking him, without words, to lay on his back. He was infinitely excited.

Adria was on fire. She was aggressive. Micah felt it, and went with it. He sat up, once, and kissed her, then lay back down, letting her lead. She needed to. He was also on fire, and excited beyond belief by her urgency, her energy.

He lay down on his back and reveled in complete ecstasy, as Adria climbed on top of him, and in moments, she began to ride him. He reached up, briefly, to touch her body, then was taken over by the pleasure of feeling her working on him, moving up and down, grinding. He went prone, closing his eyes in rapture, his hands falling at his sides, pressed down hard against the floor of the van. He could feel her all around him, holding him. She was making love to him. He was in heaven.

Adria writhed on top of him, throwing her head back, touching herself with her hands, riding him all the while, faster and faster. Micah's head spun with pleasure. When she climaxed and tightened, he went with her, exclaiming.

He grabbed her hips with his hands and pulled her down onto him, harder still, thrusting upward. She cried out in pain and pleasure. Micah was floating. Adria gasped, gulping the air. Her body shuddered, then she relaxed, and she collapsed on top of him, and he wrapped his arms around her, enveloping her. He could die, right then and there and be happy, he thought.

They lay, side-by-side, for the next several minutes, overcome. Despite completing their act of love, they kissed madly for minutes on end, lost in each other. Then, Adria simply lay in Micah's arms, smiling. Micah smiled as well.

"We're good at this," she said.

"We've had a lot of practice," Micah said. "More than anyone could ever possibly realize."

"Over a hundred years," Adria sighed.

"I'm not nearly as well endowed as John."

"Are you kidding?" Adria looked at Micah's face, blushing. "You're fabulous."

"Fabulous?" Micah teased. "Really?"

"Shut up," Adria laughed. "You're always wonderful. You know that?"

"So are you," Micah sighed.

"Was this the last time?"

"No," Micah said. "It can't be."

"What if it was?"

"Well, I can remedy that one right now," Micah said.

He quickly rolled on top of her, kissing her with passion. Within moments, they were making love, again.

They did not return to Cannon Beach until almost eight in the morning. Micah had to drop Adria off. She watched him drive away feeling a profound sense of loss. An impending feeling of doom suddenly filled her soul. Time was running out. She could feel it more than ever, now that their beautiful night together was at an end.

Adria was right, in her feelings. Micah felt it as well, as he drove away from her, and the distance between them grew. They both felt the time winding down, although, neither of them realized just how short their time truly was. They now had less than a week to live.

20. March 28-April 2, 2010

Adria spent most of Sunday sleeping. In the late afternoon, she got up and had an early supper with her dad. They hardly spoke, however. He was afraid of what they might say, so Mr. Allan felt it was better not to speak at all.

After supper, Micah came over. It was their last night to be together, since Adria would be going to her mom's house starting Monday. She couldn't very well spend the night at Sam's house on a school night. Adria would be away from Micah for the next five nights. This had been the pattern for weeks, and they'd learned to deal with it.

Micah and Adria sat on the couch and watched TV with Adria's dad. No one spoke, and Mr. Allan only stared at the screen. At ten p.m., Micah and Adria said goodnight and went upstairs.

In Adria's room, she and Micah lay in bed, awake. They did not make love. They only lay on their sides, facing each other, and stared. They studied each other's faces, and reveled in the fact that they were there, together.

On Monday, March 29, the school week began. Micah always left Adria's house and drove in his van. Sam always came and caravanned with Adria, everyone in their own, separate vehicle. This, also, was a pattern.

The school week went by slowly. Adria's first evening back at her mother's, she had dinner with her, and Emily stared at her while she ate.

"Did Dad call you?" Adria dared to ask.

"Yes," Emily said. "But, I was waiting for you to ask, Adria. You shouldn't expect your father to fight your battles for you."

"I'm sorry," Adria said.

"Why didn't you tell me you got invited to the Prom?" Emily sounded hurt.

"I only got asked a few days ago, really," Adria said. "And I wasn't even sure if I wanted to go."

"Why not? It's with Micah, right?"

Adria nodded. "But, a school dance isn't really my thing."

"Well, your Dad's right about one thing," Emily said. "It is a right of passage. Even if it isn't your Senior Prom. If you get asked, you should go."

"So, it's okay?" Adria was hopeful.

"To go to the Prom," Emily said. "But, I think you should have a curfew."

"But, there's this party, and Micah really wants to go," Adria said.

"A party? After the Prom? Adria," Emily said. "That's not something I think I want you involved in."

"Mom, I'm seventeen."

"Not eighteen," Emily said. "And where is this party at, anyway?"

"Phillip Moore's?" Adria said it like a question. "He's a Senior, really popular. Micah got invited, and he really wants to go."

"When does it start?"

"Midnight, I guess," Adria said.

"I might consider letting you go for an hour," Emily said. "Be home by one? How does that sound?"

"One? One in the morning? Mom, it goes all night. Plus, to be home from Seaside by one, we'd barely be there a half hour."

"Oh, it's in Seaside?"

"So is the Prom, mom," Adria said.

"Well," she sighed. "I guess, maybe two, then."

"Mom!"

"Adria!"

"I'm not a child! Please. Micah really wants to spend the entire night with me. We have to."

"Adria, don't push me on this. I'm not about to let you stay out all night with your boyfriend. God knows what could happen. S.E.X. could happen, you know?"

"Are you joking me?"

"No," Emily said.

"You won't let me go, because you're afraid I'll have sex?"

"Promise me you won't," Emily said.

Adria took a deep breath. She was debating what she should say next. But she felt her time with Micah running out, and she'd promised him. She'd promised to give him her time, and what he wanted of her. A dying man's last wish, he'd called it. Adria was desperate, and tired of lying and hiding.

"Mom," Adria took a deep breath. "Micah and I already had sex."

Emily stared at her daughter for several, long moments, not blinking. Then she shook her head.

"And you think I'm going to let you go out after Prom now? You think telling me that helps your argument?"

"Mom, I love him."

"I don't care, Adria! You're not going to be out all night with Micah. You should not be having sex with him, honey. You've only been with him for, what? A few months? Honey, this is crazy. No."

"Mom, I'm going."

"If you think I'm going to let you be out all night with your boyfriend, you've got another think coming, young lady. Does your father have any clue what's been going on between you and Micah?"

Adria smiled, shaking her head. She had to tell her mother.

"You think this is funny?"

"Mom?" Adria looked at her mother and prepared herself to tell her she and Micah's secret. She took a deep breath.

"Micah and I are not boyfriend and girlfriend," she paused. "We're married. Micah is my husband."

Emily stared at her daughter. Her mouth fell open. She dropped the fork she'd been holding. The kitchen was dead quiet.

"That's not funny," Emily finally said. "You're seventeen, Adria. You think I'm stupid? You can't get married until you're eighteen."

"Well, you can with a fake ID," Adria said.

She wasn't about to implicate her father, but she had to inform her mother of the seriousness of her relationship with Micah. If she did, perhaps they could spend the next few nights together, instead of apart.

"If you and Micah got married using fake ID's, then it's not legal, and we can have it annulled," Emily said.

"It *is* legal."

"Not if you lied about your age, Adria. How could you do this?"

"Mom, have you heard a word I've said? Micah and I are married!"

"No, you're not!" Emily yelled. "It doesn't count. It's not legal."

"It *is* legal," Adria yelled. "We didn't use fake ID's. Dad took us. He signed a parental consent form. It only takes one parent."

"What?!" Emily looked at Adria, her cheeks aflame. "Please tell me you're joking."

"Micah's my husband," Adria said. "My *legal* husband. And I'm going to Prom with him. And afterwards, we're going to a party. I'll be home by sunrise."

"The hell you will!" Emily yelled.

Adria's mother stood, leaving the table, and went to the phone. She dialed, and within moments, she was screaming at Richard Allan. Adria closed her eyes and buried her face in her hands. She felt awful for getting her father in trouble.

Adria stood and left the kitchen. While her mother was busy screaming over the phone, she left a note, saying she'd be home in the morning. Then she drove to Micah's, where she knew his father had already left for work.

When Micah opened the door and saw Adria's face, he did not even ask her what was wrong. He was just happy to see her, especially at a time when he hadn't thought he'd be able to. He took her up in his arms and they went to his room.

He kissed her. He hugged her. They made love. Then they fell asleep in each other's arms.

****

March 30, 2010

On Tuesday morning, Adria left Micah's house and returned to her mother's. She took a shower and got dressed for school. When she came back downstairs, her mother was sitting at the kitchen table, doing nothing. Adria sat down.

"I love you, Mom," she began. "I love you so much. You're the best mother I could have ever hoped for."

"Is that supposed to make me feel better, Adria? You lied to me. You went behind my back. All this time. If you loved Micah that much, why didn't you come and talk to me about it?"

"You wouldn't have understood," Adria said.

"But, you trusted your father to understand?" Emily was very hurt, Adria could tell. "Do you not trust me as much as your father?"

"I do, it's just. Dad found us together," Adria said. "That's the only reason he knows. I had to tell him."

"I just don't understand how in the world your father agreed to sign that consent. To take you into Portland," Emily said.

"Because he saw how much we love each other. Me and Micah."

"Adria," Emily said. "My God. You got *married?* And I wasn't even there. My only daughter got married, and I didn't even get to witness it? Don't you think I would have wanted to?"

"You would have tried to stop us."

"And you would have done it anyway, right?"

Adria nodded.

"That's what your Dad said. It's why he did it, he told me. 'Cause he said he knew you'd go around him, find a way to do it on your own. Is that true?"

Adria nodded again.

"Well, it was still wrong, what your father did, Adria."

"Please don't be mad at him, Mom," Adria said. "He only wanted me to be happy. After everything. After all the nightmares. He knew how happy Micah makes me."

"Does he?" Emily gazed at Adria, her eyes pained, but hopeful.

"Mom, yes," Adria said. "I love him so much."

"And you guys are really married," Emily mused. "Does his father know?"

Adria shook her head. She became afraid.

"You're not going to tell him, are you?"

"Well, I think he has the right to know, Adria."

"Mom, please don't. Or, at least," she paused to think. "At least wait until after Prom?"

"You're asking a lot of me, Adria. If I wait until after Prom, I'll be letting you and Micah run around behind his father's back, and I'll know about it. I'll be helping to lie. I don't lie, Adria. Don't make me."

"I know, I'm sorry," Adria said. "But, please? Mom, I'm begging you. Just do this for me, just this one thing? Wait until after Prom, and then, I swear, on Sunday night, I'll go with Micah, and we'll tell his dad."

"You promise?" Emily asked.

Adria nodded. She felt awful. She made a promise to her mother that she wasn't sure she would be able to keep. She wasn't even certain that she and Micah would even live long enough to go to the Prom, or the after party, much less, talk to Micah's dad the following Sunday night.

"Okay," Emily sighed.

"Then, I'll be at Micah's house tonight. His dad has Wednesday and Thursday nights off, so we can't be together then. But, tonight, and Friday, we will."

"Looks like you've got this whole lying and sneaking around thing down pat, don't you," Emily said.

"Mom, I'm sorry."

"I'm not sure who you even are anymore, Adria."

"I'm your daughter," Adria said. "Who loves you very much. So much, I decided to tell you the truth, and not lie to you anymore."

"You waited to tell me the truth," Emily said. "Until you felt you had no other choice."

"No, I had a choice," Adria said. "I could have just stayed out all night, and not explained to you why at all."

"Yes," Emily said. "I guess you could have."

"Please forgive me," Adria said. "I need us to be on good terms."

"Adria, I'm happy that you're happy," Emily said. "I just wasn't expecting my daughter to grow up so fast. To be married while she's still in high school. Please tell me you and Micah are being careful?"

Adria nodded. She and Micah hadn't used protection a single time. But, she had not become pregnant, just as she knew she wouldn't. There was no stopping the curse.

"Bring Micah over tonight. Before the two of you go back to his house. Let me meet my son-in-law," Emily said. "Okay?"

"Okay," Adria agreed.

Then she left for school. Sam was beside herself to hear how things were going. They walkied on the drive, and Sam could not believe that Micah was going to talk to Adria's mother that evening.

At school, Micah was nervous when Adria told him. He sighed.

"Are you certain she's not the one who might pull a shotgun?" Micah joked. "I mean, she is OSP, too, you know? Maybe that's how it's going to happen?"

"She only wants to meet you, knowing you're my husband," Adria ignored his joke. "And she made me promise that we'd tell your Dad, next Sunday night, after the Prom."

"We may not even make it to the Prom, Adria," Micah said. "You might have to break that promise."

"I know," Adria said. "But, she asked me to promise, so I did."

Micah nodded. Adria sighed.

"This isn't how I wanted my relationship to be, with my mother, you know? So near the end."

"I know," Micah said.

"I just wanted to keep my promise to you. Give you the best Prom night ever."

"I know, Adria. It's okay," Micah said.

He placed his forehead against hers and sighed. She felt comforted, and smiled.

****

That evening, Micah had dinner at Emily's house. The atmosphere was uncomfortable. The three of them ate in silence. Every once in a while, Micah would look over at Adria, and she'd flash him a smile. At one point, Micah smiled back, and the two of them were lost in each other, gazing at one another in complete rapture. Emily watched this, and although she did not want to see it, it was plain as day, in front of her face.

Her daughter had been doing infinitely better these last several months, and the reason was sitting across from her, she realized. At one point, she was certain her daughter might actually be deathly ill, and had feared for her life. Now, she looked at Adria and saw the bright color, high in her cheeks. She saw how healthy and happy Adria looked, and she couldn't help but be grateful with Micah, for that.

"Micah," Emily said. She gazed at him. "I want you to promise me something."

Micah looked at Emily Allan and nodded. She smiled.

"You'd better not break my daughter's heart," Emily said. "If she gets hurt, I will never forgive you. Do you understand me?"

Micah looked at Emily and swallowed. He looked at Adria, who only gave him a pained look of understanding. Adria nodded, telling him everything was going to be okay. Micah nodded at Emily and feigned a smile.

"Micah," Emily said, not letting him off the hook. "I mean it. You'd better look after Adria. You're her husband, which I still cannot believe. And that means you will take care of her. Understand?"

"Yes, Ms. Allan," Micah said. "I promise I'll love your daughter until the day I die… And after."

Adria began to cry then. Emily thought she was moved to tears by the beauty of Micah's remarks. She had no clue of the true ramifications and meanings behind Micah's statements.

****

Wednesday, March 31, 2010

Sam spent most of Wednesday afternoon and evening with Adria, at her mother's house. They put on their Prom dresses to show each other, and laughed like teenage girls tend to do. Later in the evening, Sam grew quiet as Adria burned copies of her music and wrote her father's name on one, her mother's on another.

Later still, the girls lay in bed together, listening to music. Adria played Feist; Intuition, and Sam looked at her best friend.

"How long?"

"Not long at all," Adria said. "I'm starting to doubt that Micah and I will even make it to Prom night."

"I can't do this," Sam said. "I can't let you go, Adria."

"You may not even be with me when it happens, Sam."

"I promised your Dad I'd stick to you like glue," Sam said. "And if I know it's going to happen before Saturday. Adria, that's three days away. I'm not leaving your side."

"You have to go home tonight," Adria said. "It's a school night. Besides, it can't be tonight. Micah and I aren't even together. It always happens when we're together."

"Well, then, it has to be Friday, then. That's the next night you'll be together."

"But, we're together at school, too," Adria said.

"You think it will happen at school?"

"Kane attacked Micah at school," Adria shrugged.

"But, Kane's gone," Sam said. "You think someone else is going to pick a fight with Micah?"

"Who knows," Adria said. "For all I know, a tree will fall over on him."

"Are you scared?"

"Terrified," Adria said.

At that moment, Adria's phone sounded. Micah was texting her. She looked at her phone, breathing a sigh of relief.

"Still here. Still breathing."

"I'm sorry, Adria."

"I know."

"I still can't believe this is really going to happen. Maybe it won't. Maybe you're wrong about what you feel?"

"No," Adria said. "Today, when I first saw Micah walking down the hall, I saw a man. With blond hair, blue eyes. Taller than Micah. Thinner. It was Justin."

"Tremaine?"

"Yes," Adria said. "Micah already remembers some of that life. The last day or so. I only just remembered today. It's getting close, Sam. I can remember pieces of our first life together, now. Before the curse."

"Adria," Sam whispered. "I don't think I can watch you die, and not do anything."

"How do you think *I* feel? Knowing Micah is going to die? I'll have to watch him."

"But, then you'll go with him," Sam said. "I'll be left all alone. I'll be left to live the rest of my life, without you. Adria," Sam began to cry.

"Sam, I'm sorry. I don't know what to do. I don't want to hurt anyone. But, I can't live without Micah. I can't let him go ahead without me. Alone."

"I know," Sam cried. "I just don't know how I'm going to do this. How I'm going to survive this."

"I'll be alive, Sam. Just remember that. I won't be dead. After I'm gone, Sam? After the funerals? I want you to look up at the sky. I want you to look out at the ocean, and feel me and Micah. I want you to know when you look at the beauty of the world, that we're out there, somewhere, living. We'll be little babies, Sam. Just beginning, starting out our lives. And when you're an old lady, in your forties, Micah and I will probably just be meeting, and falling in love. We'll just be starting out, right where we are right now. If you think about all those things, whenever you start to feel sad, maybe it will help? Maybe it will help my Dad, too? I don't know how to help my mother. If she doesn't know. Sam, please, will you look after my Mom? My Dad, too?"

"Yes," Sam said. "But, who will look out for me?"

"Just do what I told you," Adria said. "Just know that I won't truly be dead. My soul will still exist. I'll be alive, and so will Micah. Okay?"

Sam nodded. The girls sat up in bed and hugged each other tight. When it was time for Sam to go home, she left, reluctantly.

"I'll see you in the morning?" she said. Adria nodded.

****

Thursday, April 1, 2010

The school day passed with no events. Adria was on edge the entire day. She rushed to Micah at his locker between every class they didn't have together. She watched the masses of students as they walked the hallways, wondering if an attack was imminent. By the end of the day, Adria was a complete wreck.

In the parking lot after school, Sam walked with Adria and Micah, to his van. Once at the van, Adria looked around, feeling nervous.

"I'll follow you," she said to Micah. He nodded. Neither of them realized the implications of her words.

"Do you feel anything?" Adria said.

Micah shook his head.

"Nothing?"

He shook his head again. She hugged him fiercely. Sam looked away, her face contorted in pain. *This is insane.*

"Look, maybe I shouldn't bring this up, but. Do you guys really need to go to Prom? Maybe you should just stay home, sleep at Micah's house?"

"No," Micah said. "We're having our Prom. We're not going to hide."

"But," Sam interjected. Micah shook his head and yelled.

"No!" He made Sam jump. "I'm going to die, Sam. And I don't want to hide in a hole. I want my last days with Adria to be like this. In the open. I'm not going to stay home from school. I'm just going to live, like everything is normal. If I live it any other way, I'll go crazy. In a dark room."

"With me," Adria said.

"I am with you," Micah said. "But, in some strange way, Adria, I just want to get it over with. I'm tired of worrying. Waiting. Aren't you?"

Adria looked into Micah's eyes and saw the pain inside them. He was right. If it was going to happen, it was better to get it over with. It wasn't as if they had any other choice, anyhow. She nodded. Sam looked down at the ground, crying.

"I'll follow you?" Adria said. Again, not realizing the implication of her words.

Again, Micah nodded.

"Sam?" Micah said. "You'll be with Adria 'til she goes to sleep tonight?"

"Yes," Sam said.

Micah nodded. He looked at Adria.

"Nothing's going to happen tonight. It can't. It won't, unless we're together."

"Friday," Adria whispered.

"I don't know," Micah said. "Maybe."

"Jesus!" Sam said. She shook her head and walked several feet away.

Micah hugged Adria again, tightly, and then kissed her on the cheek. Then he got in his van and backed out, waiting for Adria to follow him.

Sam stayed with Adria until ten that night. Nothing happened. Every time Micah texted her, Adria breathed a sigh of relief. Sam paced the floor for most of the night, going crazy.

"I can't believe that in a few short days, this is all going to be over with," she said. "And you and Micah will be gone. It's not real."

Adria said nothing. Before Sam left, she hugged her tight. Later, Adria tossed and turned all night in her sleep. When she dreamt, it was of Charlotte Williams and Justin Tremaine. In the morning, when she awoke, she remembered as much of their life together as Micah did, and she knew the time had arrived for the final curse of death to come upon them both.

****

Friday, April 2, 2010

Adria went downstairs. She felt that today was the last day she would see her mother. Emily did not know this, of course. She ate breakfast with her mother in silence. Finally, Emily spoke.

"Are you staying with Micah tonight?"

"Yes," Adria said. "But, I'll come to say goodbye to you, first."

"Goodbye?" Emily frowned. "You mean, goodnight?"

"Yeah," Adria said, attempting to smile.

"Well, I'll see you on Saturday, honey. You have to come back here in the morning, before Micah's Dad comes home, right?"

"Yes," Adria said, although she didn't know if she would be coming home on Saturday morning or not.

"Well, I'll see you then. And I want to take pictures of you and Micah all dressed up, okay?"

"Yeah."

"Fine," Emily said. "Then you'll go to Prom, and your party. Stay out all night," Emily sighed. "And come home in the morning. And on Sunday night, we'll talk to Micah's Dad, finally. Get this whole thing over with, thank God."

"Yes," Adria said. "We'll get the whole thing over with."

"It will be a relief, honey, you'll see," Emily said.

She took Adria's hand across the table and squeezed it, trying to comfort her.

"Everything will be okay, Adria. All right?"

Adria nodded, her eyes welling up with tears. Emily frowned at her.

"Honey, what's wrong? You think I'm still mad? 'Cause I'm not. I'm over it. Okay?"

"No, I know you're not mad anymore," Adria still cried. "I just love you so much. I love you, Mommy!"

Adria rushed out of her chair and hugged her mother, almost choking her. Emily hugged her daughter back, feeling bewildered. Adria hugged her mother for several moments, before letting go.

"I'll see you tonight, okay?" Emily said. "Before you leave to go with Micah."

Adria nodded. She said goodbye to her mother, not knowing if she would even be home that night. She left and went to school for what she knew would be the last time.

****

The school day dragged on so slowly, Adria could not sit still. She sighed loudly, several times in class, and several students looked at her. Some of them smiled, for they thought she was simply bored. Micah relieved her by waiting for her outside of every class. She wasn't sure how he managed to be there, outside the classroom door, at every bell, but she didn't care. She was only grateful.

Sam met Adria at her locker between every class. The three of them sat together at lunch. Everyone was paranoid and no one could relax. Micah held onto Adria, clinging to her like mad. He held her hand everywhere they walked, squeezing it tight. He held her hand so tight, it hurt, but Adria did not care. She gazed at Micah, lost in his eyes, and infinitely afraid that she was looking into them for the last time, every moment of the day.

Finally, the last class let out. The students were wild. All the upper classmen were excited for the festivities of the weekend. Everyone yelled and cheered and whooped. Micah looked at Adria and smiled.

"Come to my house?" he asked. "I don't want to be away from you for another moment. From here on out."

"Won't your dad be home?"

"Yes," Micah said. "I want you to meet him."

"Finally?"

"Finally," Micah said. "I can't be away from you, Adria. Not now."

"It's close," Adria said. It wasn't a question.

"Yes."

"Justin," Adria said, her voice strangled.

"You remember?"

"Yes. Since yesterday morning."

"Then it's time," Micah nodded.

Adria nodded back, and Micah hugged her tight, looking over her shoulder, wondering if danger was already rushing at him. He pulled away and smiled at her, trying to comfort her. He was now in Adria-mode, his only concern, getting her through this. He only cared about keeping her safe and protected for as long as possible.

"You can get through this, Adria," he said. "We can get through this."

Adria nodded. Sam walked with them out into the parking lot.

"I'll follow you both, to Micah's house," Sam said. "You'll text me? Every twenty minutes?"

"Until we go to sleep," Adria said. "And first thing in the morning, right before eight."

"Okay," Sam said. "It's not tonight, is it, Micah?"

Sam looked at Micah, intent. Micah shook his head, shrugging.

"I don't know anymore. I can't feel anything, now."

"Adria?" Sam asked. "Do you feel anything?"

"No," Adria said. "Nothing."

Sam frowned. She looked at Adria, wondering.

"Song?"

"Sailed On, by Landon Pigg."

"That's appropriate," Sam said, but she breathed a sigh of relief. Adria had not lost this, at least. She had not lost what made her Adria.

"See you soon," Sam said.

"Yeah," Adria said.

****

At Micah's house, Adria was nervous to meet his father. She'd only seen him once, in the front office, the first day she met Micah. She barely remembered what he looked like.

Mr. Foster was in the downstairs den, frowning over some papers. The door was open, and Adria could see the man, sitting behind his desk. He looked up to see her, staring at him. He stood and walked to the door, closing it. Adria looked at Micah and frowned. He shrugged and took her to his room.

"I thought I was going to meet him?"

"Maybe later," Micah said. "If he's not busy."

"What could he possibly be busy with?" Adria said. "What was he looking at, anyway?"

"Who knows?" Micah sighed. "Anyway, do you really want to spend our last hours together puzzling over the intricacies of my father's mysterious aloofness?"

"Huh," Adria said.

"What?" Micah frowned.

"So, that's where you get it from," she smiled at him.

Micah broke out into his trademark, crooked grin and enveloped her in his arms, spinning her around. She laughed.

"I'm not aloof," he said, kissing her.

"Not anymore, but you were," she said.

"That's because I was trying not to get us cursed," he breathed, kissing her again.

"Well, it didn't work," she said.

"Yeah, well, I didn't know being away from you would almost kill me, now did I?"

"Micah," Adria breathed. "Let's run? Tonight. Let's just pack our bags and run. Maybe we can get away from it, still?"

"I'm not leaving this house, tonight," Micah said. "We're staying here, right in this room."

"Micah?" Mr. Foster called from the living room.

Micah frowned.

"Hold on," he said, going to his door and opening it.

"Yeah?" he called down to his Dad.

"Is your friend staying for dinner?" Adria heard him ask.

"Um, yeah?" Micah said.

"I'll order pizza," Mr. Foster said.

"Okay," Micah said, and closed the door.

He walked back over to Adria and hugged her again.

"Weird," he said, almost under his breath.

The two of them lay in bed together, holding each other. They gazed at one another. They kissed. They gazed some more. They smiled and laughed, and cried. Mostly, Adria cried, and Micah smiled at her through his own tears, wiping hers away.

"Song?"

"My Sundown. Jimmy Eat World."

"That's not so sad," Micah said.

"No," Adria said. "Nothing's wrong when I'm with you, Micah."

"You'll always be with me," he said.

"I know."

****

Later, Micah's Dad called the two of them down for dinner. The pizza box sat on the dining room table. Mr. Foster sat in a chair in the living room and ate his food alone. Micah sat at the dining room table with Adria and they ate while gazing at one another. Micah was smiling like crazy. Adria frowned.

"This is why I'm not afraid to die," Micah said.

Adria looked over her shoulder, into the living room, worried Micah's father might hear them. Then she looked back at Micah, who didn't seem worried at all.

"Micah," she said. "I'm sorry."

"For what?" he asked, still gazing and smiling at her.

"For how lonely your life has been," she said. Then she lowered her voice. "Maybe the next one won't be so sad."

"I'm not sad," Micah said. "I have you."

Adria looked at Micah and melted. How could he be so calm? He didn't seem frightened at all. He seemed perfectly happy. Adria was perplexed. Micah picked up on her thoughts. He could read her face, and he knew she was confused.

"Adria, I'm not sad. I'm actually happy, now, the closer it gets. It's almost all over. We're almost free of it all. I know everything's going to be better for us. Next time. I don't feel afraid. I'm sad for you, and the pain you'll go through. But, I know that will only last a short while as well. I know we're both going to a better place."

"What if our next lives are horrible?" Adria said.

"They won't be," Micah said. "Remember the seventh life of Tanook? The Nehalem blessed him in his seventh life, remember? The curse was lifted. He was a great hunter in his village, a hero. And he lived to be one-hundred-years old. It will be the same for us, Adria. Our seventh life will be blessed. The Nehalem will bless us. I know we'll have a wonderful life together, Adria. I feel it. Don't you? It's why your song's not sad. It has to be."

"My songs don't always fit the mood," Adria said, but she looked at Micah, wondering.

She closed her eyes and took a deep breath. A sudden vision overtook her. She was in a boat, and the sky was gray and stormy, but a ray of sun broke through the clouds and shot down in a straight beam, over the gray water of the ocean, like a spotlight from Heaven. That's what Justin said it looked like, she remembered. She smiled and laughed, looking down at her hand. A beautiful diamond ring was on her finger. Adria remembered, while sitting with Micah. When she opened her eyes, Justin was sitting at the table with her. She sighed and smiled.

"Justin," she said. "Remember the sunbeam, over the water?"

"Yes," Micah said. "I do, Lottie."

She smiled. He remembered. And suddenly, Adria knew that Micah was right. Their next life would be blessed. She wanted to tell Sam. Then, Micah's father called the two of them into the living room.

Adria frowned. She looked at Micah, who stood and took her hand. He was now just Micah, again. They walked into the living room and sat down on the couch, adjacent to Mr. Foster in his chair. He smiled at Adria and nodded.

"Hello," he said. "I'm Ken."

"Uh, hi," Adria said. She frowned, feeling uncomfortable.

"You can call me Mr. Foster, if that makes you feel more comfortable. Adria, is it?"

Adria nodded, looking at Micah, her face questioning. Micah smiled at her.

"If you're wondering how I know your name," Mr. Foster said, "It might be because Micah's mentioned you a few times, in passing. But, if he hadn't, then I would say I know your name from this."

Mr. Foster produced a paper from his front pants pocket. It was folded in half. He handed it to Adria, who unfolded it, frowning. She raked in a quick breath as she read it. It was a copy of her and Micah's marriage license. Micah looked at it over Adria's shoulder and frowned at his father.

"You did provide your home address when you filled out the paperwork in the county office, right, Micah?" Mr. Foster said. "What did you think would happen? You didn't think a copy of your marriage license would be mailed here, to the house?"

Micah said nothing. He sat, frozen. Adria was worried for him. She set the copy of the license on the coffee table in front of her and took Micah's hand, to comfort him. It worked.

"So," Mr. Foster said. "I guess this makes you my daughter-in-law, hmm?" He smiled at Adria.

Adria frowned at Mr. Foster, confused. She couldn't tell if he was upset, or happy. Adria couldn't guess any real reason why he would be happy, so she settled on anger, instead.

"Micah?" Mr. Foster said. "Don't you have anything to say for yourself?"

"Like what?" Micah said, his voice quiet. "I'm not getting an annulment, if that's what you want."

"I don't want you to get an annulment, Micah. Is that what *you* want?"

"No," Micah said.

"Then, why would I?"

"Mr. Foster, I'm sorry," Adria said.

"For what, Adria?" Mr. Foster asked. "For calming my son down? For getting him to finally stop beating the crap out of people? For making him happy? What are you sorry for?"

Adria looked at Micah, completely miffed. Micah only stared at his father in complete shock.

"Dad?"

"Micah," Mr. Foster said. "You've been so unhappy. There was a time when I used to come home from work every morning, certain that I was going to find you hanging in your closet, from a rope. Or in bed with an empty bottle of pills and a note. You know that? You were miserable. When I moved us out here, I even let you decide where we should go. I was trying to get you to help me, Micah. And you picked here. And I thought it was a mistake, after your first day of school, when you got in another damn fight. And later, that whole, further mess with Kane. And still, I did everything I could to try and save you. To try and bring you around. Next thing I know, you're walking around, singing songs. Whistling. Smiling. Hell, even laughing."

Adria laughed. Micah smirked at her merriment.

"Yeah," Mr. Foster nodded, addressing her. "He hadn't laughed in a very long time. Or smiled. And I wondered what could have changed my son around like that. Made him happy again, like he was, once, when he was a kid. And then, I get this paper in the mail, and suddenly, I understand why. *You*, Adria. I don't know how, I don't know why, but I don't care. Micah's not getting into fights anymore. Well, except for some residual mess with Kane, but that wasn't actually Micah's fault that time, now was it?"

Adria shook her head. Mr. Foster smiled.

"Seventeen," Mr. Foster shook his head. "Married at seventeen. And finally, he brings you here for me to meet. Why'd you wait so long, Micah? Were you afraid I'd chase her away?"

"I'm not afraid of you," Micah said.

"No," Mr. Foster said. "No, Micah. I'm afraid of you. 'Cause I let you down, son. With your mom."

"It wasn't your fault," Micah said. His voice was shaking now. Adria squeezed his hand tighter.

"I should have realized what she was doing," Mr. Foster said, his own voice beginning to shake. "How could I not see?"

"I didn't know, either," Micah said. "I never blamed you. Is that what you thought?"

"The nightmares, Micah," Mr. Foster said. "That was you, as a child, trying to tell me. Your subconscious was trying to tell me that something was wrong."

"Dad, my nightmares had nothing to do with mom," Micah said.

"Micah, they started exactly one year before your mom..." Mr. Foster trailed off, his own emotions overwhelming him.

"That's just a coincidence," Micah said. "Dad, you didn't do anything wrong. You never let me down. Never. I'm just sorry I ever disappointed you."

"Micah, you never disappointed me. Never. I only wanted to help you. I just didn't know how."

"You just did," Micah said. He released Adria's hand and stood, walking over to his father. Mr. Foster stood, and Micah embraced him tightly.

"I love you, Dad," Micah cried.

"I love you, too, Micah," Mr. Foster also cried.

Adria cried watching them. She was happy for Micah, and yet a strong wave of incredible sadness flowed over her then, as she realized the pain that Mr. Foster would soon have to endure. Then, she realized the pain would have been infinitely worse, probably, without this moment, and the knowledge comforted her.

Micah pulled away and looked at Adria. Then he looked back at his father, smiling.

"Dad? I want you to meet Adria. My wife."

Mr. Foster's chin trembled and he nodded at Adria, extending his hand for her to shake. She stood from the couch and shook his hand, but Mr. Foster quickly pulled her into his arms and embraced her. She hugged him back, then pulled away and took Micah's hand.

"How long have you known?" Adria asked.

"Two weeks," Mr. Foster said. "And if you're wondering if I knew you two were sneaking back and forth between houses, yes. I knew that, too. And I suppose you're planning on staying here tonight, after I go to work?"

Adria looked down at the floor and nodded, embarrassed and ashamed. Mr. Foster nodded, smiling and winking at Micah.

"Do your parents know you're over here?" Mr. Foster asked Adria. "Do they know you're married to my son?"

Adria nodded. She was eager to tell her mother that Mr. Foster knew. She wouldn't need to keep her promise for the upcoming Sunday night. It had already been fulfilled.

"Mr. Foster?"

"Yes, Adria?"

"Could you do me a huge favor, and talk to my mom on the phone? So she knows that you know? She made me promise we'd tell you no later than Sunday. I want her to know that you know, now."

"Micah? Were you going to tell me on Sunday?" Mr. Foster asked.

Micah nodded, although he was not the one who'd made the promise. Mr. Foster smiled.

"Sure, Adria. I'd be happy to talk to your mother. I know your father already knows, since I'm assuming he's the one who signed the consent form. Your father is Mr. Richard Allan, I presume?"

"He only did it because he knew we were going to get married, anyway," Adria stammered. "We were going to do it with fake ID's that said we were nineteen, but my Dad found out about us, and then he realized we would find a way, so he took us. Please don't be mad at him, Mr. Foster."

"I'm not mad, Adria," Mr. Foster said. "Like I said. I've never seen Micah this happy. Happy, yes, as a child, before everything. But even then, not like this. This is...I don't know what this is. But, it's wonderful, Adria. And I can think of worse trouble for Micah to get into, than getting married. Like jail, or expulsion, or both. Marriage? I can handle. Just, please tell me you two are using some kind of protection?"

****

That night, Adria and Micah lay in his bed together, holding each other and laughing. They were happy.

"Everyone's so caught up in this whole 'using protection' thing," Adria sighed. "Protection. They have no idea."

"Adria," Micah sighed, "It's Friday night and we're here, alone. I don't think anything's going to happen tonight. I think we'll be okay."

"Then, it's tomorrow?"

"I don't know," Micah said. "What could possibly happen at the Prom? We'll dance to death?"

"Maybe a light will fall on your head? Or a car will crash into us?" Adria said.

"Please don't do that. Please don't let your mind worry, spinning in circles like that."

"I can't help it."

"Yes, you can," Micah said, gazing at her. "Just be with me, Adria. I'm scared. I don't want to leave you all alone."

"You aren't."

"I will," Micah said. "I don't want to, though. You know that."

Adria nodded. Her soul was aching. He could feel it. So was his.

"Once more," Micah said. "This is it, Adria. This is the last time. We can get through this, together. We have to. It will all be over with soon."

She nodded, crying. He kissed her lips. Then he smiled at her.

"I'm taking you to the Prom," he said. "However trivial it may seem. We're going to be teenagers, for a few hours. Just, a normal night, like nothing's wrong, and everything's okay. Okay?"

"Okay," she sighed. "Okay."

****

In the morning, Adria left Micah and returned home, to her mother's house. She knew as long as they were apart, for the remainder of that day, nothing would happen to Micah.

21. Saturday, April 3, 2010

"Song?" Sam asked.

"We Will Meet Again, by Vast."

Sam sighed, looking at Adria. They were both wearing their Prom dresses. They had done each other's hair. Sam wore her red hair down, but curled. Adria's hair was swept up, off her face, held by a sparkly clip at the back of her head, but a few thin, black wisps of hair caressed her cheeks. Her lips were ruby red, her eyes highlighted with light eyeliner and the slightest hint of pink eye shadow.

Sam's dress was all black, but Adria wore a black dress with a pink, satin ribbon around the middle, that looked absolutely gorgeous on her. It was the most beautiful Sam had ever seen her look.

"Micah is going to die when he sees you," Sam said.

Her smile faded as she realized the irony of her remarks. She looked at Adria with regret.

"I, I didn't mean it like that," she said.

"I know," Adria said. "Besides, it doesn't matter. We made it, Sam. And I wasn't sure we would. We made it to tonight. And I feel wonderful. I don't feel anything. No dread, no worries. I feel relieved."

"What do you think it means?" Sam frowned.

"I don't know," Adria said. "But, I don't feel like anything bad is going to happen tonight. In fact, I'm starting to feel as if, maybe, the curse isn't going to happen."

"Adria," Sam chided with her voice. "How could that even be?"

"I don't know. Maybe that book is wrong? Maybe Tanook only had six lives? Or…what if those researchers translated it wrong? What if they translated one stupid word wrong, and it isn't six deaths, but only five? What if the curse is actually lifted on our sixth life? This one?"

Sam frowned, thinking hard. She shrugged.

"Seriously, Sam," Adria continued. "Think about it. Micah and I have been together now, in that way, for a while. Several months. Since last December. That was four months ago. Why would it take this long for the curse to happen?

"I mean, if Micah was going to die, he would have by now, right? Kane could have easily killed him, that day in the hallway. I thought that was it, when it was happening. But, it didn't happen. I mean, we got married, and nothing stopped us. For all we know, getting married really did undo the curse. Or it was undone, anyway, because our sixth life is blessed by the Nehalem, not the seventh."

"I want to believe you, Adria, I really do," Sam said. "But, you're reaching, aren't you? You and Micah said you felt it coming on, and that was only a few days ago, remember? You said you knew it was coming soon. You both remember being Charlotte and Justin, now."

"We have our memories, but so? Maybe what we felt coming on, was the lifting of the curse?"

"No," Sam said. "Tanook's curse was lifted when he was born into his seventh life. Not in the middle of it."

"But, he was only one man," Adria argued. "Remember? And we have no way of knowing how the curse might act differently, with a couple involved. The rules have already changed. I mean, were Micah and I even supposed to remember any of our lives?"

"Tanook did," Sam said. "And it made him crazy. So crazy, the villagers killed him, for fear of their own safety."

"But, Micah and I aren't crazy," Adria said. "What if we read the legend wrong? Do you have the book here, Sam?"

"Yeah?" Sam said.

"Take it out, let's look at it again."

****

The Seven Lives of Tanook the Hunter

In the time just after the great expansion, when the Clanock tribe came to live on the edges of the Nehalem, a great war was raging between the Sea Gods, who lived in the tunnels of the Great Sea Rock, and the peaceful Nehalem. The waters raged with their battles.

A great hunter of the Clanock tribe, Tanook, dared to fish one day, at the Great Sea Rock. The Gods were quieted, and many fish were to be found there. Tanook provided for his clan, for they were in a scarce season, and the fish were greatly needed.

So Tanook dared to enter the waters of the warring Gods, and the Sea Spirits were angered. The Nehalem and the Sea Gods began to fight, while Tanook sat helpless in his boat. The Tunnel Spirits tried to take Tanook, but the Nehalem fought for their people, for they were their true Gods.

The war continued, and Tanook called to both sides, for a truce. A bargain was set, and Tanook agreed to sacrifice his life. The Tunnel Spirits took his life, but the Nehalem gave it back. The Gods began to fight, once more.

The Spirits of life and death made an agreement. They drew a line in the waters, and the wars ended. The storms would die no longer at the mouth of the Nehalem, but at the Great Sea Rock. This would give more food to the Clanock tribe.

But the Clanock tribe would never be allowed to fish in the sea at the Rock, for this was the territory of the Sea Gods. Tanook accepted his curse, and the waters of the Sea Gods were also cursed, to keep the tribe away.

Tanook walked out of the sea, but the Tunnel Spirits had marked him. The Nehalem had also blessed him. The truce was set for seven lives.

Tanook returned to his tribe, and the waters fought no more. The Sea Spirits took his life, when he reached twenty years of age, for this, the waters had agreed to. When Tanook died, the Clanock named the next baby after him, and his life was restored by the blessing of the Nehalem. The truce continued, and Tanook was taken by the Sea Spirits six times, for this the Gods had also agreed upon.

The Sea Spirits always took Tanook's life. Always a baby took its first breath, as Tanook, the man, took his last. Tanook lived for one-hundred-and-twenty years. His sixth life, he recalled the others, and went mad.

The Sea Spirits cursed the villagers to take his life, for they feared for the safety of their people, for Tanook was cursed with a great rage. This was the sixth life.

The Nehalem kept their agreement with the Tunnel Spirits, and so, in his seventh life, Tanook's life was restored, and the Tunnel Spirits lifted the curse of death. Tanook led the village as a great hunter, and the curse was no more. Tanook lived to be one hundred years old, and so, he lived two-hundred-and-twenty years.

The Clanock tribe never fished at the Great Sea Rock again, for those waters were cursed with Tanook's Truce. The Nehalem and the Tunnel Spirits rested, and the waters were drawn with a line. The Clanock tribe paid their debts, with the six lives of Tanook, and so he lived to be a great hunter, once more. This is how the Clanock Tribe came to be named the Tanook Tribe.

****

Sam closed the book again. She sighed. She looked at Adria, perplexed. Adria was smiling.

"What?"

"The translation," Adria said. "Look at each separate paragraph. They don't fit. It's almost as if, maybe, several different researchers added their own translation? I mean, you said a team of researchers interviewed the last of the Tillamook, right?"

"Yeah, so?"

"Well, it's choppy. I mean, it's almost like the first book in the Bible. Genesis? It's like a paste and copy deal. The story is told, then it restarts, halfway through, with different details, you know? Like two different people tried to tell the tale?"

"Again, so?"

"Or maybe," Adria said. "They interviewed several Tillamook, and each one gave a slightly different rendering, you know? So, the researchers then attempted to piece all the differing details together. I mean, that would make sense, as to why the story is so choppy, right? It's not a smooth read, Sam. It's not very well written."

"It's not a novel," Sam said. "It's a research book. A preservation book. I doubt the translators were trying to win an award, or make it to the top of the bestseller list."

Adria ignored Sam's remarks, lost in thought.

"Tanook walked out of the water," Adria whispered. "Sam, he walked out of the water."

"So?" Sam was beginning to feel hopeful.

"So," Adria said, her face breaking out in a smile. "The bargain was set, for seven lives. The first six would be cursed with death. The seventh life, Tanook would be free to live, for one hundred years."

"Adria," Sam said. "You'd better explain what you're thinking right now, before I go freaking insane, here."

"Tanook walked out of the water. The Sea Gods didn't take his life the first time until he turned twenty. Then, they took his life six times. But, he walked out of the water, Sam. Justin and I, didn't. We didn't walk out of the water. We died."

Sam stared at Adria, thinking. Her eyes suddenly grew wide and she smiled.

"And me and Micah only just remembered our first life a few days ago," Adria continued. "We remember our first life, Sam. Just like all the others. In our first life together, we were taken. Our lives were taken. We never walked out of the water, like Tanook did."

"That was the first life," Sam whispered. "That was the first life?"

Adria nodded. "It makes sense, right?" Adria said, hoping.

Sam nodded, her eyes filling with tears. Adria sighed.

"If Justin and I drowning was the first life-taking of the curse, because we dared to be in those waters, because we broke the truce, then…" she trailed off.

"Then when you died in 1993, that was the taking of your sixth life," Sam said. "And this is you and Micah's seventh life. This is the life where you're blessed, where you're free to be together."

"Could it be true?"

"You don't feel anything, right?" Sam said. "You don't feel as if the curse is coming?"

"No," Adria said. "I feel completely free."

"Then, maybe," Sam said.

"I can't wait to tell Micah," Adria said, pacing.

"Well, it's almost six. He'll be here any minute. So will Jason."

"Do you like him?" Adria asked.

"Jason?"

Adria nodded. She'd been so caught up in her own life, with Micah, she hadn't been a very good friend. She hadn't really talked to Sam about her life, at all. Now, she felt horribly guilty.

"He's cute," Sam shrugged. "But, it's our first date, and it's Prom."

"You think he'll try to...?"

"We're not soul mates," Sam said. "He'll be lucky if I let him slip me the tongue."

"Gross," Adria laughed.

"Um, considering what I know you and Micah have done, that's not so gross, at all."

"We have our whole life ahead of us, Sam," Adria breathed. "I just know it."

Adria smiled at her friend, and Sam couldn't help herself. She broke out in her own, wide grin. The doorbell rang then, almost as if on cue. Adria sighed, growing nervous, although she had no idea why. It wasn't as if this was her first date with Micah. It was, however, the first time she'd be seeing him, believing they had forever together.

****

When Adria opened the door, she stared at Micah. The sun was behind him, and he blocked it. It gave the illusion that he was outlined by gold. A bright, yellow line of filament surrounded him. Adria saw his eyes, how they sparkled. She took in his black suit, the white dress shirt, his jacket. He looked beautiful. His hair was even slicked back, slightly. For the first time ever, Micah's bangs weren't hanging in his face, but were pushed back, to the sides of his temples.

Adria could do nothing but sigh. Micah stared at her, taking in her dress, her hair, her makeup. He could smell her perfume. She was gorgeous. His heart sped up, and he took in a deep breath and held it, forgetting to breathe out. They both exhaled at the same time, and laughed. Then, he stepped over the threshold of the doorway and took her up in his arms. Emily stood in the kitchen entryway watching. She had her camera ready.

They stood and posed, while Emily snapped several photos of them. Adria's eyes sparkled with happiness, her cheeks flushed with anticipation. She was excited for the dance, now.

Sam came down the stairs, and Adria pulled Micah up, into her room, to talk to him. Sam waited for her own date to show.

****

In her room, Adria threw her arms around Micah and hugged him tight. He hugged her back, feeling relieved. He wanted tonight to be wonderful, and he'd worried that Adria would spend the entire evening on edge. It was the last thing he wanted for tonight. He wanted them both to simply be happy, together.

"Micah," Adria breathed. "Everything's going to be okay."

"I know," he said. "It's what I've been trying to make you see all along."

"No, you don't understand," Adria said, pulling away. "We aren't cursed. This is our seventh life."

Micah frowned at Adria, his eyes looking sad. He shook his head.

"Yes,"Adria insisted. "Our first life was as Charlotte and Justin. That was the first life we paid with. Tanook walked out of the sea, he didn't die right then. But, we did."

"Adria," Micah looked to be on the verge of tears. "It doesn't matter what the book says. What matters is what we feel."

"I don't feel anything," Adria laughed. "I don't feel anything bad coming. Do you? You said yesterday, you didn't feel anything."

"I didn't," Micah said. "But, that doesn't mean the curse is lifted."

"But, we have already died six times," Adria said. "This is our seventh life."

"Adria, the book could be wrong, too," Micah said. "Did you ever think about that?"

"Yes," Adria said. "Which is why you shouldn't jump to the conclusion that we're still cursed, Micah. What if the word for six and seven, in the Tillamook language, sound almost identical? We don't know. What if the translators got it wrong?"

"What if they did," Micah said. "Huh? What if the words for seven and eight sound almost identical? Your theory could go either way. It could work for us, or against us, Adria. Don't do this. Don't work against us."

"I'm not!" she yelled. "I'm trying to work for us."

"No," Micah said. "You're filling yourself up with false hope."

"By wanting to be with you?"

"By hoping things will turn out differently than they will," Micah said. "Once more, Adria. You felt it, too, remember?"

"Not anymore," Adria said. "It's gone."

"That doesn't mean the curse is," he said. "Please. Just be with me tonight? Just be with me tonight, and be happy? Let's not even worry about tomorrow. It's all I want, Adria. To be with you, tonight."

"I am with you, Micah."

She kissed him on the lips and he closed his eyes. When she pulled away, his eyes remained closed.

"Micah, I don't want to hurt you," she said.

"You won't," he said. "I just don't want to be alone, Adria. I want you with me, by my side."

"Always."

Micah opened his eyes, then, and smiled. He wanted Adria to enjoy the evening. He didn't want her happiness to rest on false hopes, but if that's what it took for her to be with him tonight, and not think about the bad things, then he could accept that. He only wanted them to be together tonight, and be happy. Once more.

****

Jason showed up, and Emily took pictures of him and Sam. Adria sized him up and decided he might be a decent date for Sam. Sam was very pretty. Jason was a senior, and tall and thin. He was handsome enough. Sam seemed pleased.

The four of them posed for Emily, then Adria went with Micah in his van, and Sam went with Jason, in his BMW.

In the front doorway, before they left, Adria turned back and hugged her mother tight.

"I love you, Mom," she said.

"I love you, too, honey," Emily said. "Now, go. Have the best time of your life."

"I will," Adria said. "I'll see you in the morning."

"See you," Emily said.

****

"Fancy," Adria said to Sam, under her breath, as she took in Jason's car, while walking down the front steps of her yard.

Sam laughed and winked. Adria smiled.

"We're stopping at my Dad's on our way out. He wants to take pictures, too," Adria said.

"We'll sit and wait," Sam nodded. "But, hey. Everything's going to be okay, Adria. I think you're right. I feel it, too."

"Like a cloud has been lifted?" Adria nodded, and so did Sam.

****

At her father's house, Richard took photos and even some video footage. Adria rolled her eyes.

"Dad, please, we're going to be late for our dinner reservations."

"Hey, my daughter only goes to the Prom once," Richard said. His voice faltered slightly as he took in his own words.

"There's always next year, too, Dad."

Richard lowered his video camera and looked at Adria. She smiled, nodding. Richard's eyes looked to Micah, who only looked away. Richard read the disparate feelings between them, and he felt confused, conflicted. The whole thing had been a crazy notion, from the very beginning, he reasoned. His own hope began to bloom. After all, nothing had happened, yet. They had made it to Prom.

"Well, you two have a good time, then," he said.

Richard walked over to his daughter and hugged her tight.

"You be careful tonight, okay, honey?"

"I will, Dad. I love you," Adria said. "And I'll call you tomorrow morning, when we're back. Before eight."

"Baby, I'm up tonight," Richard said. "I won't be back 'til after eight. Eyes in the Sky, remember?"

Adria nodded.

"I'll leave it on the machine," she said.

"Good deal," Richard said.

He stood in the doorway of his house and watched his daughter get into Micah's van. He smiled. He felt confident he would see his daughter again. He now felt as if all the insanity of the last few months had suddenly melted away.

****

In Seaside, the two couples, Sam and Jason, and Micah and Adria, dined at a fancy restaurant. Then, they drove to the convention center, where the Prom was being held in the downstairs ballroom.

The dance was wonderful. Although the DJ did not play techno songs, strictly, quite a few fast-paced songs were played. Micah and Adria caused a scene during these songs, as they fell into full-on 'rave' mode. They jumped and danced, and even got fairly risqué in some of their moves. A small circle formed around them, and all the other attendees cheered, clapped and egged them on.

Micah and Adria only had eyes for each other. The rest of the world fell away. Sam and Jason also watched them from the sidelines, and Sam couldn't help but smile and cheer for her friend. Everyone had an absolute blast.

During the slow songs, Micah and Adria held each other, their eyes closed, their foreheads pressed together. By the end of the dance, at the last slow song, they didn't even bother swaying. They just stood on the dance floor, hands laced together, foreheads touching.

Sam danced with Jason, and he tried to put his hands on her butt, but she moved them up to her hips and sighed, watching her best friend be madly in love. It would be worth it, she thought to herself. To be in love like that, she sighed inside her own mind. It would be worth dying for.

The Prom ended, and all the students filed out of the ballroom. Many of them were heading to Phillip Moore's house, for the after party. Micah was full of energy. He smiled wickedly, taking Adria's hand. She laughed.

A long caravan of cars and SUV's honked at one another, driving from the convention center to the outskirts of town, to the posh neighborhood on Ocean Avenue. Cars lined the streets, parking for several blocks. Micah pulled up and parked on the front lawn of the house, as did several other cars. They were among some of the first to arrive.

"This is crazy," Adria laughed.

"This is awesome," Micah said.

He leaned across to Adria's side of the van and kissed her. She melted.

"Do you really want to go inside, to the party?" she asked.

Adria looked over her shoulder, into the back of the van. Micah sighed.

"I mean, we could go in a few minutes?" She looked at him demurely.

Micah quickly climbed into the back, and Adria followed him. As the sounds of screaming, laughing teens floated to them from outside, they began to kiss wildly, passionately. Door's slammed from cars around them. People whooped, girls screamed. In the darkness of Micah's van, Adria felt for him.

They were in almost complete blackness. Micah didn't dare turn on the lantern, for he didn't want anyone to see them. There was something infinitely exciting about feeling for Adria in the darkness. They fumbled, their hands finding each other. They could not see, only feel.

Adria could not wait to feel Micah. She didn't remove any of her clothes, only took off her underwear, hitching her dress up, over her thighs. Micah also could not wait. He unzipped his pants and pulled his underwear down enough to free himself. Adria sighed in desperate longing.

"Micah," she whispered.

She felt for him in the dark, and pulled him on top of her, opening herself up to him. He buried his face in her shoulder and took her, desperately, wildly. She moaned again and again, raking in deep breaths, rocking along with his body. She lifted her hips, and Micah felt wonderful to her. She wanted the moment to last forever.

But, her body was on the brink and then over, in only a few, short minutes and she cried out, every muscle in her body tensing up. Micah also cried out, pushing into her one last time, with so much force, she cried out again, her muscles now so tense, they ached. Then, they both relaxed, together, and Micah kissed her with so much passion and love, Adria thought she could die right then and there, and be perfectly happy.

Inside the house, the crowd was already building, and music boomed. Several people walking by the black Volkswagen van, stopped to listen to the cries and moans of ecstasy coming from inside. Micah and Adria had kept themselves in darkness, but in their passion, they'd thought little of remaining quiet.

Several young men went to the front of the van and one of them ran back to his car. He came back, momentarily, with a flashlight, and shone it in through the windshield.

Bright light suddenly flooded the van, and Micah looked up, seeing nothing but white. His bangs hung down in his face now, again, and Adria looked up at him, smiling. She did not care about the boys outside. She looked at Micah above her, and all she could think of, was how beautiful he looked.

The boys laughed wildly at the scene of Micah on top of Adria. Then, they whooped and ran off, into the house. Sam and Jason were already inside. Sam was patiently waiting inside the front door for her best friend. She heard the boys with the flashlight come in, exclaiming about how Micah was 'the man', and she shook her head. She turned and caught Jason smirking and gave him a dirty look. He stopped smiling and feigned apathy. Sam rolled her eyes.

Inside the van, back in darkness again, Micah felt horrible. He felt as if he'd tarnished Adria's reputation.

"I'm sorry," he said.

"For what?"

"For this. In my van. On our special night."

"Micah, every night is special with you," Adria said. "And for the first time ever, I actually feel like a carefree teenager."

"But, people saw."

"So?" Adria said. "Let them see. I don't care, Micah. I love you. I don't care what anyone thinks. That was wonderful. It was so romantic."

"Really?" he sounded surprised.

"Wasn't it wonderful for you?"

"Yes," he sighed. "It was."

She pulled him on top of her again, and kissed him. They lay together, in each other's arms.

"Sam will be waiting, inside," Adria said. "She's probably worried out of her mind, by now."

"Okay," Micah said. "But," he trailed off.

"What?"

"If that was our last time," he said. "Was it a good last time?"

"It won't be our last time," Adria said.

"Indulge me."

"I did," she teased.

"I'm serious."

"It was perfect," Adria said. "Absolutely perfect."

He kissed her then, and he trembled. Adria did not understand why. She only kissed him back, and loved him. He pulled away, sitting up, pulling her with him.

"Ready to go to a party?" he asked.

"I'm ready to go anywhere with you, Micah."

Micah's heart melted at her words. He smiled, although, Adria couldn't see it. He was comforted.

"Song?"

"I Don't Want To Let You Go," she said.

"You don't have to," Micah said, frowning.

"No," she laughed. "The song. It's by Weezer. It's just what's in there, tonight."

****

And it played for her, all night, all throughout the party. Once inside, as they entered the front door, several people turned and cheered, clapping and applauding them both. Micah smiled, embarrassed and turned to look at Adria, to make sure she was okay. She smiled back at him, and he hugged her. This made everyone cheer even more.

Sam stood by the door, and Adria smiled at her, shrugging. Sam only shook her head, smiling.

"Where's Jason?" Adria asked.

"Getting us drinks," Sam said. "But I'm not about to drink something I didn't see poured," she said. "For all I know, he's slipping roofies in my beer as we speak."

"Smart move," Adria laughed. "Are you okay?"

"Are you?" Sam nodded. "You must be. You're glowing."

"I feel like a normal person, for the first time in forever," Adria said.

Micah heard Adria say this to Sam, and his heart filled with happiness. This was all he wanted tonight. For Adria to feel this way.

The three of them went together to the keg in the kitchen and Micah filled a cup for Sam. Jason tried to bring her a beer, but she refused it, taking the cup from Micah, instead. Jason shrugged and downed the beer himself, belching loudly. Adria looked at Micah, then Sam, smiling in surprise.

Later, the four of them danced in the living room, briefly. Then, someone put on techno, and the living room exploded. Micah and Adria led the large group in over two hours of crazy dancing, before things started to die down, around three in the morning. For the rest of the night, Adria and Micah stood in a corner, kissing, or just with their foreheads together.

Jason became extremely drunk, and ended up vomiting all over the kitchen floor. Eventually, Sam was by herself. At one point, as she stood near the stairwell, she overheard two girls talking about Adria and Micah.

"God, look at her, she is so lucky," the first girl said. "She's not pretty enough for him, though."

"I know. He is so hot," the second girl said. "If I was his girlfriend, I would just die."

The girls laughed. Sam turned around and placed herself directly in front of both girls. She gave them a pissed off look, her eyebrows raised. The two girls quickly left, one of them exclaiming, 'whatever,' and Sam turned to look at Micah and Adria, sighing.

At five in the morning, Jason was passed out on the stairs. Adria was ready to leave. She went to Sam.

"Micah and I are ready to go."

"Fuck," Sam said. "Jason's shitfaced."

"You can come with us," Adria said. "Fuck Jason."

"He wished. It didn't happen," Sam said.

"Come on," Adria said, laughing.

22. April 3, 2010

The three of them left the house. Micah put his arm around Adria, smiling. It was cold out, this early in the morning. It was still dark outside.

In the van, Adria sat in the passenger seat, and Sam had to sit in the back of the cab.

"What's with all the blankets and pillows?" Sam said. Then she said, "Oh, never mind," and grew quiet for a moment. "Cool, I'm going to sleep. Okay, you guys?"

"Sure," Micah laughed.

He started the van and smiled at Adria. He mouthed the words 'I love you,' and she smiled back, leaning over and kissing his cheek.

Micah backed off the lawn, and started down Ocean Avenue, heading to highway 26, to go home to Cannon Beach. For the next ten minutes, as he drove, he intermittently looked over at Adria, smiling. She smiled back, and the two of them couldn't help giggling out loud, several times. They were both so happy. Micah breathed in deeply, and exhaled, feeling exhilarated. He looked at Adria again, his smile so wide, his face hurt.

"Song?"

Adria was smiling wide as well. She looked at Micah then, and her face froze. Her eyes seemed to dull, momentarily. She looked confused, almost shocked, as she listened for the music in her own head, that was not there. Her eyes grew wide, as her smile faded. She looked at Micah, frowning. Micah looked back at her in growing concern.

"Adria?"

Micah's heart was pounding in his chest, already. Before Adria could open her mouth to speak, to tell him she heard nothing, that she heard only silence inside her head, her body was thrown, as the entire van was rocked forward by a heavy jolt. Adria gasped. Micah's respiration came in quick bursts.

Behind his van, a black car sped up, once more, and again, struck Micah's vehicle from behind. Again, Adria's body jerked forward, and her heart leapt in her chest. She was fully aware of what was happening. Sam sat up in the back of the van, but she remained silent. She'd been asleep. She listened, as Adria began speaking in a panicked voice, and closed her own eyes.

"No! No! I can't, I can't," Adria began to hyperventilate in her incredible panic, as the realization of what was happening hit her.

"Adria, it's okay," Micah said. "Everything's going to be okay."

"No!" Adria screamed. "This wasn't supposed to happen!"

"Yes, it was," Micah said, trying to sound calm, for Adria. "Adria, we knew this was coming."

"No," Adria cried. "This is our seventh life. *This* one."

"No," Micah said, his voice was low and sad. He sounded hurt and sympathetic, at once. He was trying to comfort Adria, and she knew it. Her heart flew out to him. She loved him so much. Micah knew he was about to die, and all he wanted to do was comfort Adria. Her heart broke.

"Adria, when we drowned off Tillamook Rock, that wasn't the Sea Spirits taking our first life. That was just us, drowning. It was an accident, that's all. Just a stupid accident. It wasn't the curse. We just died in the wrong place, that's all."

Adria was crying.

"Micah, please," she sobbed. "I can't, I can't."

"You can," Micah said, and his voice was so gentle, it gave her strength. "I need you by my side, Adria. I can't do this alone."

"I won't leave you alone, Micah, I promise."

They both reached their hands out at the same time, towards each other, grasping together in a promise lock.

The van was jolted again, and Micah lost Adria's hand, fighting hard to keep his vehicle on the road. Adria looked back, over her shoulder, but she couldn't see the car behind them. Micah could, however, in his side mirror.

"It's Kane."

"No," Adria sobbed.

"He's gonna run us off the road," Sam said, appearing from the back.

"Slam on your brakes," Adria said. "This doesn't have to happen."

"Yes, it does, Adria," Micah said. "You know it does."

"We can fight it."

At that moment, however, Kane rammed his car into the van again, and Micah lost control. The wheel jerked sideways, and the van jolted. There was a loud, banging sound, as the front left tire blew out. Micah fought hard to regain control of the van, but it was impossible.

They were just passing a lookout spot, on the right. It was a photo op spot, overlooking the ocean, high up on the cliffs. Without thinking, Micah used all his strength to jerk the wheel, and he managed to turn the skid he was in, to come to a halt, parallel to the road, on the dirt, just off the pullout. The van came to a stop, rocking back and forth, now turned backwards, facing the way they'd just come. It was five-thirty in the morning, and still dark outside, but the first orange hints of light were barely visible on the horizon.

Adria's breaths came in short bursts. Micah reached for her and took her face in his hands. She was crying uncontrollably. She looked at him and her heart continued to break.

"You knew, didn't you?" she said.

Micah did not want to lie to her. He nodded his head, looking ashamed.

"I only wanted one more night with you," he said. "One normal, wonderful night. It was, wasn't it?"

She nodded, still crying.

"And you were happy?"

Adria nodded again. By now, Kane had sped up. He pulled in, adjacent to the van and screeched to a halt. He got out and stood between the two vehicles, staring the van down.

"Come out of there, you chicken shit!"

"Micah, don't," Sam said, from behind them, inside the cab.

"It's going to happen," Micah said. "Whether I get out or not."

"Then, I'm going with you," Adria said. Her voice was weak, barely above a whisper.

"Adria," Micah said. His eyes were pained. "This is going to hurt you, very badly."

"I know," she said.

"I'm so sorry," Micah said. "I don't want to leave you, you know that, don't you?"

"Yes," she cried. "I don't want to watch you die."

"Then don't."

"This is not happening," Sam said. "Micah, won't you even try to fight?"

"Perhaps," Micah said. "But, we all know how this has to end."

"No," Sam said, looking at her best friend. "Adria?"

"Come on you coward!" Kane yelled.

Westley Kane marched up to the van, and pulled open Adria's door.

"Shit!" Micah yelled.

Kane pulled Adria from the van, even as Micah opened his own door and got out. Kane dragged Adria, several feet away. While this was happening, Sam dug in her purse and pulled out her cell phone. She started to dial, then looked at her phone, screaming. There was no service here, on this bluff. She couldn't believe it.

"God dammit!" Sam screamed. She climbed from the back, into the front of the van, and got out, rushing up to where Kane still held tightly onto Adria's arm. He was pulling her, dragging her, and she was reluctantly following.

She fell and Kane dragged her body, raking it across the ground.

Micah ran from the van and rushed straight to Kane, even as Sam leapt from the van. Kane was ready. He dropped Adria's arm, and reached behind his back, under his jacket, and pulled out a gun.

It was still dark out, but Kane was lit up bright as day by the headlights of his own car. He whipped the gun out from behind his back and held it at arms length, at Adria's head, but his eyes were locked on Micah. Adria lay, panting, at Kane's feet. Sam froze where she was, several feet from Kane, when she saw the gun. Her breath caught in her throat.

"Don't move, you piece of shit," Kane said. Spittle flew from his mouth, and his eyes were crazed and red rimmed.

Adria looked up and saw the gun, and her own heart froze. She backed up several feet, on her knees.

"Adria? Are you okay?" Micah said.

Adria continued to back up, not looking at Kane. She stopped moving when she felt Micah's hand on her shoulder. She turned to look up at him. His eyes were locked on Kane's. Adria stood, by Micah's side, and he put his arm around her. Kane sneered. Sam stood by the wayside, still frozen. She watched everything that was happening while floating on gauze. Everything seemed like a dream to her.

"You ruined my life, you fuck," Kane said. His chin trembled. "Do you have any idea what you've done to me? Expulsion? No college recruiters will go near me now, you fucking shit!"

"Westley, please," Adria said.

"Letting a fucking girl fight for you again, Foster? You're nothing but a piece of shit!" Kane screamed.

He held the gun with a trembling hand, bringing it up now to point at Micah's chest. Adria stepped in front of Micah, to protect him, and Kane laughed. He pointed the gun straight at her face.

"You can't save him!" Kane said. "I will waste you, Adria!"

"Leave her alone!" Micah screamed.

He stepped away and around Adria, but Adria was in a panic. She couldn't stand by and do nothing. It wasn't in her nature, not when she loved Micah as much as she did. She couldn't help herself. The sun was just beginning to rise now, a light pinkish-orange tinge lining the horizon, blocked by the trees. They were all still bathed in a ghostly white glow from the headlights of Kane's car, and surrounded beyond this, by darkness.

"Westley, please, don't do this," Adria sobbed. She stepped in front of Micah, again, cutting off his movements to get around her. He grabbed her shoulders, gently, and she placed one hand on his, across her chest, over her right shoulder. Their fingers laced. Micah stopped moving and stood still. He let Adria do what she needed to, to feel as if she'd tried. In his heart, he knew how everything was going to end.

"Please, Westley. Please. I'll do anything. Just, please don't hurt him. I'll do anything," Adria begged. Tears streamed down her cheeks.

Westley faltered for a moment. He looked almost shocked by Adria's pleas. He frowned, looking from her face to Micah's. Then, the fire was back inside his eyes, and an intense rage that Micah recognized all too well. It was the fire of madness, and it would not relent until it was played out. Until it was extinguished, through death. It was the curse.

Westley smiled at Adria, looking her up and down. Micah could feel the fire growing inside him. His own rage was building. He was no longer afraid, just angry. He could tell what Kane was thinking, from the look on his face, even before he said it.

"Anything?" Kane said, his tone sickening and perverted. "Anything, Adria. Would you?"

Kane licked his lips and continued to eye Adria. Micah was barely able to contain himself.

"Please," Adria said. "Don't hurt him."

"I won't," Kane said matter-of-factly. "I won't hurt your boyfriend. If you'll do one thing for me."

"What? Anything!"

"Adria," Micah whispered. "No. Don't try and bargain with the devil."

"The devil?" Kane said. "I'm the devil, Foster? *Me*?! I'm not the one who just ruined someone else's life. I'm not the one who picked a random fight, for no fucking reason at all!"

"Please, Westley," Adria said, again.

"Fine. Let's make a deal," Westley said. "I'll let your boyfriend go, if you get into my car, get into the back seat, turn that pretty little ass of yours around, and let me fuck you."

Adria stared at Kane for several moments, not comprehending. She frowned. She felt Micah's hands tighten on her shoulders. She could feel him trembling with rage. She could feel the heat coming off of him, as his rage grew into an inferno.

"What?" she whispered.

"You heard me," Kane said. "You said you'd do anything, right? Well do me, then. Huh? Fuck me, you little cunt. How much do you love your boyfriend now, huh?"

"Shut...your...mouth," Micah strangled out. His voice shook with anger. Adria's eyes were wide and disbelieving.

"The only way your boyfriend walks away from this, is if you do me right here, baby," Kane said. "Why don't you get down on your knees and suck me, while your boyfriend watches, you slut."

Adria still stood, shocked and disbelieving, reeling from Kane's remarks. Micah could stand no more. He stepped around Adria, and before she even realized he'd moved, he was next to her, not behind her. He took one step forward, his face contorted in a sneer. Kane reacted in an instant, retraining the gun, the few inches he needed to, and pointed it at Micah's chest, once more. Micah took another step forward and Kane's hand jerked. A loud report rang out and echoed in the quiet around them.

No one moved. Not even Micah. Blood bloomed on the front of his white dress shirt, and his entire front was red in an instant. Kane stood, his hand trembling, his face shocked and white.

Adria stood, dazed and numb. She swayed on her feet, her ears still ringing from the loud gunshot, so close to her. Behind everyone, Sam stood, also in shock.

Kane turned and ran to his car, getting in and driving away, his tires squealing out, when they made contact with the pavement of the highway. Dust floated in the air.

Adria turned, as Micah fell to his knees, hugging himself with his arms. She caught him, and they both fell to the ground. His body lay across her lap, his head in her hands. He looked up at her face and she cried, taking in the blood, his injury finally registering on her mind.

"It's done," he said, his voice soft.

"No," Adria cried, her voice barely above a whisper.

"It's not so bad," Micah said, his voice faltering. "It doesn't hurt so much."

"Micah," Adria cried, looking down into his face. "I'm sorry."

"It's not your fault," Micah said. "This was always going to happen. You couldn't stop it."

"I love you," she sobbed.

"I know," he smiled. She couldn't believe it. Micah smiled.

"I'm not afraid, Adria," he said. "Please, don't cry."

"Micah," she said. She touched his face, cradling it in her hand.

Micah reached his own hand up to hers, at his face, and held it. He looked into her eyes, his breathing more labored now.

Behind them, Sam stood a few feet away, holding herself, sobbing her own silent tears. Her heart was breaking for Adria.

"It's all going to be okay," Micah said. "I'll wait for you, Adria."

"I won't make you wait," Adria said. "Not long."

Micah nodded, almost imperceptibly. Then he smiled again.

"I said I wouldn't ask you."

"You don't have to," Adria said. "Once more, Micah."

She nodded, a tear falling from the tip of her nose. Another fell from her chin. She smiled at him.

"I'm not afraid anymore, either," she told him. "I can feel it, too."

Micah nodded, for he knew what she meant. They'd talked about it, only the day before. They both knew they were going to a better life. A blessed life, where they would be free to be together, without the curse.

Adria could feel Micah going. She gazed at him, trying to comfort him.

"I'm here, Micah. You're not alone. I'm with you."

"Always," Micah said.

He smiled up at her, once more, and then his eyes lost focus. His smile faded as the life left his body. His hand on the back of hers, slipped away, and his head lolled to the side, toward her body. He was gone.

Adria sat, with Micah's body in her lap for several seconds, not breathing. Then, she let out a loud sob of heartrending pain. It echoed in the early morning light that now surrounded her.

Suddenly, Sam was there, standing in front of Adria, as Micah's still body lay in her lap. Tears streamed down her face as she looked at her best friend. Adria looked up at Sam and her face contorted.

"I'm sorry, Sam," she strangled out.

Adria raked in a breath. She closed her eyes. She breathed out and smiled. Sam's heart broke.

"I can feel him, Sam," Adria said. She opened her eyes to look at her best friend.

"I can feel Micah. He's all around me. He's waiting."

Sam nodded, tears still streaming down her face. Adria looked down at Micah's body, and gently moved it off her lap, standing to look at Sam.

"I'm sorry, Sam," Adria said again.

"I know," Sam said.

"I have to go."

Sam nodded. She couldn't stop crying.

"Remember what I told you," Adria said. "I won't be dead, Sam."

Sam nodded again, a strangled noise escaping from her throat.

"I have to go, Sam. He's waiting." she repeated.

Sam walked a few feet after Adria, following her. Then, she stopped, and watched Adria walk several feet further on, towards the cliff edge of the lookout. Sam didn't dare follow Adria any further. She was trying very hard, even now, to restrain herself.

Adria reached the edge of the cliff and turned to face Sam. She smiled.

"Tell my father I'm sorry," she said, her voice trembling. "And, Sam? Tell my mother...I fell. It was an accident. I tripped and fell."

"Adria," Sam cried.

"You're my best friend, Sam," Adria said. "I love you."

"I love you, too," Sam said. "Now, go, before I change my mind, or try to stop you."

Adria smiled, remembering. Sam had said those very words to her, once before.

"I have a feeling, you and I will meet again someday," Adria said.

She turned around, her back facing Sam. She closed her eyes, and breathed in deep, feeling Micah all around her. His soul was pulling on hers, she could feel it. He was waiting for her, but there wasn't much time left. She would not make him wait any longer.

Adria spread her arms out to her sides, as a bird spreads its wings. Just like she had as Sophie Prescott, Adria Allan became a bird, and leaned forward, arms spread, to fly off the cliff.

Sam's breath caught in her throat. In an instant, Adria was gone, vanished from her sight, and Sam was left to look at empty air. She did not even blink. She stood, looking at the spot where Adria had been, only moments before, and tears welled up in her eyes, spilling down her cheeks in hot torrents.

Sam collapsed in the dirt and sobbed. She screamed. She cried out in heartrending shrieks. She sounded like a madwoman. She screamed until her voice cracked, then she sat in the silence of the dawn, holding herself in her own arms, rocking on her knees, like a small child.

Then, she felt a warm breeze on her cheek. It blew to either side of her face, dividing in two, and she gasped, breathing in the scent. It was something sweet. Strawberries? She felt Adria on one side of her, and Micah on the other. She knew it was them. She felt them, all around her. She knew it was them, and she knew they were together.

Then, they were both gone on the breeze. Sam was all alone, once more. She closed her eyes and smiled as she heard Adria's voice inside her head. As she remembered the words Adria had left her with. When she saw Richard Allan later that day, she would tell him of what she felt. She would also tell him what Adria had said to her, days before she died.

"I'll be alive, Sam. Just remember that. I won't be dead. After I'm gone, Sam? After the funerals? I want you to look up at the sky. I want you to look out at the ocean, and feel me and Micah. I want you to know when you look at the

beauty of the world, that we're out there, somewhere, living."

23. Thursday, April 4, 2080

Sam kept her promise, and spent hours, days with Emily Allan. Although Emily did not know of the curse, she was comforted by Sam's explanation that her daughter had not jumped, but had fallen, while backing up in shock at seeing Micah's lifeless body. Adria's death was deemed a tragic accident, by everyone, and Westley Kane would be going to prison for murder in the first degree.

Sam kept her promise to Adria to help Richard and Emily Allan through their pain. She would become a surrogate daughter to both of them, in many ways, and they would keep in touch throughout the years, even after Sam moved away from Cannon Beach.

Sam also reached out to Mr. Foster, although she'd never promised Micah she would do so. He was not quite as receptive, for Sam was a complete stranger to him, but he seemed grateful, all the same.

Ken Foster moved away from Cannon Beach a year after Micah's death, and relocated to Miami. He corresponded with Sam for a few years, sporadically, and then, she simply stopped receiving letters from him. She received news of him over the years, however, from Richard and Emily, whom he did manage to keep in touch with, once a year, at Christmas time. Ken Foster died of a heart attack, eight years after his son was shot and killed.

Sam returned, periodically, over the years, and always visited both Richard and Emily. She wrote them long letters. She kept in touch with the Allan's for the rest of her life, and they remained extremely close with her, until they each passed away. Richard Allan died from a stroke at age 82, when Sam was fifty-four. Emily Allan died of heart failure, two years later, at age eighty-three, when Sam was fifty-six.

Sam never spoke of the curse, or the truth of what she knew about the deaths of Adria Allan and Micah Foster. Not for many years. She finally told her tale to her granddaughter, Ellie, when she was very old, and Ellie was a teenager. Ellie sat and listened to her grandmother's tale, weeks before she would die of cancer, at the age of 87. She listened with wide eyes. When Sam was finished, Ellie looked at her and stared.

Sam smiled at her and instructed her granddaughter to open a drawer. Inside was a CD. Sam instructed her granddaughter to play it on the old fashioned computer Sam still owned. She smiled as she heard Adria's music begin to play. Her smile widened as she heard her best friend's voice begin to sing.

"That's her," Sam said. Her voice shook from the years and the stress of the memories that were now too fresh in her mind, once more.

"That's Adria. She's out there right now, somewhere. With Micah. I know she is. She was born on April 3, 2010. She'd be an old woman now, herself, and Micah, an old man. They'd both be seventy years old, now. Seventeen years younger than me."

24. April 18, 2010

It was six in the morning. Sam rose early and drove to the lookout in the predawn light. She pulled off Highway 26 and parked in the dirt. The spot where Micah had died was mounded up with piles of flowers from over half the student body of Seaside High. A week after the tragic deaths of Micah Foster and Adria Allan, a candlelight vigil was held. Students still came, almost every night since then, and left candles burning in tall glass jars.

This morning, two weeks since the deaths, the lookout was empty. Sam got out of her car, walked to the edge of the cliff, and looked out at the water. She'd looked up at the blue sky, during the funerals, as Adria had told her to, and smiled at the sun on her face. In her chair, as the service carried on, she did not hear the words of the minister, but Adria's words continued to play inside her head. They were Sam's song, now.

"We'll be little babies, Sam. Just beginning, starting out our lives. And when you're an old lady, in your forties, Micah and I will probably just be meeting, and falling in love. We'll just be starting, right where we are right now. If you think about all those things, whenever you start to feel sad, maybe it will help."

Sam sighed, her heart still aching. She smiled, wiping a tear away from her cheek.

"It does help, Adria," Sam whispered. "Not much. But a little. It does."

****

Today, two weeks after losing Adria, Sam looked out at the water, and she closed her eyes, trying to feel the souls of Adria and Micah. She wondered where they were, at that very moment. Visions played inside her head, and she wasn't certain if they were real, or only her own crazy mind, doing some wishful, hopeful thinking. She frowned, hearing Adria's voice. She heard words that Adria had never spoken to her. Still, she wondered if it was all in her own imagination.

"Who do you think we'll be, next time?"

"Adria?" Sam said, looking out at the ocean. Her heart beat so fast, like a drum.

"I hope we're American."

Sam smiled. She breathed in deep, hearing music bloom to life inside her head.
"What song?" Sam said. Then she recognized the song as one of Adria's favorites.
"Stina Nordenstam," Sam breathed. "For You."

Sam's heart broke for joy and sadness all at once.

"I hope we have wonderful lives next time. I hope I have wonderful parents, like this time. And I hope we live on the same block, and play together as children."

Sam continued to hear Adria's voice, and she did not understand what she was hearing, but she knew it brought her comfort. Perhaps it was a gift from the Nehalem? Sam could only wonder, as she continued looking out at the vast expanse of ocean in front of her eyes, at the world all around her.

"I want to live on the same block. Nextdoor neighbors would be perfect. Do you think that's even possible?"

"Yes, I do," Sam sighed.

Then, she frowned. She heard Micah's voice, and she cried, knowing it was a gift, from something, somewhere, beyond her own understanding.

"Whoever we end up being, wherever we're each born, I know I'll find you."

Sam laughed.

"How can you be so sure? If the curse is the only thing that's drawn us together every time, then, once it's lifted, there won't be anything to bring us together."

Sam cried. She continued to laugh, even through her tears.

"Yes, there will. My love for you."

Sam smelled something sweet, yet again, floating on the breeze, all around her. She still did not know what it was. Strawberries?

****

It would be years before she would realize what the smell was. It was only after Sam became a mother and held her own newborn baby, that she would recognize the smell as that of a newborn's head.

Sam would finally understand this, ten years after Adria flew from a cliff, so her soul could be with Micah's. The day they both died, was the day they were born.

Once More

About the Author

Jennifer Word is an award winning poet, novelist and editor. She resides in Ventura County, CA with her two children, two cats, and a plecostomus. She holds a B.A. in Psychology from Pepperdine University, with minors in Education and English. She loves horror, both written and cinema. She has written multiple novels and dozens of short stories, half a dozen novellas, and award winning poetry.

Follow her on Twitter @jenniferword, or visit her author page at www.jenniferwordauthor.com